TILLY TENNANT

Eden's COMFORT KITCHEN

bookouture

Published by Bookouture in 2024

An imprint of Storyfire Ltd.
Carmelite House
50 Victoria Embankment
London EC4Y 0DZ

www.bookouture.com

Storyfire Ltd's authorised representative in the EEA is Hachette Ireland
8 Castlecourt Centre
Castleknock Road
Castleknock
Dublin 15 D15 YF6A
Ireland

ISBN: 978-1-83525-697-8
eBook ISBN: 978-1-83525-696-1

Eden's
COMFORT
KITCHEN

BOOKS BY TILLY TENNANT

The Summer of Secrets

The Summer Getaway

The Christmas Wish

The Mill on Magnolia Lane

Hattie's Home for Broken Hearts

The Garden on Sparrow Street

The Break Up

The Waffle House on the Pier

Worth Waiting For

Cathy's Christmas Kitchen

Once Upon a Winter

The Spring of Second Chances

The Time of My Life

The Little Orchard on the Lane

The Hotel at Honeymoon Station

My Best Friend's Wedding

The Cafe at Marigold Marina

A Home at Cornflower Cottage

Christmas in Paris

THE VILLAGE NURSE SERIES

A Helping Hand for the Village Nurse

New Dreams for the Village Nurse

2 99 ①

THE LIFEBOAT SISTERS SERIES
The Lifeboat Sisters
Second Chances for the Lifeboat Sisters
A Secret for the Lifeboat Sisters

AN UNFORGETTABLE CHRISTMAS SERIES
A Very Vintage Christmas
A Cosy Candlelit Christmas

FROM ITALY WITH LOVE SERIES
Rome is Where the Heart is
A Wedding in Italy

HONEYBOURNE SERIES
The Little Village Bakery
Christmas at the Little Village Bakery

For all those who try to make a difference, however big or small

CHAPTER ONE

For the first time since she was fourteen, Eden Sherwood stood on the clifftops and looked out over Sea Glass Bay. Thirteen years had passed since then, thirteen years filled with growing up and making her mark in the world, becoming who she was today – whoever that was. Right now, she wasn't sure who that was, only that she didn't much care for her.

The weather was as kind as it had been that day – at least as she remembered it. But then, in her memory of those days, the sun was always warm and gentle, the breeze cooling and the clouds as white as white. Perhaps it hadn't always been so, but that was the image she recalled now, of a postcard scene in vibrant, happy colours. It was uncanny how little had changed, except for the feeling of dread in her heart that she now carried wherever she went. As a child standing here, she would have been dimly aware that the glorious fortnight of family time would come to an end and she'd go home, disgruntled but already looking forward to the next one. But this time, she stood and looked out over the ocean in the knowledge that she could never go home.

The memory of this place had always been a happy one. So

what was she doing here now? Why sully it? Why taint those perfect recollections with her current sense of desperation? What had she hoped to find here? Happiness? To be transported back to those carefree days? Standing here now, she saw how silly that notion was. She wasn't going to find happiness here – it was too late to find happiness anywhere; things had gone too far for that. All she'd done was ruin one of the few pure memories she still had. Looking out over this perfect bay with eyes that were tired and dry and puffy from weeping wasn't doing anything to lift her spirits. It had been foolish to hope it would, and, in the end, nobody could say she had anyone to blame for that but herself. Certainly not her family who, rightly so, would never forgive her for the trouble she'd caused.

The black sheep, the bad penny, the wayward child; she'd heard it all over the years, and she'd laughed because, yes, she was all those things, but she was also the youngest daughter, the doted-upon baby of the family, the last surprise for an older couple who had never expected her arrival but had loved her all the more for it. She'd never treated them the way they'd deserved for that love – she finally saw that with painful clarity. And now there was no way to put it right, because her mum was dead and it was all Eden's fault.

Had it really been a month since the funeral? The images of that day were still seared onto her brain so that it felt like yesterday. Would it always be like this? People said time healed, but was that just a lie they told to make the grief more bearable?

Everyone had been in black – that was the thing that struck Eden straight away as their procession arrived at the chapel. Her mum would have hated that. Whenever Eden pictured her mum, she was in pastel florals: pinks, lilacs, baby blues and soft greens. She loved gentle colour, and she'd filled their home with it. Eden and Caitlin used to joke that their mum could never walk past a fringed lampshade in a store window without going in to buy it. She never wore black – Eden remembered that distinctly – and she wouldn't have wanted all these people to be in black. Perhaps if her death hadn't been so sudden, if there had been warning and time enough to prepare she'd have said so.

'Peonies everywhere.' Eden's older sister, Caitlin, had looked around at the floral tributes arranged outside the chapel for their arrival. 'That's nice. I'm glad people thought about her favourite flowers.'

'I don't ever want to see another peony as long as I live,' Eden had replied. 'They're horrible flowers.'

Caitlin had thrown her a sideways look – weary, beaten, almost impatient. 'You don't mean that.'

'Don't I?'

Of course she hadn't. Eden only hated seeing the peonies because she was seeing the flowers her mum had so loved there, of all places. She'd never see them the same way again.

She recalled now the feel of Caitlin's hand as she'd wrapped it around hers, and the now familiar guilt stabbed at her as she also recalled how she'd pulled so savagely away. At the time, she'd felt patronised somehow, but looking back, she realised Caitlin had needed the comfort as much as she'd sought to give it. Why had Eden really done that? Was it because of the burning shame, the sense that she deserved no comfort or understanding, only punishment and blame? Because forgiveness somehow made her guilt even worse?

As if that hadn't been bad enough, her dad, following the coffin into the chapel, in the midst of his sorrow had sent the smallest yet sweetest, saddest, most desperate smile her way. He'd sought to somehow reassure her, to let her know it would be OK, that he didn't blame her in the way she blamed herself.

How could he do that? How could he simply let her get away with it? How could he forgive so easily? It almost angered her. She wanted his hate, she wanted his blame because this was worse. How could he still love her after what had happened? That was the moment when the first seeds of her plan had been sown. She had to leave. She had no right to her father's affection when she'd never done anything to earn it. Wouldn't her family be better off without her?

Eden had looked at the coffin, dressed in yet more peonies and decided yes, they would be.

On the cliffs overlooking Sea Glass Bay, Eden lifted her phone from her pocket and checked her diary. Not that she needed to – she had the name of her accommodation burned into her brain. She'd recognised it immediately in the listings online, and she'd looked at her handover instructions with the owner more times than she could count during the previous few days, anxious to get here but dreading it too. Satisfied that the arrangements were as she remembered, she locked it again and turned away from the sea and towards the building that would be hers for the next six months.

Four Winds Cottage. As a child spending two weeks of most summers in Sea Glass Bay at a charming but regular hotel, she'd been enchanted by the sound of the name, a house she only usually saw from afar whenever she and her dad would trek up the cliffs to take advantage of a good wind to fly her kite.

But now the name sounded forlorn, like her happiness, scattered to the four winds, and it felt all too apt for her current mood. But it had been the only long-term rental on the website – the beekeeping, chicken-rearing owners of her childhood long since gone. Perhaps they'd died or moved away. Eden didn't know, and perhaps it didn't matter. For the next six months, this was going to be her home. After that, who knew, but perhaps that didn't matter now either.

The sun was climbing higher as she began her walk to the cottage, standing alone on the clifftop as if it had always been a part of the landscape. After a few minutes, she was forced to take off her jacket – despite the stiff breeze coming in from the sea, the June sun was strong enough to burn through, and the extra work the uneven path was making for her was hardly helping her keep cool. The taxi that had brought her here from the train station in the neighbouring town had gone as far as it could but couldn't make it right to the front door. There was no road to speak of, only a rough path that perhaps a car could do at a pinch – though this driver clearly had concerns for his suspension – and this made Four Winds Cottage relatively inaccessible. But that was fine with Eden. In fact, it was good. It meant no impromptu visitors.

The path hugged the clifftop for a way before branching off – one direction continuing along the cliffs, the other leading to steep steps and the beach below, and a third taking the walker close to the front gate of Four Winds Cottage. The ivory rocks of the cliff face swept down to a golden ribbon of sand and the sparkling seas below. The grass that carpeted either side of the path was new and sweet and untouched, starred with daisies, clover and buttercups. Gulls swooped overhead, and a sudden change in direction to take them out to sea made Eden look to see what might have been a trawler, going through its catch. At least, whatever the boat was doing, the gulls were keen to crowd around it.

It was then that she caught a flash on the water, something breaking the surface to whip up a spray of sparkling foam, only to disappear again. Dolphins were common in these parts – the pub in the village was even called the Darling Dolphin, as far as Eden remembered. During every childhood visit to Sea Glass Bay, she'd been desperate to catch a glimpse of one, but she never had. Eventually she'd given up the quest, content to swim and play amongst the dunes and trust that if she was meant to see a dolphin, she would, although it had always irked her. Even a few weeks ago, the activity she thought she'd seen out on the water would have stoked more than a little excitement at the thought of finally seeing one, and she wished she could feel that excitement now. But even if she could tell from this distance, even if she could be sure of what she was seeing, in her current mood, she doubted she could have got excited about it.

At the cottage, Eden stopped at the gate. The garden was wild, wind-blasted, and it was clear the proximity to the ocean had some bearing on what grew there, but it was somehow all the more charming for its unruliness. The owners had lain gravel where the lawns had once been, and hardy succulents poked out from it. There were more mature trees and shrubs that seemed well established – a honeysuckle clinging to the trellis around the front door, some gnarled trees shading the windows and a couple of unwieldy rose bushes. It all looked low maintenance – not that Eden knew a great deal about gardening. She supposed it would have to be considering how many people came and went – it was a holiday let, after all, and Eden didn't imagine many of the visitors who had come before her stayed for as long as she planned to.

It was then the front door opened, and a lady in wellies and a sturdy wax jacket came out, smiling broadly.

'Eden?'

'Yes...' Eden offered her hand, and the lady shook it. 'Margery?'

'That's me. How are you? Good journey down? Remind me again where you travelled from.'

'Essex. A bit of a trek but not too bad.'

Margery glanced at the path beyond the garden gate.

'I didn't come by car,' Eden said, guessing at her thoughts. She didn't see the point in adding that she'd sold her car, along with many other belongings, to fund this... what was it? An escape? A new start? Hiding?

'Just as well, I suppose,' Margery said cheerfully. 'It's a devil to get a car up here. I get no end of complaints even though I've made it clear on the rental site. I've contacted the authorities about getting a proper road laid, but there's some mumbo jumbo about planning rules getting in the way. I live in hope, but I don't think it will be any time soon.'

'Well, I certainly won't complain.' Eden forced a smile she didn't much feel like making.

'I suppose it does look prettier the way it is,' Margery said. 'And it's such a stunning view up here – when I bought it from a local family, it needed a lot of work – and I don't mind telling you I was worried at first that it would be too much – but how could I view a house like this and refuse it? Especially as it was on the market at such a good price. I plan to live here myself when I retire, but I might as well make some money from it in the meantime, eh?'

'So you live nearby?'

'Salisbury. I don't come to meet everyone who rents it from me, of course, because, goodness, that would be a trek every week, but I thought as you were taking it for such a long time, I'd pop over to say hello and talk you through one or two things.'

More like to be nosy, Eden thought, but she didn't say so.

'You're sure you don't want my cleaner to come in every week and go over the place? She normally does changeover days anyway so it would be no bother.'

'It's fine – I can manage it.'

'Well…' Margery shoved her hands into the pockets of her wax jacket and nodded. 'It will save me some money if I don't have to pay her.'

Eden paused. When it had been discussed during the email exchange, it hadn't occurred to her she might be making someone's life more difficult. She'd only wanted to be left alone. But if she didn't let the cleaner in, the woman wouldn't get paid. Would that be just another thing Eden had managed to screw up?

'Actually,' she said slowly, 'perhaps it's a good idea if she comes up every now and again to go over things. I won't have to worry about it then, will I? And she'll be keeping an eye on things for you at the same time, won't she?'

'Just as you like. I have a good instinct, and I'm sure you're perfectly trustworthy, but I'll ask her to come up every Saturday if it suits you. Let me know if you change your mind at any point.'

'I will.'

'So... six months in Four Winds, eh? I must admit I was surprised by your email asking to take it for so long. Are you working from here? Artist or writer or something? Looking for inspiration?'

'No,' Eden said. 'Just looking for some peace.'

'Oh, you'll find that here. Do you know Sea Glass Bay was voted the friendliest resort on the south coast last year? There's peace up here if you want it, of course, but the people are so lovely you might decide you want to spend a lot of your time in the town. Lots to do too – the beach, some darling little cafés and restaurants, a good pub with great food. I wouldn't worry a bit about being alone either – it's a very safe place.'

Eden nodded and tried to look impressed. First impressions of Margery were good – she seemed stoic and practical and a bit like a teacher Eden had been fond of in high school. She felt like Margery was the sort of woman who would sort any problems with the house immediately and with no fuss. In any other circumstances, Eden might have been inclined to chat with more enthusiasm, but she was finding enthusiasm for anything difficult these days.

'That's all good to hear,' Eden said. 'I used to come here as a young girl with my family. We used to stay in a little hotel in the town... don't remember what it was called but I believe it closed down a few years ago.'

'That'll be the Sandpiper, I expect. Don't know much about

it but I believe the owners retired. Of course this was before I bought Four Winds.'

'How long have you owned this place then?'

'Gosh, now you're asking! Time goes so quickly but... perhaps four or five years.'

'When I used to come to the bay as a girl, my dad used to bring me up to the cliffs with my kite because it was so windy. It was brilliant. I remember seeing this place and thinking it was lovely. We bought eggs from here once too.'

'How long ago was it you last came?'

'About thirteen years or so.'

'I believe the owners at that time did sell eggs, yes. They kept bees too and sold the honey. Don't worry...' Margery chuckled. 'There are no bees or chickens now. You can get all that from the shop in town like normal people do.'

Eden's mind went back to that day with her father, and it almost felt as if she was that girl again, standing in wide-eyed wonder at the threshold as they bought honey and eggs from the owner of the cottage; she'd always been entranced whenever she'd seen it. She'd never been inside before, though, only wondered from afar, but the interior hadn't disappointed, seeming as romantically fairy tale-ish to her young eyes as the name had suggested, like the scene of an old smugglers' tale, or the home of the humble and sweet girl who would one day capture the heart of a prince. She might get her eggs from the shop like normal people now, but she was strangely saddened by that notion.

'I expect you'll want your keys.' Margery's brisk tone broke into Eden's thoughts. Perhaps it was just as well, because the misery spiral she fell into far too often these days had been looming again. 'Would you like me to show you around the boiler and whatnot before I go?'

'I suppose that might be a good idea, though I'm sure I could figure it out.'

'There is a file in the living room that explains everything, but as I'm here anyway, I'm quite happy to go over it with you. I've left you a few bits and pieces to get you started too – washing-up liquid and that sort of thing.'

'That's brilliant, thank you.'

'No problem at all. After all, you are renting from me longer than anyone ever does. I should thank you that I won't have to worry about empty weeks for the rest of this year. I don't mind telling you, it makes life a lot easier.'

Margery handed the key to Eden and moved aside to let her open the front door before following her in. As Eden entered, she was disappointed but also strangely relieved to find that it wasn't as she remembered from her one visit.

She and Margery moved along the hall into the kitchen, Eden vaguely aware of Margery's constant brisk chatter as they went but not really taking much notice. She was far too distracted by Four Winds itself. The low ceilings and small, sturdy-framed windows didn't let in as much light as she'd have liked, but they did combine to make it feel cosy and safe. It was hardly the stuff of fairy tales, more a relic of a bygone era, traditional panels of dark wood and stone flooring with dried flowers and pots hanging from exposed beams in the kitchen and an inglenook fireplace in the tiny parlour. It was furnished in solid wood – every cupboard and dresser looked as if it had been lifted from the set of a period drama. But for all that heaviness, it was pretty, and its solidness had a sort of dependability to it that made Eden feel immediately comforted and protected.

She went straight to the windows to let the sea air and warmth in. Despite the fact that it must have been recently occupied by someone on holiday and that the cleaner had obviously been in, there was a faint mustiness and a fine layer of dust on every surface, but nothing that couldn't be blown out with a good gust and some furniture polish. Eden supposed it was an old house and next to the sea, and so perhaps it would get musty and damp from time to time.

Ten minutes later, Margery had gone, and the house was suddenly and profoundly silent. Eden was alone. Completely and utterly alone, perhaps for the first time in her life. She'd lived by herself in London for a time, building her career, enjoying what she now realised was a privileged life, but she'd always had someone to fall back on. She could go home whenever she liked with a ton of washing and her mum would do it, or drop in unannounced when she felt like it and her mum would always cook her favourite meal. Or if she needed to be at an airport somewhere or other, her dad would always chauffer her there. Those days were gone. Eden was alone now, and she'd have to get on with it.

In her jeans pocket, her phone began to vibrate. She lifted it out to note the name on the caller ID.

Caitlin, her older sister. Ten years older, in fact, and the age gap had always made her seem like a disapproving auntie rather than a sister. Eden watched the display. Just seeing the name hurt. Eden had done many bad, selfish things over the years, and many of those things had been done to Caitlin. The worst of it was, far too often Eden hadn't cared. Caitlin interfered and lectured and chastised, and Eden had hated her for it. She couldn't change any of that, but neither did she want to be reminded of it – she wasn't ready to face her mistakes yet. Even then, her mind went unwillingly back to one of the last times, perhaps the time that had been the beginning of the end.

'Eden...' Caitlin's expression was one of barely contained fury as Eden opened the door to let her into the flat. 'What's wrong with your phone?'

'Nothing.'

'Maybe you'd like to answer it once in a while then.'

Eden waited for her sister to be in the hallway before closing the door and folding her arms. 'I take it from your tone this isn't a social call?'

'Did you take Grandma's gold watch?'

'I borrowed it; I didn't take it. And Mum said it was OK.'

'Mum would.'

'What's that mean? It's her watch to lend out, isn't it? Grandma left it to her.'

'Yes, Grandma left it to her and it's valuable. It's also one of the few things Mum has left of Grandma's.'

'Mum said it was OK. If it was that valuable—'

'Mum also says you've had it for a month and not taken it back.'

'If she wanted it, she only had to ask.'

'She shouldn't have to ask. You said it was for a wedding reception – you'd only be wearing it for a few hours.'

'What is this – CSI? Yes, I wore it for a wedding and I haven't got round to returning it. What's it got to do with you? Mum's not bothered.'

'Of course she's bothered. And it has everything to do with me. I'm her daughter too, you know. That watch is a family heirloom. One of us one day will pass it on to one of our children.'

'Well, it won't be you, will it?'

A sudden, sharp look darkened Caitlin's features. 'What are you trying to say?'

'You don't have kids.'

'Doesn't mean I'll never have kids.'

'You've got to get a man to put up with you for long enough first for that to happen.'

'Classy as ever, Eden. I can always trust you to say the most hurtful thing and not even break a sweat. Do you actually care about anyone but yourself?'

'You're the one crashing my house to tell me off about something you've no need to be involved in – what did you expect? I'd just curtsy and be like, sorry, sis? If Mum wants the watch, she only has to say. And she hasn't said, so how am I supposed to know? I suppose she did that passive-aggressive thing of not telling me but complaining to you so you'd do her dirty work?'

'Don't be so childish; of course not. I noticed she hadn't worn it in a while, and I asked her. She did nothing of the sort, and I'm here because I know she'll never ask you no matter how much she wants to. I love you both but, dear God, where you're concerned, she's a doormat, and you take far too much advantage of how much she adores you. Someone's got to say it.'

'And you feel like that's your job?'

'There's nobody else who will.'

'Still don't see why you have to. I don't see why anyone has to. If it doesn't worry Mum, then it's a non-issue.'

'Here's an idea – why don't you take it back and save everyone going round and round in circles over something that ought to be a non-issue?'

'Here's a better idea – why don't you keep your nose out? Nobody is going round in circles over anything apart from you. But then you've got nothing better to do, I suppose.'

'What? I might not be a city darling like you, but I have a job and a home. I certainly don't have time to chase after you.'

'But you're here anyway. I think you're a bit obsessed with me, quite honestly. Always have been – hated that I came along and spoiled your party when you thought you were always going to be the only child.'

At this, Caitlin balled her fists. Eden saw the movement from the corner of her eye and she knew instantly she'd gone too far. But would she back down? Say sorry? Admit she was out of order? No, Eden would do none of those things. Instead, she'd do what she'd always done and revel in her meanness. She couldn't understand why she felt the need to taunt her sister all the time.

Perhaps because deep down, she knew that all the things her sister had said about her were true and it hurt to acknowledge. So she kicked back rather than try to understand, rather than try to change. It was stupid and pointless and later she would come to understand that.

'I know what you're trying to do,' Caitlin said, so obviously fighting the urge to slap Eden. 'And I'm sure you think it's hilarious, so I'm not going to give you the satisfaction of rising to it. I'm going to leave, and I'm going to trust that at some point during the next few days, you'll have an adult response to this conversation and take Mum's watch home to her.'

'I will. I said that, didn't I? Go back to your sad spinster life and stop trying to run mine, eh?'

Caitlin looked pained as she turned to go. Eden wanted to pull her back, to say she was sorry, but stubborn pride wouldn't let her. So she simply watched her sister leave. Then she went to get her phone and sent a text to her friend, even though she knew it was a vain hope.

Hey, sorry to ask but could you have another look for my watch?

There was an instant reply.

Didn't you think you'd lost it in the taxi?

Yeah, but could you look anyway? My sister is asking about it. It's kind of an heirloom.

Not to be funny, but I spent an hour last week looking and it's not here, not gonna look again, no point. Guess you'll have to buy her another one.

Eden locked her phone and sighed. It was just another thing she'd screwed up. She never meant to upset the people she loved, but somehow she always did.

The watch never did turn up, and when Eden finally owned up to it, her mum didn't get upset. She only looked so desperately sad that Eden didn't know what to say. So she did what she always did in those situations – she skipped off back to her flat and took no blame at all. She removed herself from the visible consequences of her actions and hoped that they would be gone by the time she visited again. Until the day would come when there would be no hiding, when the consequences would be so big she'd never be able to escape them.

Eden dropped her keys onto the table and slumped into one of the chairs, looking around the silent kitchen of Four Winds Cottage, not seeing the charm of it, only the misery that had brought her here. She tried to hold on to the hopes that she'd also brought with her. The events of the past month had to mean something. She didn't know how or what, but she knew something had to change.

CHAPTER TWO

After finishing a quick wipe of the surfaces and eating a bag of crisps she'd had in her handbag for the train journey, Eden needed some air.

She lingered for a moment at her phone on the table, hand hovering over it as she headed for the door, and then decided to leave it there. Nobody was going to be phoning her – at least, nobody she had the strength to talk to right now. It felt odd to leave the house without it but strangely liberating too. She could barely remember a life where she didn't carry one everywhere she went – even around her flat – and yet there must have been one. Perhaps going without now would help her to connect to that girl again, if only for a short while. After all, wasn't that what she'd been hoping to do by coming back here?

The path down the cliffs to the beach was steep, but she enjoyed the exertion, and having to concentrate on where she was walking helped to clear her mind. Yes, this was absolutely what she'd come to Sea Glass Bay for, and she decided as she clambered down that she would do this every day for the next six months.

It was midweek and the cove was a secluded one, out of the

way of the main tourist spots further along the coast, and so while it had always been less lively, today it was quieter than Eden had expected. There were a few older couples snoozing away on deckchairs at the foot of the cliffs, some bodyboarders out at sea, and a young woman playing football with two small children, buckets and spades acting as goalposts while the children – perhaps five or six – squealed with laughter as they raced up and down the sand with the ball. Eden found a spot on the sand and settled there, closing her eyes to tune into the sound of the waves, matching her breathing to them and letting the sun warm her. It was as close to contentment as she'd had for weeks.

She'd zoned out when a sudden blow to the head made her eyes snap open, and she leaped up with a yelp. A colourful plastic ball rolled away from her, and as she looked up, the woman was running across the beach, the two children racing after her.

'Oh God I am so sorry!' she panted. 'Are you all right? I didn't... totally my fault. I didn't realise I'd kicked it so hard!'

'It's OK.' Eden forced a smile. 'No harm done. You'd have to kick harder than that to damage this nut.'

'Lucky the ball's a bit flimsy too, not a proper football, eh?'

The woman scooped up the ball, and as the children arrived by her side, they stopped and studied Eden with a mixture of shyness and curiosity.

'Hello,' Eden said, with some shyness of her own.

'What's your name?' the boy asked.

'Eden.'

The boy nodded and the girl wrapped a hand around the woman's leg. Eden gave them all a closer look. She'd have guessed the children were around the same age – twins? How old? She was a bit rubbish at this sort of thing. Six? Seven? Nine or ten? She felt stupid for not being able to tell. And was the woman their mum? She looked young – Eden would have said younger than her own twenty-seven – but certainly old enough to have children.

'You on holiday?' the woman asked.

'Sort of.'

'Ah...' The woman stroked an absent hand over the girl's hair, and the action was so natural and unknowing that Eden was now convinced she was their mother. 'Well, sorry again about the ball. We'll move a bit further down the beach so it doesn't happen again.'

'Sorry,' the boy said.

'Sorry,' the girl added.

Eden couldn't help but smile. They were cute, even if she didn't know how to talk to them.

They began to walk away, but then the little girl turned around and ran back to Eden. She stopped a few feet short and pointed to the beach dress she'd changed into before coming out.

'You look pretty.'

Tears welled in Eden's eyes, springing from nowhere, so sudden and violent she was almost overwhelmed.

'Thank you.'

The girl looked taken aback, confused by the reaction, but as she turned to run back to the woman, Eden called to stop her.

'Hey. You don't have to move down the beach for me, you know. You were here first, after all.'

The woman smiled and nodded, and Eden was glad she'd persuaded them to stay in their spot, because as they continued their game, she didn't close her eyes but curled her arms around her knees to hug them close and watched. There was such joy in their squeals and laughter, and while she loved to hear it, there was a bittersweetness to the moment too. Not so many years ago it would have been her racing up and down this beach, carefree, careless of a tragedy in her future looming silently, invisibly, but far too quickly.

Before ten minutes had passed, the ball came flying in her direction again, but this time she was ready to catch it neatly before throwing it back. And now the woman started to collect the buckets and spades up as if to move, shouting an apology at Eden as she did.

Eden got up and went over.

'Honestly, don't move on my account. It's been nice to see them having so much fun.' She smiled at them both.

'I'm Nancy,' the girl said with a mixture of shyness and eagerness.

'Hello, Nancy.' Eden glanced at the boy, but when he missed his cue, the woman spoke for him.

'And this little...' She roughed the boy's hair, and he grimaced, squirming out of her reach. 'This is Levi.'

'Cute names,' Eden said. 'So are you on holiday?'

'No, we live here. School's out today, teacher training day, so I'm the entertainment.'

Eden looked at them again. 'How old are you then? Let me guess... about thirty-seven?'

Nancy started to giggle, and Levi groaned.

'Six!' Nancy laughed. 'We're six!'

'Both of you?' Eden asked. 'No, I don't believe it. I was going to see if you wanted to go to the pub later.'

Nancy's giggling grew even more uncontrollable, and Levi wore a broad grin.

'We can't go to the pub!' he said.

Eden frowned. 'Why not?'

The woman started to laugh too. She turned to Eden. 'How long are you on holiday for?'

'Actually, I sort of... well, I'm sort of on holiday, I suppose, but technically... I'm here for about six months. Does that count as a holiday?'

'A decent one, as far as I can tell,' the woman said. 'Are you here with your family? Friends?'

'On my own. I'm staying at the cottage up there...' Eden pointed at the cliffs, and the woman's eyes widened.

'Four Winds?'

'Yes, you know it?'

'My great-uncle and aunt used to live there. This was years ago, mind... He died just before I got these two, and my aunt died not long after. They had once promised...' She looked suddenly wistful but then seemed to shake it. 'Never mind that. It's a great spot, isn't it?'

'Lovely,' Eden agreed. 'I suppose you must know it well.'

'I spent a lot of time there as a kid, of course, but haven't been in since it was sold.'

'Who bought it?'

'Not a clue. Someone from outside the bay, I think.'

A sudden idea occurred to Eden. She'd wanted to be alone, but something about this woman suddenly made her feel more open. And this woman had a connection to the house, so surely she'd like to see it again after so many years of it being gone from her family? It was in her power to do a nice thing for someone, and wasn't that part of the change she wanted for herself too?

'Would you...? What I'm trying to say is, if you wanted to come and look around for old times' sake, I'd be more than happy. I haven't got much in the way of drinks or anything – just arrived today and not been shopping, but you're welcome to snoop.'

'Oh, I wouldn't want to...'

'You wouldn't be.'

'Livia...' The little girl tugged at the woman's hand. 'Where are we going?'

Eden smoothed away a frown. So this wasn't their mum?

The woman – Livia – smiled at Eden. 'It's really lovely of you to offer, but maybe another time.'

'Well, you know where I am,' Eden said. 'And I'm not just

saying it – you'd be really welcome to pop in any time. And it's not like I'm going anywhere soon.'

Livia looked at the twins. 'Right, you two. I suppose we ought to be wrapping up this game anyway. Your gran will be expecting us for tea.'

There was a groan from both of them, and they were still complaining about cutting their game short as Eden watched them pack up. When the last thing was in a bag, Nancy came racing over to Eden. She held out a pink-and-biscuit seashell.

'I found this.'

'It's lovely,' Eden said.

Nancy put it on the sand next to her. 'It's for you.'

'Thanks!' Eden said, those strange and unwanted tears pushing up into her throat again. 'Don't you want to keep it?'

'No, I have one. Livia says to only take one from the beach each time or the creatures will have nowhere to live.'

'Perhaps I ought to leave this one for the creatures then? Because with your one and this one it's two.'

Nancy shrugged, and before she could find a suitable reply, Livia called her from across the beach, and she raced back to her family. All three waved at Eden before making their way up the steps to the clifftop.

Eden watched them go with a faint smile. And then her attention was caught by the sight of a man walking the promenade in formal trousers and a shirt. At this distance, she couldn't make out his face but there was something oddly familiar about him. In the next moment, he got into a car parked in one of the spaces overlooking the beach and started the engine, and Eden dismissed the incident almost as soon as he'd pulled out of the space.

Closing her eyes, she let the sound of the waves rolling in soothe her. Already, she felt more at peace than she had in a long time.

CHAPTER THREE

Breakfast the following morning was non-existent. And it would have to remain that way until the food delivery Eden had ordered the day before arrived. She'd slept well enough, the rhythmic booming of the waves against the cliffs morphing into a comforting white noise as she'd dropped off. The sound of the gulls at dawn was a different matter. If she hadn't known better, she'd have suspected some kind of conspiracy to wake her with the sunrise, so insistent were their cries. Once she was awake, she decided she might as well be up and ready for the day, even if that meant having to wait for her breakfast to arrive.

The taps in the bathroom were inexplicably the wrong way round on the bathroom sink, so the cold was where the hot ought to be and vice versa. She supposed that would take some getting used to; thankfully the boiler wasn't efficient enough to produce water that would scald her when she got it wrong.

At least she had coffee in the kitchen cupboards – perhaps left by a previous guest – and though there was no milk, she didn't mind drinking it black. It would wake her properly if nothing else, and she only had to wait a couple of hours for her online shop to arrive.

It was quickly becoming apparent to Eden how impractical life at Four Winds Cottage was going to be. While the beautiful, windswept and romantically remote location was everything she needed right now, for everyday considerations like getting deliveries and shopping up there, the spot was less than ideal. Her first taste of this was a phone call from the driver who was meant to be bringing her online delivery, who – like the taxi driver the day before – had refused to take his van down the path right to the house.

It was also becoming apparent, by virtue of this inconvenience, why the cottage had been the only one on the rental site. It was likely that the more accessible ones had been taken already, leaving only the remote and difficult Four Winds for a last-minute request such as the one Eden had made. Anyone with any sense would have rented something in the main village or down at the foot of the cliffs rather than on a windswept perch that might look like something out of *Poldark* but was about as well serviced as any home from that century would have been too.

On a more positive note, the weather was doing its best to be on her side. This June day was as glorious as the one before. Much as she needed to sit down and plan how she was going to make the next six months work, having quit her job at a property development company and sold just about everything she owned to come here, she decided it would wait. The beach, the balm for her soul, was calling. And then maybe she'd take a walk into the town to see if that was still as comfortingly familiar as the clifftops had been on her arrival the day before. She recalled the ice-cream parlour that had been a favourite – not even a parlour so much as a window opening on to the street with a jumbled collection of old tables and chairs outside.

. . .

'There! There it is!' Ten-year-old Eden bounced up and down as the parlour came into view, candy-striped awning shading painted wooden furniture, families filling every table as they sat in the sun with their banana splits or knickerbocker glories or tubs with mini mountains of different coloured ice cream. It was the first holiday she could recall where Caitlin wasn't with them, but she was twenty now and preferred to escape to some Spanish costa with friends than join her parents and little sister in a British seaside resort. Eden had loved being the only child that week and all the attention that had come with it. 'Can we get one?'

'Eden, wait, we have to—'

'Please! Please, Dad! Can we get one now? It will be closed when we come back!'

'It's not going to close in the next half hour. I promise we'll come back just as soon as we've had lunch.'

'I'm not hungry.'

Eden's mum had let out the most beautiful laugh at this. Years later, it would still play in Eden's mind when she thought of the moment, like a tape recording. 'You're not hungry? Then you can't want ice cream.'

'It's different,' Eden pouted.

'Is it?' her dad asked wryly.

'I promise to eat my dinner.'

Eden's mum shared a look with her dad, and at that moment Eden knew she'd won.

'All right,' he sighed. 'I suppose we're on holiday, after all. To hell with it – who needs nutrition anyway? Let's all get ice cream for lunch.'

Trips to the ice-cream parlour had invariably been followed by a visit to the shop that sold beach toys, or, as she grew older, the souvenir shop that sold bead necklaces and bracelets and seaside-themed trinkets. She recalled now a fish and chip shop that her dad was fond of, and the pub where she'd sat in the beer garden with her mum and sister, a bottle of pop with a straw bobbing about in it on the table in front of her, while her dad went and rubbed shoulders with the locals inside. Her dad would talk to anyone – still would, even now – and the thought of him sitting at home, lonely and bereft without her mum, forced the ever-threatening knot of emotion up into her throat again.

Part of her longed to call him to see if he was OK, but she was the last person he needed or wanted. Caitlin would be there for him, and her support would be far more welcome than Eden's was. Caitlin always knew what to do and what to say, while Eden always managed to put her foot in it. At her mum's funeral, people had marvelled at the job Caitlin had done organising everything and consoling their dad; she'd heard them remarking how well Caitlin would take care of him.

You've always been spoiled.

Caitlin's words that afternoon had replayed in Eden's head almost every day since.

Never accepted a minute of responsibility in your life. Always had everyone dancing to your tune, always wanting more and more, no matter how much you've got.

And so on. Eden had heard it all before, of course. She'd often found it funny, funnier the angrier Caitlin got, which enraged her sister even more. When Eden was little, Caitlin had indulged her too, just as their parents had, and perhaps that was partly why Caitlin couldn't stand it now, conscious on some level of her part in the ruining of her little sister.

Not that Eden thought for a minute what she herself had become was anyone's fault but her own. Her family may have reinforced her sense of entitlement, but in the end, she had to accept responsibility for it. It had taken twenty-seven years, but finally, she had. Too late for her mum, too late to rebuild their destroyed family, so what was she meant to do with this revelation now?

She spent an hour on the beach, as soothing today as it had been the day before. There was no sign of Livia, Nancy and Levi, and Eden was oddly disappointed by that. What she did enjoy was the notion that there was no pressure to spend all her time here thinking that she had to squeeze every drop out of it because she'd be going home in a few days. This – for all intents and purposes – was home, for the next six months, and so she had all the time in the world to sit in this spot and no desperate rush to cram those moments in.

Then she got up and brushed herself down, and by the time she'd walked to the town with its cluster of shops and houses crowding the curve of the bay, she was hungry and thirsty.

The chip shop was more or less as she remembered it, but she hadn't for a minute expected the chips to be as good as she'd recalled. They were, however, and as she ate them, she was tempted to phone her dad, just to tell him so. Perhaps she would, she promised herself, instantly realising that she'd have to drum up the courage first and doubting she'd be able to. She wanted to. Perhaps that was a good enough start.

After her chips, she had just enough room for ice cream. She was hopeful as she made her way over to the window that this wouldn't have changed either. Sure enough, it looked exactly the same: the ramshackle collection of tables and chairs out on the pavement, the silver freezers lined up, the pink and blue stripes of the sign over the hatch. The sight encouraged her to hope that the ice cream might be the same too. There was a queue – which was also encouraging because that invariably meant people knew it would be worth queuing for. When it came to her turn, she looked up from counting the coins in her purse and stared straight into the face of the woman she'd met on the beach the day before.

'Hello!' Livia said brightly. 'Having a good day? What'll it be?'

'Oh, er... hi. I didn't know you worked here...'

'Well, you wouldn't, I expect. I never said so.'

'Oh God...' Eden flushed. 'That's such a stupid thing to say.'

Livia smiled. 'Aww don't worry about it. It's the sort of daft thing I say all the time so you're not alone. What would you like?'

'Um, do you still do that sour cherry one you used to have? I mean, I used to have a sour cherry thing in a chocolate-coated cone when I'd come here years ago.'

'Oh yes, we still do that. While Mum's in charge we'll never change the flavours!'

'So your mum owns this place?'

'Dad used to run it, but he died earlier this year, so it's just me and Mum keeping things ticking over.'

'He died? I'm sorry to—'

'Thank you,' Livia said. 'I expect Dad would have served you if you came here... how long ago?'

'About thirteen years ago, if not more.'

'God, yes, it would have been Dad. Me and Zoe – my sister – used to help him a bit on weekends back then, but I think we probably made things worse rather than better.'

'Does your sister still work here?'

At this Livia's open and warm expression seemed to darken. 'No,' she said, the sparkle gone from her voice too. 'Not now. It's just me and Mum. I expect Levi and Nancy will want to get involved when they're old enough, but that's a few years off yet.'

'Oh, I see.'

Eden fell to silence as she watched Livia put together her order and wondered what had happened to make her suddenly so obviously sad. Was she like Eden? Was there some tragedy she was struggling to come to terms with? Livia had mentioned losing her father – was it even more than that?

Eden handed her a note, and Livia got her change while Eden licked at the ice cream. This was exactly as she remembered, and it was all she could do not to sigh with happiness.

'That's stunning,' she said, bringing Livia's warm smile back.

'Glad to hear it.'

Eden moved away from the window to allow the next customer to order and took a seat on one of the chairs arranged in front of it. She wanted to talk to Livia some more, but it looked as if she'd have to wait until the queue died down. She couldn't put her finger on what it was, but something about her felt right, as if she was a kindred spirit, and she wanted to know more about this woman who seemed to be able to light up a room as soon as she walked into it. The long chestnut hair that had streamed behind her in the wind of the beach the day before was tied up in a ponytail today, and though her face was round, it was freckled and pretty, and her smile was infectious. Eden somehow knew, without having to know anything about her, that she was kind and generous and a good person to have around.

As quickly as the queue shortened, it lengthened again as new customers joined. The tourist season was in full swing, and Eden supposed it was like this all the time for the ice-cream parlour. When her ice cream was finished and she had no need to take up a seat, she wondered whether she ought to leave Livia to it. She looked busy, and Eden didn't want to come across as her new best stalker. But there was some irresistible pull, something that made her want to stay, like being in her orbit somehow promised some kind of healing. It was difficult to explain, even more difficult to understand, and yet Eden felt it.

Forty minutes passed in this way, Eden losing patience each time she spied an upcoming opportunity to talk to Livia again, only to see new customers join the queue. Eventually she decided to leave. Perhaps it would be calmer later in the afternoon, though looking at the weather, she doubted it. People would be milling around the pretty bay and its town well into the evening, no doubt.

Just as Eden was getting up, an older woman who was unmistakably related to Livia appeared at the counter. Eden racked her brain. The woman seemed familiar – maybe she'd served them once on one of Eden's childhood visits. It seemed reasonable to assume as Livia had told Eden the parlour had been in the family for years. They had a few words, and then Livia took off her apron and emerged from a door at the side of the building with a cold drink. As she looked up, she caught Eden's eye and smiled.

'Still here?' she asked, making her way over. 'Thinking about getting seconds?'

'I would,' Eden said. 'It was so good, but I'd regret it later.'

'I don't think you should ever regret something that makes you happy. There aren't enough of those things in life – grab the ones that come to you, that's what I say.'

'If that's a pitch to sell more ice cream, you ought to copyright it.'

Livia laughed gently and then sucked on the straw in her drink.

'Are you finished for the day?' Eden asked.

'God, no! Mum's just come to take over for a bit so I can have a break.'

'Must be hard to run this place, just you two, I mean.'

'It keeps us busy, but we don't mind. After all, it's only really this busy for a few months of the year, and the rest of the time it's far quieter. We do the work now so we can bank the money and survive the winter – that's how a lot of places round here manage.' She sat down on a chair at the table Eden had just vacated. 'Got something nice planned for today?'

'Not really...'

Eden wondered whether Livia would mind if she sat down again to join her or whether it would interrupt some well-earned downtime. But then Livia took the question out of the air and answered it for her.

'You don't have to leave on my account. Sit down if you like. How are you settling in at Four Winds?'

'Well, I've got some food in now, so that's a start.'

'Sounds like a very good start to me. Have you come across the old beehives in the garden yet?'

'Oh, the lady who owns the house now said there had been bees, but they're not there now, and neither are the hives... at least, I don't think so. Quite honestly, I haven't thought to look. Maybe I should.'

'The hives were still there last time I was there, but that was a few years ago. I don't suppose they are now. The new owners probably got rid of those and the chicken coops if they didn't need them.'

'It's a shame. I might have been a bit scared of the bees, but the idea is kind of cute. I definitely would have been excited to have chickens in the garden.'

Livia nodded. 'The bees used to fascinate me. I used to watch my great-uncle doing all his bits through the window. I'd have got stuck in, but he never wanted me to get stung, and he didn't have a suit that would fit me back then.' She took a sip of her drink, her eyes somewhere far away. 'Often thought I might get some hives of my own once I got my own house...' She shook herself. 'Like that's ever going to happen.'

'You live with your mum?'

'Yes. Me and the kids and Mum, we all live together. I mean, it's nice, but... anyway, you don't need to hear about all that.'

'You have a partner?'

'Not now. You?'

'No. So we're both single.'

'Two women in the prime of our lives with no partners – where did we go wrong, eh?'

Eden knew exactly where she'd gone wrong, but she wasn't about to tell Livia. The more she talked to her, the more she wanted to be her friend, and telling her about the events that had sent her running to Sea Glass Bay was not going to make anyone want to be her friend.

'Listen...' Livia sucked up the last of her drink before putting the glass on the table and smiling at Eden. 'If you're at a loose end later, you could come up to the Darling Dolphin... the local pub. It's a good night in there – would get you out of the cottage for a few hours.'

'You'll be in there?'

'Oh, I'm there most nights.'

'I don't... I wouldn't want to crash... I'm sure you'll be having a laugh with your friends, and I wouldn't want to muscle in...'

'Oh no, it won't be like that. I work there. I've always got time to chat in between serving customers, though.'

'You work there as well?'

'From time to time when Ralph gets busy. Ralph's the landlord. It helps him out, and the money helps us and I like it. More like a social thing than a job really.'

'Yes, but you must be exhausted doing a full day here and then going to work there.'

'It's a long day, but it's not all the time. Ralph's the same as us – far busier in the summer than the winter – mostly locals in the winter, and there aren't so many of us once all the second-home owners and tourists go. I don't mind – like I said, we get the money in where we can. You've got to round here; it's the only way to survive for a lot of people.'

'I feel lazy now.'

'You have a job, though?'

'Not at the moment. I mean, I did, I had... well, I'm taking some time out so I can be here. I was hoping to get something to do here. Just need to get myself organised.'

'Oh, well, if you wanted something just here and there, I bet Ralph would snap your hand off. I know it's a bit menial and you probably don't—'

'It'd be nice. The job I've just left was really stressful, and mostly I was miserable there, so actually I think it would be nice to do something more...'

Mindless, Eden thought, something where she could just switch off and forget who she was and why she was here, a chance to reinvent herself. But she wasn't sure saying all this was a good idea.

'I mean,' she continued, 'I do have a bit of money saved, but I think that will probably get used up on the cottage... well, the point is that I don't think it would be a good idea to rely on savings all the time. I probably ought to think about earning some money – six months is a long time to keep dipping into that pot.'

'Sounds sensible to me. I'll put a word in with Ralph if you like. If you come up later, you could talk to him yourself and see what you think. He's lovely to work for, and the regulars are great. You'd be surprised what a good night you can have just working.'

While Eden was grateful, she was confused. Livia didn't know the first thing about her – why would she want to help like this? Why would she put in a word at the pub for a woman she'd only met the day before? It was lovely, but in the fast-paced, stressful job for a high-end property developer that Eden had just left, someone like Livia would have been eaten alive. She didn't know whether to be charmed by her trust and open-ness or alarmed. But in the spirit of embracing her new start, she decided not to let it worry her. If everyone in Sea Glass Bay was going to be this welcoming, perhaps the happiness she was craving was in reach. And even if it wasn't, she'd be surrounded by nice people, and perhaps that in itself would be enough.

'What time should I be there?'

Livia stood and scooped up her glass. 'Um... I don't know. Whenever you feel like it. If you want to talk to Ralph about work, I'd say earlier is better, before he gets busy. But if you're just wanting a few drinks, then come whenever you like.'

'I will, thank you. And I think I would like to see Ralph about some work – as long as he can cope with an incompetent out-of-towner. I've never worked a bar before.'

'You'll soon pick it up. The regulars will lecture you on how to pull their pints so you won't have much choice!' She laughed lightly. 'I'll tell him you'll be coming. What's your name, by the way, I don't think...'

'Eden. Eden Sherwood.'

'Oh, like Robin Hood. I'll definitely remember that! See you later then, Eden.'

As Livia went back to the parlour, Eden watched as Livia's mum gestured at Eden and seemed to be asking Livia about her. Why did she suddenly feel anxious again? Like somehow the older, more experienced woman would see right through Eden in an instant, would see exactly who she was, would catch her out as someone with a black secret who shouldn't be trusted. But as she watched, Livia looked across and gave her a bright smile, so warm, so genuine, that suddenly Eden didn't want to be that person with that past. For a taste of this new friendship, this new start, for the trust Livia seemed to be placing in her already, she was going to do her best to be worthy of it.

CHAPTER FOUR

It had taken far too long to decide what to wear. Eden was used to having to go the extra mile in her appearance. Her circle of friends back in London had been good fun, but she was under no illusions about how superficial those relationships had been – in fact, she'd been as guilty of that as they were. It was all about image, about fitting in, about wearing the right brands and being seen at the right places. It was part and parcel of the life she'd built there. It was a world she was trying to leave behind, but she still didn't really know how to.

And so, while her instinct was to dress the way she'd always dress for a night out, in a way that showed a successful woman, she realised that this was no longer the version of herself she wanted to present to the world. Not here in Sea Glass Bay, and certainly not going to the local pub in the hopes of getting a job behind the bar. She'd changed her outfit half a dozen times, alternately dressing up and feeling it was too much and then dressing down to worry it wasn't enough.

In the end, she'd settled on the dress that little Nancy had been so enamoured of, reasoning that if Nancy had been taken enough to say so, it was probably something that spoke of the real her.

As she pulled a comb through freshly washed hair that was still a salon shade of blonde, she noticed the phone she'd tossed onto the bed vibrating with an incoming call. Her sister, Caitlin.

As she'd done all the times since she'd arrived in the bay, Eden watched for a moment, letting it ring out, afraid to pick up, not knowing what to say even if she did pluck up the courage.

Once it had stopped, she sniffed back her tears, put the radio on and tried not to think about it.

The wind had picked up since Eden had sat outside the ice-cream parlour with Livia, and the hair she'd carefully combed and smoothed was tangled and wild by the time she'd left the clifftop path. Eden did her best to tidy it before she got to the pub but eventually gave it up as a bad job.

As the pub came into view, she paused and drew in a deep breath. It looked welcoming enough: a rose-covered arbour shading a wide front door, yellow bulbs strung across the tables and chairs that dotted a pretty beer garden. She could see from the outside that it had changed since her dad had taken her there, but she supposed that was to be expected, even if it was a little disappointing. The dark wood of the bar that used to be visible from the sash windows had been painted a parchment colour so that it was far brighter and more modern, and chalk-boards hung on the walls announcing food specials or drinks offers. The lights of the garden were new, as were the patio heaters hanging from outside walls. The signage had been repainted too – gone was the old-master-style seascape with a dolphin leaping from the waves that had once hung outside, to be replaced with something brighter and more cartoonish – a grinning dolphin standing on its tail and beckoning the customer in. Eden's dad would have something to say about this as a sign of progress, and she guessed it wouldn't be complimentary. She wondered what her mum might have said, and the thought made her immediately sad, so she tried to banish it.

Inside, the air was humid. Most of the tables were already full, but there were a couple next to the bar still available. Eden wondered whether it would be better to sit at one of those or simply stand at the bar. If she stood at the bar, would it seem as if she expected Livia to talk to her all night, even if she was busy? But if she sat at a table, would that give the impression she didn't want anyone to talk to her at all?

'Eden!'

Eden looked round to see Livia bringing in a large bottle of rum. She set it on the bar and waved her over.

'I wasn't sure if you were coming or not. I did mention to Ralph that you might. Hang on...'

She turned to a row of optics and slotted the new bottle of rum into one of them. When she seemed satisfied it was plumbed in, she turned to Eden again.

'Sorry, just had to get that in – Elsie's due in at eight, and she always wants a rum and cola, and it has to be that rum.'

'That's all right;, I don't want to stop you working.'

'I'm glad you came. Ralph's keen to meet you. He says he might not have loads of shifts, but he'll certainly have some spares until September if you want them.'

'Doesn't he want to interview me first?'

'Oh, I expect so. Though his idea of an interview will be: what's your name and when can you start? He's pretty informal like that.'

'He might not like the look of me.'

Livia blew a stray hair from her face and frowned with some humour. 'Why not? You look normal enough. Or are you secretly a *Doctor Who* monster?'

'Nothing as interesting as that,' Eden said with a smile, at ease once again. Livia seemed to have a knack for putting her at ease with very little effort.

'Although Levi would have been made up if you were. He's nuts about that programme. You want a drink?'

'Have you got a nice gin?'

'I've got about twenty gins – any in particular?' Livia stood back to let Eden see a row of colourful bottles lining the shelves behind the bar. 'The orange one is nice – at least I think so. Or if your thing is more spicy, we have one with cardamon in it.'

'I'll have the orange one. With lemonade, please.'

'Can't go wrong with that. Double?'

'I...'

'Go on, have a double. Life's too short for single measures, that's what I say.'

'Double then.' Eden smiled. 'No wonder Ralph wants you to work for him – you're a good saleswoman.'

'I know, that's what I keep telling him, but he still doesn't put my wages up.'

While Livia was busy making her drink, Eden took a moment to glance around the room. There were mostly couples and families at the tables. Some were eating casual bar-snack-type food, though there was a menu on the wall, it seemed the Darling Dolphin's dining options were quite informal. It wasn't a big menu either – Eden counted a choice of eight dishes, all traditional pub grub like steak and ale pie, lasagne, and fish and chips.

'Does your food do well?' Eden asked.

'Oh yes.' Livia put the drink down in front of her. Eden got her card out, and Livia fetched the machine. 'Especially in peak season. There's a dining room out back – Ralph's got separate staff for that. I don't have much to do with it unless he's really up against it; I prefer to work the bar. Quite honestly, I think Ralph wishes he didn't have to mess around with that bit of the business, but it brings too much money in for him to get rid of it.'

Eden was about to reply when Livia nodded at a man coming into the bar from a door at the side of the room. He was large in every way – tall and broad with the biggest, fullest beard Eden had ever seen. His cheeks were flushed and his movements confident, but there was a gentleness about him, despite his size.

'Here he is,' Livia said. She beckoned him over. 'Ralph... this is Eden come about the job.'

Ralph came over and offered a huge hand. Eden shook it, suddenly feeling like a child visiting Santa's grotto.

'Livia tells me you've taken Four Winds.'

'For the next six months, yes.'

'God help you in the winter up there. Pleasant enough now, I expect.'

'I can't say I thought as far ahead as winter,' Eden said, feeling foolish that it hadn't even occurred to her what winter might be like in her remote outcrop.

'You're looking for work then?'

'If you've got some. I don't have any bar experience – does that matter?'

'Won't take you long to pick up. How do you feel about waiting tables? Not that I need anyone on there just now, but from time to time, Livia picks up the slack in the dining room for me.'

'I haven't done that before either, but I'm a fast learner.'

'What did you do before?'

Eden hesitated. She could have told the truth: she'd come from a job where she'd sold luxury properties in the city dealing with clients with bank balances that dwarfed the economies of many small countries, and she'd made a lot of money doing it. She'd also spent a lot of that money too, on things she'd never needed. She'd spent so much of it she was constantly trying to find it from other places. Now that she considered it, she realised it was quite ridiculous. But this didn't seem the moment for that kind of honesty.

'I was in admin,' she said, seizing on something that was a half-truth. 'A bit different to this, I suppose. But I'm a hard worker, and I'll have a go at most things.'

Ralph nodded thoughtfully. 'Could you start this weekend? It wouldn't be guaranteed shifts, but there's usually plenty over the summer, so you won't go short.'

'I'm not doing anything at all really; I can start whenever you like.'

'The weekend will do just fine.'

'Brilliant! Thank you! So are there rules... I mean, like a uniform or anything?'

'God, no!' Ralph threw back his head and laughed. 'Just wear whatever you don't mind ruining with spilled beer. Don't dip your fingers in where they're not meant to be, get here on time, don't complain when you have to clean sick from the toilet walls and we'll get on just fine.' He looked at Livia. 'Have I covered everything?'

'More or less,' Livia said, beaming at Eden. 'What do you think?'

'That's all good with me,' Eden said.

Ralph nodded and started to make his way round to the serving side of the bar. 'Welcome aboard. Let's have a tot to celebrate – what are you drinking? On the house, this one.'

'Oh, well... I just got this gin, so...'

'Another gin then.'

Eden watched as Ralph discarded the measure and poured some gin into a glass. There had to be a treble or even quadruple in there.

He turned to Eden. 'What's your mixer?'

'Lemonade,' Eden said. 'Thank you.'

With a broad, beardy grin, he plonked the finished drink

onto the bar in front of her before helping himself to a neat measure of the rum Livia had fixed into the optic earlier. Knocking it straight back, he nodded at Eden and Livia before heading towards the door he'd come in through not ten minutes before.

'I'm going to be plastered after this lot,' Eden said, looking with some bewilderment at the two glasses of gin in front of her.

'He might look a bit scary, but Ralph's a sweetheart,' Livia said. 'He'd do anything for anyone, and if you work for him, he looks after you.'

'I got that impression. I only hope I don't let him down – I wasn't joking when I said I'd never done any work like this before.'

'Not even when you were a teenager?'

'Unfortunately not. You don't think it will be a problem, do you?'

'Like Ralph said, it won't take long to get the hang of it. Actually' – she nodded towards the entrance – 'here's little Elsie. You could have a go at doing her rum and Coke for her if you wanted to pop your bar cherry.'

'Would I be allowed? I haven't officially started yet.'

'Ralph wouldn't let a little thing like that bother him. I reckon if you'd said so, he'd have set you on tonight – he was just being polite.'

Eden took a swig of her gin and coughed. She'd picked up Ralph's nuclear measure and it was just as strong as she'd feared. 'Maybe I won't just yet,' she said as her eyes watered.

Livia laughed. 'Chicken! Don't worry – come the weekend, we'll make a proper barmaid of you.'

CHAPTER FIVE

Four more doubles on top of Ralph's freebie and Eden was more than tipsy.

'Hang on...' Livia called as Eden pulled her jacket around her shoulders. 'If you hang on for half an hour, last orders will be up and I'll have the clean-down finished. I'll be able to walk home with you.'

'Yours or mine?' Eden slurred.

Livia smiled. 'Yours, dafty.'

'Then how will you get home?'

'In exactly the same way.'

'You can't walk me home and then walk all the way back to yours... I don't know exactly how far that is but still, it's got to be a bit out of the way.'

'It's not that bad. I can be pacey when I want to. Long legs, you see. Sprinter's legs, my dad used to say.'

Eden shook her head. 'Nah. That's stupid. Not your legs, they're not stupid. They're probably nice. I mean, going up the cliffs for no reason is stupid. I can get home – it's fine, I know the way.'

Livia started to laugh. 'Yes, but you don't usually have to go up there drunk.'

'I'm not drunk.'

'You're not sober either.'

'I am. A bit.'

Livia laughed again as she turned to a customer. While she was busy, Eden took her cue to sneak out. Much as she appreciated Livia's offer, she wasn't about to have her walk all the way up to Four Winds Cottage and then have to walk down the cliffs back to her own place in the dark.

As soon as she'd made it home, Eden had fallen into bed with a face full of make-up, taking advantage of the fact nobody would be around to see what she looked like when she got up. She had gone straight to sleep – the first time she'd done that since her mum had died. She'd woken with warm recollections of the night before, of laughing more than she'd laughed since her mum's death, just for a short time able to leave that past behind and live for the moment. It had been lovely but all too brief. This morning, despite having those wonderful new memories, the old ones weren't going to be banished so easily.

It didn't help that Caitlin had called again. Early this time, as if to catch Eden out. Eden was drinking her first coffee of the day as the sun burned in through her kitchen window. She watched as her sister's name flashed up, the ringing somehow more insistent, more urgent with every second that Eden tried to ignore it. And then it ended abruptly, almost as if it was a mirror of Caitlin's mood at the other end, an unseen and impatient huff. She'd give up soon, wouldn't she? She hated Eden now – she'd made that clear enough – so why spend so much time trying to speak to her?

As she tried to put it out of her mind, her gaze took in the kitchen. The house was hers for the next few months, but it didn't feel like home yet. Perhaps something of her own taste would change that. She couldn't decorate, of course, but she could buy some soft furnishings and knick-knacks and then perhaps it would feel more homely. There weren't many shops in Sea Glass Bay that weren't geared specifically for the tourists, but she'd seen a fabric shop and she'd also seen a charity shop on the little high street. She might be able to get what she wanted in one of those. Of course, whatever she got in the fabric store would have to be made into something useful, and Eden couldn't sew, but she'd bet that the owners of the shop would either be able to sew it for her or know someone who could.

An hour later, she was wandering down the narrow aisles of the shop, bolts of fabric stretching ahead like the marvellous patterned columns of a Roman temple. There was every colour and every style, from minimalist geometric designs to bold and sumptuous foliage, to pretty cottage-inspired florals. Eden didn't know what she wanted or what she was going to do with it;, she only knew that she wanted to surround herself with things that felt like they were hers.

She stopped in front of a roll of William Morris-inspired cotton and ran a hand along it. Gorgeous as it was, perhaps it was a bit too vibrant for her. She moved along to something more subtle. There was still a hint of Victoriana about it, but the colours were muted and cosy. It was unassuming at first, but the more Eden looked at it, the more she liked it. As she was pondering what she might want made, a voice from behind made her jump.

'Lovely, isn't it?' The shop assistant smiled. 'I've got some of it in my bedroom at home.'

'It's gorgeous.'

'What are you thinking of making with it?'

'Oh, I don't know... cushions maybe?'

'I'd say it's a bit flimsy for that to be honest. I mean, I wouldn't want to tell you what to use, but I feel it's more suited to bedding.'

Eden's gaze went back to the fabric. She really liked it, but if it didn't work, then it didn't work.

'What do you have that would be suitable for cushions?'

The woman glided down the aisle, and Eden followed her. She stopped at a section where the shades went from biscuit to claret to leaf green, all of them with similar patterns to the one Eden had originally been looking at.

'One of these would do nicely. What machine are you working with?'

'Oh... well, that's the other thing – I don't actually sew, and I'd need someone to make it for me. You don't do that, do you?'

'We do when we have time, but we're pretty busy at the moment. There is someone locally who'd do a good job and sometimes picks up work for us. I could give you her number; you could get the fabric and see if she could do it for you.'

'That would be brilliant, thank you.'

'How much fabric do you need?'

'Sorry, I don't know...'

'Don't worry. I'm sure we can figure it out,' the woman continued. 'Let me just get a card for the seamstress...'

Eden inspected the racks while the woman went to the counter.

A moment later, she was back. 'Here we go...'

Eden took the card. The name on it was Julia Sims, and for a moment, Eden was certain she'd heard it somewhere before. 'Is it far to go to take the fabric to her?' she asked. 'Only I don't have a car.'

'Oh no, she lives in the village. And if you can't get her at her house, you can always drop it in at the ice-cream parlour on the seafront. Do you know it?'

'Yes!' The answer came to Eden in a flash. 'Julia! She owns

the ice-cream parlour? Runs it with her daughter? I know Livia!'

'That's Julia.'

'But if she runs the ice-cream parlour, how does she sew as well?'

'Search me, but she makes the time somehow. Does a good job too – lovely neat stitching. I wouldn't recommend her if she wasn't good.'

Eden reflected for a second on what a strange coincidence it was – yet another one – that the thing she'd decided to buy on a whim that morning would somehow lead her back to Livia and her family. And then another thought occurred to her – just how many jobs did Livia and her family do? Both Livia and her mother had two jobs that she knew of; they seemed to be working every waking hour.

She put her hand on a fresh green fabric with a golden song-bird and trellis motif.

'I think I'll take this one, if you can help me with the measurements.'

'Not a problem. Do you want me to work out the price before I cut?'

'No, that's fine. I like it – I think I'll take it anyway.'

The woman looked faintly doubtful but nodded. 'Right you are then. I'll go and get my shears...'

There didn't seem much point in walking all the way to Four Winds Cottage only to go back down to the town again, so Eden decided to go straight to the parlour to see Julia and then get some lunch. She'd noticed a sandwich shop on the way in, a specials board outside announcing rolls containing freshly caught crab, and her tummy growled at the mere thought of them. If she was lucky, perhaps Livia would be around and able to spare half an hour to go with her.

Eden was beginning to realise that at any given time there would be a queue outside the parlour window. Today was no exception, and despite not wanting to order ice cream, she waited her turn to talk to Livia's mum about her sewing.

'Can't stay away, eh?' Livia said, smiling, as Eden reached the counter. 'What's it today?'

'Actually, I was hoping to see your mum. The lady at the fabric shop says your mum can make stuff.'

Before Livia could answer, Julia turned from where she'd been rearranging the tubs in a freezer and wiped her hands on her apron. 'What's that, my love?'

Eden held up the carrier bag that contained her fabric. 'I was hoping you could make some cushions for me out of this. I just bought it in the shop down the road.'

Julia came out of the door and took Eden to one side so that Livia could continue serving ice cream. 'I'm sure I'd be able to fit it in. When would you want it for?'

'There's no rush.' Eden opened the bag and showed Julia the contents. 'Does that look all right? She said that was the best material to get.'

'If Mary sold it, then I'm sure it's fine. I could have it ready a week today – how does that sound?'

'That's brilliant. Thank you so much.'

Julia took the bag from her and gave Eden a curious look. 'They don't have furnishings up at Four Winds then?'

'Yes, some. But I thought... well, as I'm going to be there a while, I wanted something that felt a bit like mine. I know that sounds silly, doesn't it? But I can take it back with me when I leave.'

'Not silly at all. If it makes you feel more comfortable, then why not?'

'I'll come back next week then? Shall I come here to get them?'

'You can do. Or I can ask Livia to give them to you when

she sees you, if that's not convenient – you're going to be working at the Dolphin, aren't you?'

'Yes. I'm looking forward to it.'

'Come on holiday and get yourself a job,' Julia said with a light laugh. 'Not the sort of holiday people usually want.'

'It's not really a holiday. I mean, it is, but it's sort of not.'

Eden felt the weight of that curious scrutiny again. She didn't suppose she was making much sense to Livia's mum. She wasn't making much sense to herself for that matter.

'Right, well, I'd better get on,' Julia said. 'Queue's growing.'

Eden looked to see that half a dozen people had joined the line in the few minutes she'd been talking to Julia. 'Will Livia be having lunch soon?' she asked, feeling like a kid asking her friend's mum if they could come out to play.

'I doubt there'll be much time to stop today, to be honest. I couldn't say, though.'

'Oh, right. Well, if she...' Eden shook her head. 'Never mind. Could you tell her I'll see her up at the Dolphin tomorrow if I don't manage to catch her before?'

Julia nodded and went back into the parlour, leaving Eden to go on her way.

In the end, she'd decided to go back to the cottage and get lunch there. During the first couple of days, being here had been new and welcome, but now she was beginning to feel like a spare part, rattling around the town by herself and not really knowing what to do. There were only so many hours someone could spend on the beach staring out to sea. She'd never appreciated just how much structure having a job created. Faced with six months of very little structure, it was starkly apparent that if she wasn't careful, the peace she'd come here to find would end up driving her mad. She had a few shifts at the pub to look forward to, but she would have to fill her days with more than that.

After eating a cheese sandwich and an entire family pack of crisps, she went out to explore the cottage's back garden. As with the front garden, most of the plants were hardy and weather-resistant trees and shrubs, but while the front lawn had been replaced by gravel, here at the back there was still grass. It was a bit unruly and dotted with dandelions, coltsfoot and daisies, and Eden assumed that Margery – the owner – didn't get time to do a lot of gardening. She couldn't see the sea from the shaded rear garden, but she could hear and smell it – the boom of the waves hitting the cliffs below echoing on salt-tanged air.

Her delight at finding the old beehives Livia had mentioned was immediately tempered by the fact that they'd obviously been out of use for a very long time. Moss and mould grew over their wooden fronts, and one even had a section missing. Seeing these abandoned dwellings made her sad. A further search revealed the chicken coops similarly destitute. Eden pulled away some of the long grass that obscured them, daydreaming of an alternate universe where she might own Four Winds and live here, with bees and chickens, a dog and a handsome husband and a life that was like something out of a romance novel. But a life like that wasn't for people like her.

She was snapped from her daydream by her phone vibrating in her pocket. She pulled it out and frowned, ready to throw it across the garden in frustration. Caitlin again. Why couldn't her sister leave her alone? Why was she so keen to twist the knife? Hadn't she already told Eden exactly what she thought of her? Wasn't Eden carrying enough guilt? She certainly didn't need Caitlin adding to it. But Caitlin seemed to have other ideas.

Uninvited, the image of Caitlin's face came into Eden's mind. Not the Caitlin she'd grown up with, the older sister who'd looked out for her, who'd patiently endured her whims, who'd been resigned to her caprices and her place as the obvious favourite child. Not that Caitlin, but a Caitlin who'd looked at Eden the day of their mother's funeral with a mix of confusion, sorrow and blame.

Eden closed her eyes. She didn't want to remember that day.

The ringing stopped, but it was followed moments later by a text message. Eden's finger hovered over the icon. She wanted to open it, but at the same time she didn't. What if the message was something she didn't want to see? Once she'd read it, it would be too late to undo. Then again, it might be something she needed to see. If she didn't look, she'd never know.

Where the hell are you? What's going on? Dad's worried sick.

I can't say, but I'm fine. I'll message him.

Eden locked the phone again and slipped it into her pocket, absently taking a seat on a bench that hardly looked as if it would take her weight. If this was meant to sound as if she was forgiven, it wasn't very convincing. And Eden didn't feel as if she deserved forgiveness anyway, even if it was on offer. How could it be forgiveness? How could they forgive what she'd done when she couldn't even forgive herself? In any case, Caitlin had made her feelings clear in the days before Eden had left London, and none of them suggested someone who was ready to make peace any time soon. She'd have to message her dad, of course, and she would, just as soon as she could decide what to say.

Her gaze went back to the mouldering beehives and the half-buried chicken coop. Someone had once been blessed with an idyllic life in this place. But all good things came to an end, and just like that time in Four Winds, the charmed life Eden had once led was over too. For what she'd done, she was on her own now, and that was the way it had to be. But did it have to be that way for her dad? She had to admit, Caitlin had a point. More than a point, and it wasn't like Eden hadn't already felt like ignoring her dad wasn't entirely selfless.

She got out her phone to send him a message. She'd call at some point, but she needed more courage than she had at that moment. But a message to let him know she was OK and would phone – that was fair enough, wasn't it? It would put his mind at rest, which was what Caitlin had asked for.

Hi, Dad, hope you're OK. Don't worry about me. I'm fine. I need...

She paused, read the message again and then deleted it.

Hi, Dad

Eden stopped again, finger hovering over the keyboard. Was she overthinking this? The situation called for nothing more than a brief note to let him know she was OK, and yet, at the same time, it seemed to demand so much more than that. Her gaze went to the beehives and the chicken coops. She thought for a minute. And then began again.

Hope you're OK, Dad. I know you're not OK, but I hope you're as OK as you can be. I know I said I'd call, but I haven't been able to yet, and I'm sorry about that. I promise I will soon. Caitlin said you were worried. Please don't worry about me. I'm fine, and I'm safe. I hope you're not upset if I don't tell you where I am. I will, but I don't want to yet. It's nothing you've done – please understand that. I need time, and I think you do too.

Eden read the message back. She wasn't entirely happy with it, despite it being the third attempt. It didn't convey the depth of what she felt, and it didn't address his concerns either – at least, not in any meaningful way. But she didn't have the words that would do either of those things the justice they deserved. This, as imperfect as it was, would have to do. She supposed it was better than nothing. And surely her dad understood why she'd had to leave?

Caitlin had called her selfish, but Eden still maintained that, while some of her motives might have been selfish – even if unconsciously so – her absence was best for everyone. There would be a time when things were less raw and she would be able to see them again, but in this moment, she felt as if she was the last person her dad wanted to see, even if he had told Caitlin he was worried. So the text would give him some reassurance, and perhaps that would be enough.

She pressed send and then waited. No reply came, but she wasn't surprised by that. Her dad wasn't one of those people who had their phones attached to their palm. In fact, he probably didn't even check it more than two or three times a day, so perhaps Eden would have to wait a few hours for a reply. With that in mind, she dropped the phone into her pocket and went inside.

CHAPTER SIX

The following day, Eden woke later than she'd meant to. She'd struggled to get to sleep, and though she wasn't entirely sure why, it didn't take a genius to guess that perhaps family matters had been on her mind. It hadn't helped that her dad hadn't sent a reply that evening, and though she knew he often took a while, that was on her mind too. When she woke, there was a reply, one he must have sent when he'd got up.

> *I'm glad you messaged. I don't know what's going on, and I'm sad you don't feel like you can be here with us and you don't want to say where you are, but I understand. Please know you always have a home here and we love you. Keep us updated. Dad*

Eden wiped away a tear as she read it. She'd have to phone him soon – she realised it wasn't fair not to. And while she felt undeserving of his concern, she was glad of it. He still loved her, after all she'd done. She couldn't quite believe she deserved that either, but the thought made her happy.

Thanks, Dad. I love you too. I'm OK here. I'm kind of working on myself, and I need to figure some things out. I will see you soon, I promise. I'm actually starting a new job today – at a local pub, believe it or not. I'll phone as soon as I can. E x

Livia had told Eden it was probably best to wear something she didn't care about for her first shift at the Darling Dolphin, but Eden hadn't brought much like that with her to Sea Glass Bay. So she wore some expensive jeans and a blouse she'd bought on Oxford Street because she figured if she was doing this, she might as well make a good impression.

'You look lovely!' Livia said, admiring the blouse as Eden went to the bar. 'That colour really suits you... Is it silk?'

'Yes.'

'Hmm...'

Livia might have had thoughts on Eden's choice, but, if so, she didn't voice them. Eden supposed she'd sort of ignored her advice and that she might well spill something over the blouse before the night was out, but it didn't worry her.

'Is Ralph going to show me the ropes?' Eden asked, searching for his huge frame.

'He's in the kitchen, but I'll get you started. Come on...' Livia lifted the hatch that opened to the area behind the bar so that Eden could get to it. 'First thing's first – I'll show you how to use the till. It's not complicated – if I can use it, then any old idiot can.'

'What about a young idiot?'

Livia laughed. 'It'll be fine. Look – there are big fat buttons with almost every drink already programmed in. We don't get asked for much fancier than a gin and tonic. If there is the odd thing not on here, we have a few random buttons here...' She gestured to a big square that simply said 'cocktail' and another that said 'fancy cocktail'.

'I like the logic there,' Eden said with a grin.

'That was my idea. I couldn't see the point in pricing everything up differently when we only do a couple of basic-level cocktails. So push your buttons for what the order is... for instance, a pint and a Guinness and a lager dash, or whatever, and then total up. Dead easy.'

Livia moved to where the steel drink measures were kept and began to talk Eden through those. But before she'd got halfway, they were interrupted by a nervous cough from behind them. Eden turned to see a slight woman of perhaps forty standing at the bar.

'Debs.' Livia smiled. 'You're after Ralph?'

'Yes, he said he had some' – the woman shot a furtive glance Eden's way – 'you know...'

'Right,' Livia said cheerfully. 'He's doing the menus with the chef, but he put some stuff out for you. Come through and I'll get it for you.'

Livia left the bar area, gesturing for Eden to wait, and the woman followed her to the kitchens. A couple of minutes later – minutes where Eden was slightly panicky at the thought of getting a customer while her friend was missing, they came back out. The woman – Debs – had a basket on her arm.

'I don't know what we'd do without—' she began, but Livia put a hand up.

'Don't think anything of it, Debs. We look after each other, right? And it would only go to waste.'

'Tell Ralph I said thank you.'

'I will, but he'll only say he doesn't need any thanks.'

Debs hurried out of the pub, leaving Livia to return to Eden.

'Sorry about that,' she said, coming back to the business side of the bar.

'Is she all right?' Eden asked.

Livia smiled at her puzzled look. 'Yes, she is now. At least, she will be for a day or two.'

'What does that mean?'

Livia shook her head. 'It's nothing... it's just...'

'I didn't like to pry,' Eden said, catching on that Livia was reluctant to say more.

'You didn't. I'd be curious too. It's my fault – I said too much in the beginning, and it's natural you'd want to know the rest. But it's not fair to Debs to say – I don't think she'd appreciate it.'

It had been a long time since Eden had felt nervous at work. In the job she'd left to come here, she'd been confident in her knowledge and skills. She'd been good at it and knew she was. But this was something entirely different. Livia kept reassuring her that it was all perfectly straightforward and that anyone could do it, and how she'd have picked it up by the end of the night, but Eden was still unfamiliarly apprehensive as Livia let her loose on her first patron. She'd pulled a pint that seemed more head than beer, apologising so profusely that whatever complaint the customer might have wanted to make didn't come. Perhaps he'd felt sorry for Eden, because he'd only smiled and acknowledged that everyone had to start somewhere and took his drink without making a fuss.

'There you go,' Livia said, smiling. 'You've broken your duck. It'll get easier from here.'

It did get a little easier as the hours ticked by, so long as the customer wanted something straightforward. Whenever she got asked for something a bit odd, or something she hadn't come across before, her gaze went straight to Livia, who seemed to have a second sense for it and came to her aid as soon as she could. It hadn't taken long for Eden to start enjoying the work, as Livia had promised she would. The customers were mostly pleasant, and the time flew by so quickly she could scarcely believe it when she looked at the clock to see her shift already halfway through.

'You're doing really well,' Livia said during a rare breather. She poured herself some lemonade and looked up at Eden. 'Want one?'

'Is it OK?'

'Oh yes, Ralph doesn't mind us having a drink. I don't take the booze unless a customer tells me to get one for myself – don't want to take the Michael. But it's all right to have a soft drink whenever you like.'

'I'm sweating – I'd love one.'

Livia gave Eden the glass she'd just poured and then got herself another. As she looked up from the tap, she smiled at someone coming into the pub.

'Hey, Liam. Come to get your mum's parcel?'

The young man nodded as he made his way to the bar. He didn't look very old – perhaps eighteen or nineteen at most, skinny and full of nervous energy.

'Ralph will be in the kitchens,' Livia continued. 'Just go on in and give him a shout.'

Just as Debs had done earlier, Eden watched him go through the doors to the kitchens beyond. She sipped thoughtfully at her lemonade, hoping not to get a customer until he came out again. She couldn't deny her curiosity had been piqued. What was going on here?

A few minutes later, he came out with a carrier bag – not down at his side as it might be with shopping, but wrapped around something and cradled in his arms. He nodded at Livia and then left the pub. Eden looked to her new friend, wondering if she might offer more of an explanation this time, but she didn't seem to have noticed. Instead, she popped her empty glass into a tray ready to be washed with the next load and went to top up the bar snacks.

An hour later, an older woman – perhaps in her sixties – came to speak to Eden at the bar. Livia was serving a customer with a large order and didn't notice.

'Sorry...' the woman began. 'But... well, someone told me you were giving out... you know... parcels to people. Of stuff you don't want. I just wondered if there were any left.'

'Parcels of what?' Eden asked, immediately realising that her question had been far too blunt for the situation. The lady was clearly embarrassed that she was here at all, and Eden probably hadn't helped her feel any better.

'Um... food...'

Eden frowned. 'You want to order...?' she began, but then the pieces of the puzzle slotted together. The parcels she'd seen people leaving the kitchens with that night – they must be what this lady meant. So that was it? Food? Were they paying for this? Was it a takeaway service? If so, why all the secrecy? Eden quickly decided the takeaway theory made no sense.

'Hang on a minute for me,' she said, sidling over to Livia and speaking quietly.

'Food parcels... I send her to the kitchen, right?'

'Huh?' Livia looked up from measuring a brandy.

'The food... is that what everyone's been coming in for? I mean, the people you sent to the kitchens?'

Livia looked at the woman standing awkwardly at the counter and then back at Eden.

'Yes,' she said finally, perhaps realising there was no point in keeping it a secret. 'Could you take her to the kitchen to see if there's anything left?'

'Where do I find... I don't know where I'm supposed to look.'

'Ask one of the staff – they'll show you where we keep the tubs.'

Understanding the need for discretion, Eden went to the front of the bar and gestured for the woman to follow her.

'I'm sorry, this is my first night working here,' she said cheerfully. 'I'm not sure what's what yet, but hopefully someone on the kitchen staff can help us.'

'That's all right. Thank you. I wasn't going to come, but someone said...'

The woman trailed off. Eden didn't push for anything more.

The kitchens were like any industrial food area – mostly white tiles and stainless steel, full of heat and steam and people in chef's whites yelling at one another. Eden asked the woman to wait while she searched for Ralph. Unable to see him, instead she went to the nearest member of staff.

'Can you tell me where the spare food is?'

'None left,' the man said.

'Oh...' Eden's gaze went back to the woman, waiting at the doorway and looking as if she wished the floor would swallow her up. She went back over. 'He wants to know how many portions you want and what you'd like.'

The woman gave a nervous smile. 'Oh, only one if you have it. I don't mind what it is.'

Eden's mind went to the specials board in the bar. 'Lasagne? Would that be all right? Or a pie?'

'If you've got a pie, that would be lovely, thank you.'

Eden went back to the cook and lowered her voice. He spun to look as she began to speak, as if outraged that she was there at all. 'If you put me a pie with the bits together in one of the takeout trays, would I be able to pay for it out of my wages later?'

'You want a pie? Right now? Put a ticket in the queue.'

'No, I don't want...' Eden frowned. 'Not for a diner. Can't you just do it?'

'No, I can't just put you a meal together just like that! You'll have to wait.'

Eden cringed as he raised his voice, certain that the woman must have heard him.

'Not even just this once?' she asked, and as he began a reply, she glanced quickly towards the doors to see the woman slip out.

'Great!' Eden said, throwing the cook a look of disdain and going after her.

But the woman had moved quickly, and by the time Eden was back in the main bar, there was no sign of her. She'd obviously heard the altercation and perhaps understood what was going on. Either way, it must have made her feel like a nuisance, and she'd probably decided it wasn't worth it.

As the night went on, Eden couldn't stop thinking about her. It must have taken courage for her to come here and ask for food like that, especially as it seemed she'd come on a recommendation and hadn't been before. She wouldn't have known what to expect or what sort of reception she'd get, or whether she'd be sent away empty-handed – which wasn't exactly how it had happened but near enough. What kind of need must have driven her to that course of action? And she hadn't wanted much – just one meal. Were her own cupboards really that bare that she couldn't make something out of what she had in? The notion pulled at Eden's spirits, dragging her down, so that she struggled to enjoy the last hour of her shift in the way she'd enjoyed the first few. And the idea that Eden herself might have handled it badly and made it worse hardly helped her feel better.

Eventually, Livia rang the bell for last orders and then, gradually, the pub began to empty. Ralph appeared and poured himself a neat whisky, which he drank as he cashed up.

'Where have you been hiding?' Livia asked him as she emptied the drip trays down the sink.

'Away from you, nosy parker,' he said with a laugh.

'Charming.' Livia grinned. 'I don't have to come here to be insulted, you know – I can go home and get that from the kids.'

'Kids won't pay you for the privilege, though.'

Eden mopped the floor, listening as their banter went back and forth and wondering if she'd ever have a relationship like that with Ralph. She supposed not – Livia had told Eden earlier that she'd been born and brought up in Sea Glass Bay, and so she knew almost everyone in some capacity or another. Not only was Eden a newcomer, but she wasn't planning to stay forever. Ralph seemed like a decent enough boss, but she didn't suppose he'd want to waste time getting to know her in the circumstances.

Actually, thinking about what she'd seen tonight, he was more than a good boss. He had to be a very good person. She wanted to ask him and Livia about what had been going on, but she wasn't sure they'd welcome it – even though Eden herself had ended up getting involved. She felt as if her newness to the community made her a stranger and that somehow it waived the right to be involved in the things that went on in that community.

But as Ralph left them again to take the money from the till and put it somewhere safe, presumably in his flat above the pub, Eden's curiosity got the better of her.

'I didn't manage to help that last lady who came in for the food parcels,' she said to Livia as she squeezed the water from the mop. 'We had none left, and the bloke in the kitchen... well, he wasn't very helpful.'

'Oh? Which bloke?'

'I don't know his name. Tall, cheekbones, sort of gingery hair.'

'That'll be Greg. He's all right, just gets stressed, and when he gets stressed, he gets rude. You just have to make certain to catch him in a good mood if you want anything – although once service begins that's a rarity.'

'Next time I'll be sure to ask someone else. You do that a lot – Ralph letting people have... Where does the food come from? Just so I know for next time. I wasn't sure what I was supposed to do.'

'Sorry...' Livia paused, studying Eden thoughtfully for a moment. 'That was my fault – I don't know why I didn't mention any of that at the start of the night. Should have known someone new might come in and ask you. Most people who come know the drill. It's usually the same ones.'

'What is the drill then?'

'It's nothing complicated. Ralph just keeps his leftovers for anyone who needs them. Not for long, obviously – it'll be stuff from the day before; he won't keep anything that wouldn't reheat safely. He always says he'd only be binning it anyway. I think it's a brilliant idea.'

'Is there a lot of need for that sort of thing?'

'Oh, there's a need, all right. That's the thing about places like this – to outsiders it's all pretty and everyone's on holiday, but it's not like that when you live here. I mean, of course it's an amazing place and we're all lucky to live by the sea and everything, but it can be tough making ends meet.'

Eden watched as Livia sprayed the bar and began to wipe it down. She and her mum both did two jobs. Was that because they found it tough to make ends meet? Eden would have thought the ice-cream parlour would be a little goldmine in a place like this, but perhaps that wasn't how it really was. Perhaps even then it wasn't enough – it can't have been if they were forced to do all this extra work, could it?

'Trouble is,' Livia continued in between panting breaths as she scrubbed at a sticky spot, 'a lot of people feel embarrassed about coming in here for Ralph's bits. Which is a shame. Some of them try to pay a bit towards it, but we can't take the money because of all the food rules – Ralph can't be seen to be selling it. Quite honestly, we have to keep the whole thing on the down-low because we might get in trouble just for giving it away. The law is daft like that. But as long as we all keep it between ourselves, we might be able to help a few out. You've got to do your bit for your community, haven't you?'

Eden leaned on her mop. 'Yes,' she said absently, a plan already forming in her mind. Wasn't that what her mum had always said? And her mum did do her bit for her community, for many years. She'd baked and cooked for all sorts of charities and events. All that had only stopped when Eden had…

She didn't want to think about that now because it still hurt to remember the pain she'd caused her mum. Yet another selfish and thoughtless act she'd rather forget.

'What if…' she began slowly. 'What if there was a proper place they could go? One that wouldn't have to be secret.'

'What do you mean?'

'Like a subsidised café or something?'

'That'd be great, I'm sure,' Livia said briskly as she put the spray away under the counter. 'Are you volunteering?' she added with a grin.

'I don't know,' Eden said, her mind racing with possibilities. She wouldn't even know where to start, but the idea was suddenly so strong and so appealing, it was as if it had grabbed her around the neck and wouldn't let go. She had some money, and she had time on her hands. Why couldn't she do it? It would be something to take her mind off her own recent tragedy, to atone for her mistakes, and maybe, just maybe, if her mum could somehow see her from wherever she was, she might look at Eden making a difference for the first time in her life and be a little bit proud.

CHAPTER SEVEN

Eden got up early the following morning, despite her late bedtime, and went out exploring. She'd gone to bed thinking about the entirely off-the-cuff idea she'd mooted to Livia the night before about a community kitchen. At first it had been almost a throwaway remark, but it had quickly taken hold. She'd fallen asleep with her mum on her mind too, and they were bittersweet memories of her baking for charity coffee mornings at the local church, cooking pies and casseroles to take to the local shelter, helping prepare Christmas lunch for the lonely and vulnerable old people in their neighbourhood, those who didn't have family to spend Christmas Day with. She recalled one winter's day when she'd been revising for exams while her mother baked, and the memory was so alive, so vivid, it was as if she was back there.

'There you are! Just in time to taste-test!'

Her mother set a tray she'd just taken from the oven down on the counter. It had been snowing outside, the windows framed by a thick frost, the bare branches in the garden heavy with it, but the air in the kitchen was warm and sweet. Eden had slammed closed a textbook and marched down from her bedroom to find something to drink, certain that she didn't care one bit about passing a single exam no matter what anyone said.

'I'm on a diet.'

Eden's mum wiped flour from her hands and turned to her with a vague frown. She was wearing one of her favourite blouses – baby-blue florals – covered by a pink apron – Eden had always thought she looked so pretty in it. 'What for?'

'Because...' *Eden said, going to the fridge. She wanted a cake, of course, but there was a school disco coming up, and she had to look her best.*

'You have a lovely little figure coming; I don't know what you're worrying about. Look, I've made some chocolate-and-cherry muffins. You always said you loved my chocolate-and-cherry muffins. One won't hurt you.'

'One is like five hundred calories or something.'

'Eden...' *Her mum looked serious.* 'I don't like this diet talk; it worries me. You really don't need to be dieting, especially at your age. You're perfect as you are.'

'I only want to lose half a stone.'

'All right...' *her mum replied slowly.* 'If you don't want to taste-test, then maybe you'd like a break from your books and sit with me here a while? We haven't chatted for ages, and I could do with the company.'

'You're baking.'

'You could help. You used to love helping me.'

'Mum, I was about five.'

'Older than that.'

'Not much.'

'Still, I miss those times. You'd be doing me a huge favour too – I've got loads to do, and the coffee morning is tomorrow.'

'I've got to revise – you know that.'

'You're not revising now. You can take a short break, can't you?'

Eden could. She wanted to but still... she wasn't a little girl any more. She was too old to measure out ingredients with painstaking care as she looked up at her mum's delighted smile, soaking up the adoration and praise. She was too old to lick the mixture from the spoon or ask to go in the car to help deliver the cakes. She was too old to hang out in the kitchen with her mum.

The memories had sent Eden to sleep with tears burning her eyes, but she'd woken with renewed determination to somehow make up for all the times just like that one where she'd disappointed her mum in some way or not been the best version of herself, the daughter her parents had deserved.

Plans were forming in her brain, but they were still small and uncertain and not fleshed out enough to discuss with anyone. She didn't even know who the best person would be to talk to – though Livia and Ralph were the two most obvious to start with. Putting all that aside, it seemed to her that the logical starting point must be a venue. Perhaps when she had that the rest would start falling into place.

Her wanderings took her to parts of the bay she'd never seen before – mostly because, quite naturally, she'd stuck to the tourist traps on her previous visits as a child. There was no need to go any further than those for anyone who didn't live there, after all. But off the main row of shops and cafés on the seafront, away from the high street, the town spread like tentacles into roads where the permanent residents lived. Here the houses were still lovely, full of character, but more worn, like old shoes that had once been expensive but hadn't been resoled in a long time. Here was where the arteries of local life pulsed. The streets were quiet; it was daytime and midweek, so Eden assumed most people were out at work.

The rows of houses – some semi-detached thirties builds, some a little newer, some terraced streets that dated from the early twentieth century, the odd outlier standing alone – were all very interesting but not what Eden was looking for. In fact, she'd just about given up on finding any building that wasn't a house when she passed a gap between a row of houses on an inconspicuous road and stopped. At first it looked like it was waste ground, but then she noticed that set back, sheltered by two trees that met in the middle like a huge umbrella, was a hut with a corrugated roof. The hut itself was weather-beaten and ramshackle – but the ground it sat on was lush with wild grass, hidden rose bushes and trees of varying sizes. An overgrown asphalt path snaked from the front fence to the entrance door. Eden got out her phone and checked the map. After a moment working out exactly where she was, she concluded that this must be the scout hut.

'Excuse me!'

Eden seized the chance to question a passer-by who was out walking a grizzle-mawed old dog. She rushed across to where he'd stopped, eyeing her curiously.

'Sorry to bother you, but is that the scout hut?' She pointed to the building.

'Yes. Nobody there at this time of the day, though.'

'Do you know if it's in use all the time?'

'Not sure.'

'Can anyone use it? I mean, could someone maybe rent it for blocks of time or something? Like to do community stuff?'

'Couldn't tell you…' The man rubbed his chin. 'But there's a number you can ring on the gate there. Would that help?'

Eden looked to see a sign she'd missed. It was hardly surprising, considering how dirty and green with moss it was. If this building was in regular use, there didn't seem to be a huge amount of maintenance going on. The notion filled her with a sudden misgiving. Perhaps this wasn't it, after all. It might not be suitable, and even if it was, she was assuming she'd be able to use it, and that might have been jumping the gun just a little.

'Yes, thanks. Sorry – I didn't even notice it.'

'That's all right.'

The man continued on his way, and Eden went back across the road to take a photo of the sign. She could have dialled the number there and then, but she hadn't really figured out what she was going to ask for if there was an answer. How many days a week did she want to do this? How many people could she cater for? Where was the food going to come from? Who would cook it? Eden was a competent enough cook when it came to throwing some fish fingers in an oven, but that was about it. She'd need help, and who would be able to spare the time? There was still so much to work out, and she didn't know where to start. Today's search had seemed like the first step, but standing here now, she realised the journey hadn't started at all. She'd been carried away on the fantasy, excited by her plans, but they hadn't been plans to speak of.

Instead of dialling the number on the sign, she decided to see if Livia was free. It was a working day for her, of course, and she'd be at the ice-cream parlour as she always was, but perhaps she'd be able to spare half an hour so Eden could run some things past her. And if she didn't know the answers, perhaps she'd be able to point Eden in the direction of someone who did.

Livia sat on the low wall that separated the parlour's seating area from the promenade and licked at her ice cream. Eden had been lucky enough to catch her about to go on her lunch break. She'd laughed when Livia had emerged from the door of the parlour with two ice creams.

'Is that your lunch?'

'It's got protein and carbs. I'd call that a balanced meal.'

Eden laughed as she took one of the cones. 'I always imagined if I worked selling ice cream all week, I wouldn't want to see one on my breaks, let alone eat them.'

'Well, they're right there, so it's quick and easy. Mum says I ought to make the most of the years when I can eat like this and not put on weight.'

'Sounds fair enough.'

'So what's all the excitement? You've not come to tell me you hate the job at the pub and you're leaving already? You'd better not, not when I've only just trained you up.'

'No, I loved my first shift. Although it is about something that happened there. You know Ralph's scheme for his leftovers?'

'Yes...' Livia said uncertainly.

'I've been thinking about it all the time since. You said a lot of people needed it.'

'But they won't all use it.'

'I suppose because it sort of feels like begging and nobody wants to feel like that. I know I wouldn't.'

'True, but we do what we have to, don't we?'

'I don't know about that, but I was thinking how humiliated I'd feel if I had to—'

'I get the feeling,' Livia interrupted, and for the first time since Eden had known her, she seemed less than patient, 'that you're someone who has never struggled to make ends meet. Humiliation doesn't come into it when you've got two kids at home who'll go hungry if you don't swallow your pride and go get that food. There are some people who don't have a choice.'

'I didn't mean... You're right, I've never had to do anything like that before, but I don't think that just because someone is in need, they should have to be shown less respect than anyone else.'

'That's not exactly what I said.'

'In a way, it is. Yes, they do what they need to, but that doesn't mean it doesn't sting. The lady who came in last night when all the food was gone... you didn't see the look on her face. She hated being there, and she hated having to ask. She did a runner rather than have me— Never mind, it doesn't matter, that's not the point.'

'OK...' Livia caught a drip of ice cream as it ran down her cone and fixed Eden with a questioning gaze. 'I can get on board with that, I suppose. But where is all this leading?'

'I just think, brilliant as Ralph is, there must be a better way of doing it. A way to reach more people and make it seem like a social thing rather than begging.'

'It's not begging, but go on.'

'No, it's not... I can't figure out how to say this in the right way, sorry. I'll hold my hands up – I've had a decent life with a good job and good money. I don't know how all this works. And I don't want to come across like some middle-class saviour; I don't want to patronise anyone – that's the last thing I want. But I do want to help. I *can* help. I just don't know where to start.'

'Do you even have a clue what it is you want to do? "Help" is a bit vague. I think it has to be more than just wanting to help.'

'I know. That's why I wanted to ask you. If you could have everything you needed to make a community thing work – like a soup kitchen or something – what would you do?'

'I wouldn't call it a soup kitchen, for a start. Makes it sound like a van ladling out gruel on a street corner in Gotham City.'

Eden was thoughtful for a minute. It might seem at first that Livia was being a bit brutal, but in a way, this was exactly what Eden needed.

'How about... community café? A place where people can come and get a nice meal. No day-old leftovers from—'

'There's nothing wrong with leftovers – some of us eat them a lot.'

'Sorry, that didn't come out the way I meant. I know there's nothing wrong with leftovers, and I wouldn't want people to stop going to Ralph for those. After all, you said it yourself: it's a good way to use them up and save them going to landfill or whatever. But wouldn't it be nice if people could come and sit down somewhere and have a plate of something fresh, have a chat with their friends and not worry about the bill? Like, not just food, but so much more?'

Livia looked sceptical as she swallowed the top from her ice cream. 'You want to open a free restaurant?'

'No, not...' Eden sighed. 'See, I was worried this would happen. I don't really know what it is I want to do, but I know I want to do something. I just thought... Well, you said about the soup kitchen idea being a bit grim, and I just thought a café is a nicer thing. I don't know how it's going to work.'

'Where would you even open it?'

'Ah, well, I don't know that either, but I did see a scout hut today on Shingle Street that might do the job. I'd have to phone them to see if it's available and whether they have facilities to cook and stuff, but it looked big enough from the outside.'

'I know it. Could work.' Livia nodded slowly. 'This isn't a whim, is it? Because you've been here less than a week and you're already making plans for... Well, something like this, you can't just set it up and then get bored a week later. Once people start relying on you, that's it, you're in it for the long haul. Otherwise it's just not fair. And I don't want to be involved if this is just something to stop you getting bored while you're here.'

'You'd be involved? I didn't think—'

'I'm not making any promises, but it does seem to me you need someone local to help. And I haven't forgotten that you're only here for six months. What happens to this community café of yours after that?'

'I don't know. Maybe I can find someone to take it on.'

Livia shook her head. 'I'm sorry, but it wouldn't be me. I

want to help as much as you do, but I have Nancy and Levi and my mum, not to mention two jobs. I'd love to, but—'

'Of course – I get that. They have to come first.'

'I think the thing to do is get a plan together. Decide what it is you actually want to do, something concrete to work with. Maybe we can go and talk to Ralph about it – get his take.'

'Wouldn't it be better to ask Ralph first? He might be able to steer me in the direction of a workable plan rather than me go to him with something that's clearly stupid in the first place.'

'That does sort of make sense,' Livia agreed.

'I don't want to hassle him, though. I've only just started to work for him, and he doesn't know me, and the next thing I'm asking him for this.'

'I don't think he'd see it as hassle. He's busy, yeah, but—'

'Could you ask him? Explain what we're trying to do? He might be more willing to help if it comes from you.'

'He'd be willing to help anyway. Ralph's like that.'

'Even so, he doesn't know me from Adam. And you said yourself you thought it might be a flash in the pan when I first mentioned it. Ralph might think the same.'

'I can ask if he's willing to talk to you, if you really want me to, but I honestly think you ought to do it. He'll want to know more than I can tell him, so you might as well.'

Eden wasn't used to feeling doubtful – at least, not in this sort of situation – but she did now. In her old job, she'd come up with brilliant ideas and have no problem articulating them to her bosses. But this was something entirely different. This wasn't some money-making proposal, and she wasn't dealing with hard-headed corporate types. This was emotive, personal. What she did here had the potential to make a difference for many people. It was an unformed and as yet unrecognised hope, but somewhere in the back of her conscious thoughts there was almost a hope to change lives. Too grand, perhaps, arrogant and foolish, but what if it didn't have to be? What if she could change lives? Wouldn't that be a wonderful thing? Even if that was a step too far, what if she could make someone's life easier for a short while? Wouldn't that be a bit wonderful too?

The more she looked at the proposal, the more she agreed with Livia that Ralph's input would be invaluable. But approaching Ralph was something that made her strangely nervous. The way people viewed her mattered to Eden in a way it had never done before. She was painfully aware of her status as a newcomer, as someone the locals might not even trust. They knew nothing about her – and perhaps if they did, they'd trust her even less. She was trying hard to change that, to be a better person, but none of them would know that.

'I suppose you're right,' she said finally.

'So we're working tonight.' Livia popped the end of her cone into her mouth. 'I can ask Ralph in the meantime, but if I were you, I'd get there early and try to grab him before the pub gets busy.'

'I'd love that, if it's not too much bother. I know you've got work here and—'

'It's no bother at all.'

Eden gave her a grateful smile. 'That's great, thanks.'

CHAPTER EIGHT

Eden spent the rest of the afternoon in a state of agitation. She couldn't help but feel she needed to get something straight in her head before she talked to Ralph. She couldn't waste his time on vague notions of doing something a bit nice; she needed to present something viable, even if it wasn't a fully formed plan. So she'd bought herself a pretty notebook from the charity gift shop at the lifeboat station and then headed back to Four Winds Cottage to doodle spider diagrams with all sorts of ideas hoping to inspire a eureka moment. When she'd got to the point where she was confusing herself rather than teasing out anything useful, she took a walk along the clifftops to clear her head.

The wind had picked up, and it was colder than it had been during her first few days in Sea Glass Bay, but it was still beautiful, only now there was an added romance about it. Eden allowed herself to feel like a Regency heroine as the wind caught her hair and sent it whipping around her face and the sun skimmed the sea, catching the waves like scattered crystals. Shielding her eyes and staring out towards the horizon, she watched as boats zigzagged across the bay, and every so often, a dark shape would break the surface, but from here it was impossible to see if it was one of her elusive dolphins. It looked as if the closest she was going to get to a dolphin was the pub she'd just started to work at.

As she made her way back to the cottage, her phone bleeped the arrival of a message. It was Livia, telling her that Ralph was happy to talk to her later. He'd make time for them before the evening rush if they wanted to pick his brains.

When Eden got there, Livia had already fixed all three of them a drink from the bar.

'Orange gin, right?' she asked, pushing one across the table to Eden as she took off her jacket and sat down with her and Ralph.

'Wow, that's what I call service! Thank you.' Eden took a sip. After a sweaty walk from her house on the cliffs, it was icy and fresh and very welcome.

Ralph reached for his pint. 'So what's this about? Livia says you've got some ideas for something or other you want to do while you're here in the bay. It all sounds a bit mysterious, but I've always been a sucker for a mystery.'

Eden took another sip of her drink and then a breath.

'So... the other day when I was on shift, you had people coming in to get food parcels – which is completely brilliant, by the way – but it got me thinking. Livia says there are people round here struggling a bit, and I thought... I know you're doing something to help, but I want to do something too. I was thinking about how it might be nice if there was a place to go and eat like a soup kitchen. Only not a soup kitchen,' she added quickly, glancing at Livia. 'Because that sounds all wrong and too Victorian, you know, but somewhere to get a meal for free that was also a nice place to be. There might be places like that already, I don't know, but when I asked Livia, she didn't think so, and so...'

Ralph looked at her with some amusement. 'And you thought this would be your job?'

'I know I've only just got here and already I'm like, "I know what you all need". It must seem as if I'm being patronising, but that isn't my intention. I just...' Eden let out a sigh. 'Cards on the table, I've not been a nice person over the past few years, and I want to be a nice person. I want to be better, and I think making life better for others is the way to go. It might sound self-ish. I suppose it does, but the way I see it, even if helping others is for selfish reasons, it's still helping them.'

'Hmmm.' Ralph was silent as he reached for his glass, but his eyes didn't leave Eden. She could see the cogs turning. 'What do you propose?' he asked finally.

'I thought...' She looked at Livia, who gave her an encouraging smile. 'We were talking about it earlier, and we were thinking like a community café type of thing.'

'And how would it work?' Ralph asked.

'I'm not sure yet. That's why I wanted to ask you about it. You run a restaurant here, so you must know all about that kind of thing. I don't expect you to tell me how to do everything, but if I can get some idea of the basics, where to start, that would be a great help.'

He nodded slowly. 'You know this could be a big commitment. Unless it's just a one-off event you're thinking about?'

'No, I want it to be there all the time, whenever anyone needs it, otherwise there's hardly any point.'

'But you're not going to be here past the end of the year,' he reminded her.

'I know, and I've been thinking about that.'

'And?'

Eden shrugged. The details of this were unclear to her too, but perhaps if this thing worked as she hoped it would, perhaps if it became the thing to give her life meaning and purpose in a way it had never truly had, it might become a reason to stay in

Sea Glass Bay for good. It wasn't like anyone back in London was going to miss her, but here she could be a new person, untainted by who she'd been before, and people might like her without judging her for bad things she'd once done or because she wore the right clothes or went to the right places with the right people.

'I think it depends on what happens over the next few months,' she said. 'This thing might amount to nothing, and I don't know what I'd do then, but if it was a success and people wanted to come, then maybe I'd want to stay and keep running it.'

'And you've got the funds to do that?'

'I have some savings. I know they won't last forever, but I had a well-paid job in London and I have a decent amount. I suppose I'd have to earn more at some point, but I'll work that out.'

'More than I pay you?' he asked with that look of faint amusement again.

Eden flushed. 'Oh, that didn't come out right. I wasn't making out like your job here is... I enjoyed my first shift, and I don't think it's beneath me, if that's what you're getting at.'

'I was teasing you. Sorry,' he said. 'But I couldn't resist. I knew about all that when I took you on, and I wouldn't have given you the job if it bothered me. I'm throwing practical obstacles in your way for your benefit, so you can see what you face and what you might need to do to make this thing work. And I'm trying to make you see clearly just what it is you might be getting into, because I'm not sure you understand.'

'I suppose it looks that way,' Eden admitted. 'Perhaps I don't. I haven't thought about everything, and even when I feel like I have, I'm sure more stuff will crop up. I only know that I want to do some good, and I think this could be it. If I try and I fail, isn't it better that I've tried? If we only manage a few weeks, isn't that better than nothing?'

'It depends on what we get a few weeks of. There's no point in a few weeks of a scheme that proves to be no use to man nor beast, is there?'

'No, you're right. So what do you think? What would you do if you were starting something like this?'

'Start at the beginning. What are your resources? What's your budget? Your time constraints? Your support network? What can you realistically achieve when you take all those things into account? Is that anything like what you want to achieve and, if not, do you still want to go ahead and do it?'

'Yes,' Eden said.

'Yes what?'

'I still want to do it.'

'So you've already got the answer to all those questions?'

'No, but it won't matter. I want to do it anyway.'

Ralph raised his eyebrows. Eden could guess what he was thinking. Here was a silly young woman who knew nothing about anything, living in cloud cuckoo land. He might well be right, but that didn't mean she was going to back down. Something deep inside was telling her she needed this. She couldn't understand it and couldn't explain to anyone else why it mattered so much, but the more she dreamed it, the more it did.

'I just need practical advice,' she said. 'And maybe some help to get started. I'm not so stubborn that I don't realise I won't be able to do everything alone.'

'OK...' he said slowly. 'How many days a week are you planning on doing this?'

'Every day?'

'So when will your life fit into that?'

'I don't have much of a social life and—'

'Maybe not, but you have to rest; you're not superhuman. Even I don't work seven days a week, and I'm making money from it. Are you also thinking you can be open eight hours or more for every one of those seven days a week?'

'I hadn't thought that far ahead, but I suppose I ought to be there around the same sorts of hours as other cafés are open.'

Ralph shook his head. 'It'll never work. You'll crash within weeks and you won't keep it up. You've got to pace yourself from the start, be realistic about your energy levels. Especially if you're in it for the long haul like you say you want to be.

'Make it an event – you can't be open all day. And if the goal is to bring people together, then make it a couple of hours at lunchtime and a couple in the evening. One or two sittings. You'll have to subsidise, unless you can foot all the costs yourself for all that food for months on end. How many are you expecting?'

Eden looked blank. 'I haven't a clue. I don't know how many people would want to come.'

'Then how do you know you can manage the costs, or that your venue will be big enough?'

'I suppose when we're full we're full.'

'So you'd be using a booking system. And you run the risk of having to turn people away – people who might be in need. Is that what you want?'

'Not at all.'

'I might be able to gauge interest for you. I could probably have a word with my suppliers as well, see if they could supply you at cost or close to it. You might have to charge a little, but you could set the cost so there's just enough profit to cover over-heads. That way you have a fighting chance of being able to keep it going – as long as you're not looking to make a wage.'

'I wanted to make it free. What if some people can't afford to pay?'

Ralph was thoughtful for a moment. 'All right,' he said after a pause. 'Make it "pay what you can afford". An honesty box or something. They can put donations in on the way out.'

Livia nodded. 'I suppose we could try to get donations from the businesses around here too – that might help.'

'It couldn't hurt to ask, but they'd want to know it's a genuine thing, so I think you have to run it for a week or so first and prove that there's a point to it,' Ralph said.

'I could do that,' Eden said.

Ralph regarded her steadily from beneath bushy eyebrows. 'All by yourself?'

'I realise that's a big ask, but...'

Eden glanced at Livia. Her friend had already made her position clear – she didn't have time for this project, and she probably didn't have the inclination even if she did. But Eden didn't know anyone else, and Ralph had a point – she'd understood very early on that she wasn't going to be able to do it alone.

'I suppose I could try to help,' Livia said.

'It's OK – I get that you won't have time.'

Livia shrugged. 'The parlour shuts around five on weekdays. I'd have the kids – unless Mum could do it – but even then I suppose they could come with me. They might enjoy pitching in.'

'You'll still need more than that,' Ralph said. 'Who's going to do all the cooking, for a start? Then there's cleaning and serving.'

'I don't know.'

Livia sat up in her chair with a bright look. 'What about the diners? Make it a sort of cooperative? If they come and help, they can have their meal for free? If not, they pay what they can afford. I bet loads of people round here would enjoy that – it would be the social angle you were looking for. And, Ralph... I don't know, but...' Livia gave him a coy look that was almost comical. Eden couldn't help but think it was a look she'd given him many times before and one that probably got her what she wanted. 'Maybe your chefs wouldn't mind doing a bit extra from time to time. Like here in your kitchen. Dishes that could be prepared in advance?'

Ralph looked doubtful, but he didn't reject the idea. 'You'd want to keep your menu simple and cheap,' he said. 'Good filling meals with easy-to-get ingredients, dishes that are difficult to cook badly, especially if you're involving people where you don't know what kitchen skills they have. Some people think they can cook and they're very wrong about that. Big pots of goo – that's what you want.'

Eden couldn't help but laugh. 'Big pots of goo – got it. Like stew and curry and stuff?'

Ralph nodded. 'Don't complicate things. If you can cook it in the one pan and you don't need to be a trained chef to make it, then you're on to a winner.'

'I was actually wondering about things that come ready made to put in the oven too. Like breaded chicken and chips and that sort of thing.'

'I suppose you could, but then you run the risk of having too much going on. How many things are you planning on having on your menu?'

'How many do you think I should have?'

'I'd keep that simple too – in the beginning, at least. No more than three options, and I'd say make one of them vegan. When you know where you are with reliable volunteers and cashflow, you might be able to branch out. But even then I wouldn't go mad. The main aim is not cordon bleu, right? The important thing is to bring people together and feed them a good hearty meal, so there's no need to get too fussy.'

Eden nodded. 'I should have come to you straight away – you seem to have it all worked out.'

'To be perfectly honest, it's an idea that's crossed my mind more than once, but I've always been too busy to do much about it. I had thought of having a few one-off events here at the pub in the same vein. But the pub's always too busy, and my biggest problem has been finding a time to do it when I wouldn't be losing a lot of money. It's all very well being community-minded, but if you go bankrupt in the process, you're in no position to help anyone, are you?'

'So I suppose there's no way we can do it here in the dining room then?'

'No.'

'I thought that, but...'

'It was worth asking anyway.' He smiled. 'If you don't ask, you don't get. Well, I'm sorry to disappoint you, but much as I'd like to say yes, it's simply not an option.'

'So she asked, and she still didn't get,' Livia put in.

Ralph chuckled. 'Livia, you know I would if I could, but even your big brown eyes aren't going to get round me this time. It's not practical. From what I've seen of it, your scout hut might be a good place to start. I should warn you, though, I've heard the land might be going up for sale. If that happens, I don't know what you'll do.'

'It might be up for sale for ages,' Eden said, dipping into her property knowledge. 'Lots of plots are, especially when they're a bit off the beaten track. It's not like we're in a prime bit of London or anything.'

'True, but I don't know what it being up for sale means for the scout hut either. You might not be able to use it.'

'Won't it stay in use until the land is sold?' Livia asked. 'Where are the scouts going to meet?'

Ralph rubbed at his beard. 'That's something you'll have to ask them if you decide the hut's your place. I think it's got everything you need, so if you can get it, it's as good as anywhere, but...'

'There's only one way to find out, I suppose,' Eden said. And even though she was still doubtful, she was beginning to form a plan, and that had to be a little bit exciting.

CHAPTER NINE

Eden and Livia spent the rest of the shift discussing her plan in between customers. By the end of it, Eden was sure Livia was more excited than she was. Every suggestion came with the caveat that she wouldn't be able to spare much time but then became an enthusiastic proposal that always involved quite a lot of this time she didn't have. And when the same people came in for their leftovers as they had during Eden's first shift, Livia went with them to the kitchens, questioning them as they walked, and came back to Eden with their suggestions too – and the news that every one of them was thrilled at the idea of the café. They almost all promised to donate what time they had to helping out, even young Liam, which surprised Eden most of all. Growing up, all the teenage boys she'd known wouldn't have been seen dead somewhere like that, let alone volunteer their services.

The following morning, she phoned the number she'd taken from the sign outside the scout hut to be told that she could only have it three days a week because there were meetings on the other days, and the land was being put up for sale and they didn't yet know what that would mean for the building.

However, they'd promised that while they could help, they would, and Eden decided to take the offer. Three days a week wasn't what she'd wanted, but it was a start, and she couldn't help but recall Ralph's warning that she ought to pace herself. With that in mind, perhaps three days a week was for the best. The man she'd spoken to told her she could go down there at the end of the next scout meeting to have a look around and see about access, but that wasn't for another couple of days. Until then, she'd spend her time trying to put a plan together.

Buzzing with thoughts of the next step, she began a text to Livia but then paused halfway through. There was too much to say and she wanted opinions. Livia would be busy working at her mum's ice-cream parlour and so wouldn't have time for back-and-forth texts. No, the best thing would be to go down at lunchtime and see if she could spare half an hour to chat again. Eden was aware she ran the risk that Livia might start to groan every time she caught sight of her sitting on the parlour chairs waiting, but she hoped that wouldn't be for a while yet. She was also aware that Livia had many other claims on her time, but she was fast beginning to see her as a valuable ally.

'Hello! You've just missed Livia. Hang on for me a tick, though.'

Livia's mum, Julia, gave Eden a warm smile. Eden had always felt Julia was a bit suspicious of her up until now. There hadn't been any concrete evidence of this, only a vague feeling, but today she seemed more welcoming than she had since Eden's arrival in the bay. Perhaps Livia had told her all about Eden's plans – it seemed a fair assumption – and perhaps Julia approved.

For once, the queue was small and it only took Julia ten minutes to clear it so she could get back to Eden.

'Your sewing is ready,' she said as she slurped at a cup of tea she'd picked up from a shelf at the back of the kiosk. 'I could bring it down here for you to collect or give it to Livia when you're next on shift at the pub together – whatever suits you.'

'Wow, that was quick.'

'I always think it's better to get things out of the way as soon as you can – you never know what other little jobs are going to crop up. It doesn't do to be behind before you've even begun.'

'My mum used to say that to me all the time, especially where homework was concerned. I never listened to her...'

Eden tried not to let a sudden sadness at the thought of her mum take over, but perhaps Julia saw it anyway.

'She used to say that? Is she...?'

'She died,' Eden said. 'A month ago.'

'Oh, my love, I'm so sorry to hear that. She can't have been very old.'

Eden shook her head. 'Too young.'

'All our mothers are far too young to be taken from us when they go, whatever age that is. We're never ready. The trick is to hold on to the happy memories. It's a cliché, I know, but it's really all we can do. May I ask... was it expected? Was she ill?'

'No, it was sudden. She had a heart attack. They said afterwards she'd always had a heart defect, but nobody knew about it, not even her. I feel... I wish I'd known, because then...' Eden shook her head. 'I'm sorry... listen to me. I know you lost your husband this year too and I'm going on about my mum.'

'That's all right, my love. Your loss is as hard to you as mine is to me; it's only natural.'

'But I'm sorry for yours.'

'Thank you.'

Julia glanced at the counter to see a family arrive. 'Sorry, my love, I'd better get back; I can see a queue starting. No rest for the wicked, as they say. If you're looking for Livia, she's popped over to the charity shop on the high street. She shouldn't be long.'

Eden nodded and watched as Julia went back to work. And

then she decided to walk along to the high street to see if she might meet Livia coming back.

By the time Eden had got to the shop, she hadn't met Livia coming the other way as she'd planned. She peered through the window and noticed her going through a rack of clothes, a bundle already in her arms. After a pause, where she was uncertain whether to go in or not, she pushed open the door and made her way over.

'Oh, hi.' Livia smiled. 'Didn't expect to see you here. After a few bargains?'

'No, I came to see...' Eden glanced at the clothes in Livia's arms. 'A bit small for you, aren't they?'

Livia laughed lightly. 'They're for Nancy and Levi. I can't tell you how fast they grow out of stuff. These things are hardly worn, a couple of quid each. They'll do us for the next few months... at least, I hope so. Levi especially seems to have a growth spurt every week.'

Eden let her gaze rove the shop. If she said out loud what she was thinking, she was certain Livia would either laugh or be horrified, but Eden had never before set foot in a charity shop. She'd imagined them to be messy places full of other people's old rubbish and was surprised to see that this one was far from the image she'd always held. There were things she would not have wanted to buy, but there were things that – like Livia had just said – looked brand new. It was clean, fresh smelling and well organised. Her eye was caught by a vase over in the home section. Livia must have noticed her looking.

'You should have a nosy while you're here.'

'Oh, I don't really...' Eden turned back to her. 'I only came to find you to tell you that the scout hut said we could have three days a week. I thought... well, I was hoping you might help me make some proper plans for the opening. Maybe put me in touch with the people who said they'd help. If you've got time, that is.'

'I've got to get back to work after I'm done here. Maybe later? You could come up to the house. Mum's done your cushions anyway so you could collect them at the same time.'

'She said so... I saw her a minute ago when I went to the parlour to look for you. I'll walk back with you anyway, if that's all right.'

'If you like. I'm almost done here.' She pulled out a T-shirt with a race car on the front and showed it to Eden. 'What do you think? Cute?'

'Yes,' Eden said, not entirely sure whether it was cute or not. 'For Levi?'

'It might still be a bit big, but that's not a bad thing – we'll get longer out of it. He won't care if it fits or not; they both love new stuff. They'll go nuts when I take this lot home later – anyone would think it was London fashion week in our house the way they dive into the bag.'

'I bet they love that you bought it for them.'

'Maybe. I love that they get excited, so I'm probably just as bad as them.'

'You're brilliant with them. I've only seen you with them the once, but I can tell they adore you.'

Livia smiled as she put the T-shirt with the other clothes on her arm. 'If that's true, then I'm glad. Mum and me do our best, but we're not...' She paused, the smile fading from her lips. 'Anyway, I'll get this lot paid for and then I'll be ready to go. Are you sure you don't want to have a quick look before we leave? I can wait.'

'It's all right – I've got all day to do this sort of thing and you haven't. I can come back if I want to.'

'Rub it in, why don't you?' Livia said, the smile back on her face.

The darkness had been banished so completely that it seemed quite miraculous to Eden, as if it had never been there. But she was beginning to see that Livia had a light in her soul, a glow that seemed to draw everyone to it. It was obvious there was tragedy in her past, and Eden didn't know the full extent of it yet, but it didn't seem to drag Livia down a bit. While she might be sad, she didn't heap it on others, and she tried to be happy and strong for everyone around her. Eden wished she could be a bit more like that, but she found it harder not to dwell. Then again, perhaps the tragedies in Livia's past didn't come with quite so much guilt attached. Perhaps the awful things that had happened to her weren't her fault. It was harder to be optimistic when you were forced to face the fact that being a better person could have prevented it all in the first place.

'Give me a minute then...'

Eden watched Livia go to the till, chatting easily with the assistant as she paid for her bundle. The notion of belonging in such an obvious way was one that felt alien to Eden. It had always done so, even in London, even in the place where she'd grown up and sometimes even with the family who had doted on her.

There was a sudden pull, a longing to hear a familiar voice, and for a moment, she considered returning Caitlin's calls, if only just to have one more taste of her old life, to feel a part of something, however fine that thread of belonging had been.

But as she painted on a smile for Livia's return, she dismissed the idea. It wouldn't make her feel better. It would probably make her feel worse.

As they left the shop, Livia opened her bag and peered inside. 'I'm chuffed with all this. I can't wait to get the kids from school and let them go through it.'

'I didn't realise you had to pick them up from school; I thought you had to work at the parlour until five.'

'We're open until five, but someone has to do the school run before then. Mum and me take it in turns. It's my turn today. If you're at a loose end, you could come with me. We'll only be heading back to work after – the kids stay with us for the last hour until we close – but you're more than welcome if you fancy the walk.'

'I would, if you didn't mind. What time would that be?'

'Oh, not for a couple of hours yet.'

'Right...' Eden was thoughtful as they walked slowly back to the seafront, the sun warming her face. All around them were people in bright clothes, eating chips from trays or ice creams or fudge from the shop just along from Livia's, or clanking down to the beach with buckets and spades and windbreaks and deckchairs and all sorts of other holiday paraphernalia.

It was funny, seeing Sea Glass Bay from the other side. She'd always been one of those holidaymakers, only there during the bright, warm months where life was jolly and carefree and money was to be spent and not worried about. But although to all intents and purposes she was on a very long holiday, she felt more of a resident here than she ever had before. She was having to think about money – not in the way Livia and her mum and many others did, but she couldn't just splurge for a week and put off worrying about it until she got home. She had to budget and consider how to make the money last, and she had chores to do and a job to go to.

And then there would be the kitchen – when she eventually got it set up. The responsibility of that would add another weight of worry. She understood that people would come to rely on it or – at the very least, she hoped – look forward to it enough to miss it when it went. But then, it would go, eventually. Eden would leave, and unless someone else wanted to take it on, then it would leave with her. Would anyone be up for it? Was it fair to expect anyone else to take it on? And if it wasn't, then what did that mean for Eden? Was it her responsibility to stay and see it through? She tried to picture herself living in Sea Glass Bay for good, but she couldn't imagine what that might look like.

'Are you all right?' Livia asked, breaking into her thoughts.

'Oh yes. Just thinking.'

'About your kitchen project?'

'Yes. It's all I've thought of the last couple of days.'

'I suppose there's a lot to consider. I don't suppose... Don't take this the wrong way, but it does seem like a very sudden decision. You've only just arrived in the bay, and you're not planning to stay all that long. Do you think this thing is a good idea? It's a lovely idea, of course, and it would do a lot of good around here, but it's a tall order for someone at the best of times, and you...'

Her sentence tailed off.

'I what?'

Livia shook her head. 'I don't know what's going on with you, but I can tell there's something. You don't have to share it with me, but if you wanted to, I wouldn't judge. At least, I don't think I would. Was it a bad break-up or something? You lost your job in London?'

Eden wondered how much to say. She didn't even know where to start.

'Ignore me,' Livia said into the brief pause. 'I'm being far too nosy.'

'You're not. There's just...' Eden hesitated. She wanted to tell Livia something, but she was afraid. She had no doubt that Livia was sincere and wasn't looking to judge her, but she couldn't take the risk. She didn't think she could bear Livia's judgement, because she was sure it wouldn't be good. 'There's nothing much to tell,' she finished lamely. 'I felt like I needed some time out of the rat race, and here I am. A first world problem, I suppose.'

'If you can do it, do it. I don't blame you for that – if I had the money and nothing to tie me down, I'd probably want to do the same. Travel or something, you know?'

'But you have Nancy and Levi? Is that what stops you?'

'Yes. Mum too. They all need me. It's not that big a deal,

you know; I don't feel like I'm missing out that I can't go off. There are far worse places to be stuck than Sea Glass Bay. In fact, I know I'm lucky to live here.'

'How come… if you don't mind me asking, how come you have Nancy and Levi? What happened to their mum?'

'She died.'

'How did it happen? Or is it too painful to talk about?'

'It's fine – I can talk about it. She had a rare type of cancer. It was aggressive and over quicker than you would ever have thought possible. Some days I still can't believe she's gone, even though it's been four years.'

'She's your only sister?'

Livia nodded. 'Yes.'

'Were you close?'

'God, yes, like best friends. Not even two years between us – she was the oldest. Before she died, she made me promise I'd take on the twins. As if she needed to ask – I would always have done that.'

'What about their dad?'

'Oh, he's never been interested, not since the twins were born. We did get in touch to see if he might feel differently with Zoe's death, but all he did was visit once or twice. He sends a Christmas card when he remembers, but that's about it. Maybe one day when they're older they'll try to build some kind of relationship with him – that'll be up to them, I suppose.'

'Wow, that's harsh, considering they lost their mum.'

'Maybe, but there was no way we would have given him custody without a fight, even if he'd wanted it. Luckily he didn't, and I was allowed to adopt them.'

Eden's eyes widened. 'So they're yours?'

'Legally, yes. Mum wasn't sure, but it seemed like the best thing to me, so we went ahead.'

'But they don't call you mum.'

Livia shook her head. 'Why would they? They had a beautiful mum and they lost her. I don't want to take her place; I just wanted to be their legal parent so there'd be no question over who would take care of them, make decisions about what's best for them. Until they're eighteen, it's down to me.'

'That's kind of amazing.'

'Is it?'

'God yes! What are you, like twenty-five, twenty-six?'

'Twenty-seven.'

'And you've been looking after them for the last four years? Even adopting them? I don't know anyone back in London who'd have done something so... well, not at that age. I don't think I could have even looked after myself at that age, let alone two children.'

'I didn't see it that way. There was never any question – I was always going to care for them. Those two are everything to me, just like they would be if they were mine. And they are mine now. They don't call me mum, but they're my children.'

'You might not think it's anything to be proud of, but I think it's amazing. They're lucky to have you.'

'They'd have been luckier to have their mum, but thank you.'

The time had passed so quickly that Eden didn't realise they'd already reached the ice-cream parlour.

'I'd better get back to work,' Livia said. 'I've been longer than I meant to be. So don't forget, if you want to walk up to school with me, be back here in' – she looked at the clock on her phone – 'about an hour and a half. No pressure, of course.'

'That sounds nice. I'd like to see Nancy and Levi.'

'OK, so I'll see you then.'

Eden grasped the hand of each child tightly, aware with every fibre of her being of just what she was being trusted with and determined to repay that trust. Livia had already told her that

Nancy and Levi were everything to her, but after picking them up from school, she'd allowed Eden to take them off for an hour. The children had been beyond excited by this new and unexpected turn of events, which had made Eden feel happy and wanted.

Nancy was chattier than Levi, fascinated by everything but mostly by the novelty of their situation and with Eden herself. Her questions were endless, and barely had Eden given an answer than there was a fresh one to contemplate.

Have you got a little girl? Where do you live? What's in that bag? Who's your best friend? Do you have a dog? Do you like ice cream? What's your favourite sweet? Do you eat burgers? Are you Livia's friend? Do you work at the Dolphin?

Levi was quieter, humming to himself and content to let his sister do the talking, but from time to time he'd chime in with something of his own: *Can you swim? Do you have a car? Who's your favourite – Batman or Spider-Man? Have you ever seen an alien?*

If she'd been less stressed, Eden would have found their interrogation funny. If they were always like this, then it was no wonder Livia loved spending time with them. They were both bright and lively and lovely company, but then, knowing Livia as Eden was beginning to, that was hardly surprising. It made Eden wonder what Livia's sister – their mum – had been like. How much influence had she had on the children in the short time she'd been with them, and how much of who they were now was down to Livia and Julia?

As soon as they arrived at the beach and stepped onto the sand, both children bent to kick off their shoes and socks, dumping them on a nearby rock.

'Can we paddle?' Nancy asked.

'I suppose so,' Eden said, taking off her own shoes. But when she looked up, both children were watching her. 'It's all right – go ahead.'

'You have to come with us. We can't go to the water without you – Livia said so.'

'Livia says we have to stay with you all the time because you don't know your way around,' Levi said with such sober maturity that it was all Eden could do not to laugh.

'I suppose I might get lost,' she replied, playing along. Livia had probably framed it that way so they didn't wander off from her, not the other way around, but Eden had to admit it was an inspired bit of parenting. 'It's probably for the best. Come on then – let's go and get our feet wet.'

'I can run fastest!' Levi cried before haring off in the direction of the sea.

Nancy took off after him, leaving Eden – who considered herself fit – to bring up the rear. With a huge splash, Levi and Nancy landed in the surf and began to leap about, spraying each other with water, scooping it with hands and kicking it up with feet and laughing the whole while as if nothing could ever be as funny again. Eden joined in, indulging her inner child and marvelling at how something so silly and simple could be so freeing. It wouldn't last, but for this moment, it was a wonderful thing. If these children could still love life after all they'd been through, then why couldn't Eden?

While she caught her breath for a moment, she decided to take a photo of them playing and send it to Livia. There was an immediate reply.

Glad they're keeping you entertained!

Eden grinned as she stuffed the phone back into her bag and covered the bag with her jacket. This bit of the beach wasn't so busy, and she wasn't worried about theft, but it didn't hurt to be a little bit cautious. Then she joined the twins again, who were still running about in the waves.

Levi barrelled towards her and slapped a hand on her arm. 'You're it!'

'Aww!' Eden laughed. 'Nobody told me we were playing tag!'

She lunged forward and got him back, and then tore off down the beach, glancing behind to see them hot on her heels. As she turned back, she lost her balance, and before she knew what was happening, she was face down on the sand, swallowed by an incoming wave and soaked to the skin.

'Eden!' Nancy yelled, and Eden looked up to see a look of alarm on the little girl's face.

'I'm all right,' she said, hauling herself up and starting to laugh. 'That was rubbish, wasn't it? Serves me right for running too fast.'

There was no such sympathy from Levi, who coolly tapped Eden on the arm, announced that she was 'it' once again and took off in the direction he'd just come from.

'It's time out!' Nancy shouted after him. 'Eden fell over!'

'See,' Eden said with a wicked look. 'That's very kind of you, but...' She got to her feet, touched Nancy on the head and started to run. 'If you snooze, you lose! You're it!'

Nancy squealed, at first with indignation, but then she started to giggle. She chased Eden for a way, but then seeing Levi had stopped running and was suddenly fascinated by something he'd found on the sand, she turned her attention to him, sneaking over. He looked up but too late – Nancy tagged him and tore away.

'Nice one, Nancy!' Eden shouted. 'That's how it's done, girl!'

She didn't have long to congratulate Nancy, however, because Levi wasted no time coming for her, and he was shockingly fast. Eden panted as she dodged out of his way, forced to stop for a moment as she was laughing so hard. And as she glanced across the beach, she noticed them being watched. At least, he seemed to be watching, though he walked off as soon as she took notice of him, back towards a car parked in a bay over-looking the beach. Had he been laughing? At this distance, Eden could have been mistaken, but it certainly looked that way. She supposed it might have looked funny, her getting trounced by Nancy and Levi. What she could see was that he was dark-haired and broad shouldered, a dressed-down sort of formality to his outfit, but not suitable for where they were at all... He looked like someone she'd seen on the beach the day she'd arrived in the bay. She'd felt a familiarity then, and she felt it again now, and he was closer this time so that she could almost make out his face. But surely it couldn't be...?

Levi tagged her while she wasn't looking, and she jumped, all thoughts of the man instantly forgotten.

'Right!' she said, putting on a mean face. 'That's it! I'm going to get you good and proper!'

The game came to a natural end in the way all unscripted children's games do, where nobody had really announced it was over but everyone just moved on to something new. They went from splashing and chasing each other to poking about in rock pools and then searching the sand for shells and the sea glass that was often so abundant it had given the cove its name. Eden expressed surprise at how many pieces they did find, but when the children questioned her on why, she couldn't answer. She found that happened a lot. As many of their questions were as difficult to answer as there were easy ones. Their curiosity was never-ending and seemed to have no rules. Discussions covered just about everything, from school dinners to spaceships. It was entertaining to Eden but also a bit bewildering. As fun as it was, having small children around was exhausting. How did Livia do this and hold down two jobs?

Livia herself appeared an hour later, just as the three had sat on the sand to examine all the bits they'd collected.

'There you are,' she said, smiling broadly as she marched across the sand. 'Looks like you've been having fun,' she added, looking at the ropes of damp hair that Eden usually wore smoothed and glossy. 'Have you been swimming?'

'Not intentionally,' Eden said.

'She fell in,' Nancy cut in, and Livia's grin spread.

'Did she? I bet you laughed your heads off at that.'

'I didn't,' Nancy said solemnly.

'Well.' Livia glanced from one twin to the other. 'Time for tea. Grandma's making sausages and mash.'

'Yes!' Levi pumped the air with his fist. 'I love sausage and mash!'

'I know you do,' Livia said. 'You'd eat it every day if we let you.' She looked at Eden. 'Mum says you're welcome to join us.'

'Oh I wouldn't want to—' Eden began, but Livia stopped her.

'I think she'd really like to get to know you a bit more. And she wants to hear about your plans for the community café. We don't stand on ceremony around here – if she's inviting you to tea, she's not just being polite; she actually wants to feed you. Unless you don't like sausages, of course, but I'm sure we could find—'

It was Eden's turn to interrupt. 'I'd love to! No problem with sausages.'

'Good,' Livia said. She handed each child the socks and shoes she'd picked up from the rocks on the way over. 'Get these on and let's get marching. We don't want to keep Grandma waiting, or she might give up and eat all the sausages herself.'

Nancy giggled uncontrollably as she pulled her socks on, while Levi stuck his tongue out in concentration. But the more he concentrated, the more twisted his socks became until Livia bent down to lend a hand. As she did, she tickled his toes, and he burst out laughing. Eden smiled as she watched, filled with a warmth she'd never thought she would feel again.

Unlike Four Winds Cottage, there was no dramatic clifftop location or brooding isolation with Livia's house. There wasn't even an evocative name – it was simply number three Sea Glass Parade, but what it lacked in drama, it more than made up for in welcoming cosiness. It stood on a row of terraced cottages with low-framed, pastel-painted front doors and higgledy walls and roofs. Each house opened directly onto the pavement, though Eden would see as she took a seat in the warm kitchen, the air fragranced with cooking, a larger than expected garden at the back to make up for it. There was a circle of lawn bordered by lush shrubs and summer blooms, beyond that a bird table and a vegetable patch, with insect hotels nailed to the back wall and a bright wooden Wendy house in a shaded corner.

Livia's mum, Julia, was busy at the stove. She turned to Eden with a broad smile. 'Did you enjoy the beach? The twins weren't too much for you, were they?'

'Oh no, we had fun, didn't we?' Eden turned to the children, who nodded. Livia ushered them to the sink to stand on a chair she'd just placed so they could reach to wash their hands.

'Can you take us again tomorrow?' Nancy asked as she splashed water over not just her hands but a good deal of the surrounding surfaces.

'You can't be asking Eden every day,' Livia said with a laugh.

'I don't mind.' Eden moved her elbows from the table to let Julia set a place for her. She looked up. 'Can I help? I could set the table.'

'No need. Won't take me a tick, and everything else is done.

Sausages are just staying warm in the oven, and gravy's on the stove. Do you want a drink? I don't have wine or anything in, I'm afraid.'

'I'll drink anything,' Eden said. 'A glass of water is just fine. Thank you.'

'I'm sure we can do better than water,' Julia said. She looked at Levi, who was drying his hands. 'Could you run and fetch a bottle of Grandma's lemonade from the outhouse?'

Levi duly went through a door at the side of the kitchen and returned a few seconds later with an unlabelled bottle.

'You're honoured if Mum's opening the home-made stuff for you,' Livia said, smiling at Eden as she moved the chair from the sink to wash her own hands. 'I think that's the last bottle as well.'

Julia waved a vague hand as she opened the oven. 'I can make more easily enough.'

Levi looked up at Livia. 'Can I pour it out?'

'If you're careful,' Livia said. 'Don't want to spill any of Grandma's special drink, do we?'

'I won't.'

Eden watched as Livia opened it and steadied each glass for him. The lemonade trickled slowly into each one as he held it with the utmost concentration, barely letting it flow from the bottle at all.

'That's it, carefully does it,' Livia said. 'Brilliant job.'

'Thank you,' Eden said. She lifted the glass to her lips and took a sip. It was tart, and at first, it was all she could do not to purse her lips. But a hit of sweetness followed and a rush of citrus that made her mouth water. 'That's amazing! You should bottle that up and sell it!'

'I keep telling her that,' Livia said. 'It would go down a storm at the ice-cream parlour.'

'I don't know about that,' Julia said, clearly delighted with the praise but trying not to show it. 'I think people might have more sophisticated palates than that these days. It's all slushies and energy drinks people want. Besides, I don't have the time to make gallons of the stuff for the parlour – it's far easier to buy it in to sell there.'

'I think once people tasted this, you could stop selling ice creams and make a mint from lemonade,' Eden said. 'It's that good.'

'Well, thank you for saying so.' Julia took the lid from a crock she'd just taken out of the oven.

'Have you made pudding?' Nancy asked.

Julia laughed lightly. 'We haven't had a mouthful of our tea yet and you've already moved on. You know the rules – no pudding until we've made a dent in this.'

'But did you make pudding?' Nancy asked.

'I might have done.'

'Is it chocolate cake?'

'It might be.'

'With the bit in the middle...? And the custard?'

'If you're lucky and you've been a good girl.'

'I have!' Nancy beamed at Eden. 'Haven't I?'

'Brilliant,' Eden replied, that strange but not unwelcome warmth spreading through her again. For a fleeting moment, sitting here with this remarkable little family, she felt a part of something wonderful.

Julia put a bowl of mashed potatoes and another with mixed vegetables onto the table while Livia lined up two sausages onto each person's plate.

'So, Eden, Livia tells me you're keeping Four Winds for the next six months,' Julia said as she put a jug of gravy down. 'It used to be in our family, you know.'

'Yes, Livia did mention it,' Eden said. 'Your uncle?'

'My husband's uncle. It was meant to come to us when he passed, but... well, things changed, as they often do.'

'Oh...' Eden frowned. 'You were supposed to inherit?'

'Livia's father was, and he would have passed it straight down. As I said, things changed. I'd hoped it would be somewhere for Livia to have as her own one day—'

'Mum,' Livia cut in. 'Don't bring all that up. It's gone, and that's that.' She shot a look of apology at Eden.

Despite it, Eden suddenly felt guilty that she was currently enjoying the house that was meant to be Livia's. She knew it wasn't her doing, but it didn't make her feel any better. What was worse was that she didn't even need the house – for now, of course, but not beyond that – whereas Livia clearly did.

'I didn't know that,' she said, wanting to ask how things had changed in such a way but aware that Livia wanted to change the subject.

'And you're keeping it until the end of the year?' Julia asked.

Eden nodded. 'That was the original plan.'

'Oh? So you might not?'

'I don't know. I think it depends... That's what I'm doing at the moment, but I suppose it depends on how things go.'

'Like your community café idea?'

Eden was thinking of that, but she was also thinking of what else might change. There were things back home, things in her recent past that she had still to face fully. Whether she had the strength was another story, but she was beginning to realise that those things weren't going to go away simply because she was here ignoring them. Caitlin's calls and messages hadn't stopped, for one thing. If Eden knew one thing about her sister, it was that she'd always want the last word; being unable to contact Eden to have it would be driving her to distraction.

'That's all a bit unknown at this stage.' Eden helped herself to vegetables. 'I'm still trying to get my head around it.'

'Hmm...' Julia was silent for a moment, allowing Livia to jump in.

'But it's a brilliant idea, isn't it, Mum? You were saying so earlier.'

'Yes. I think it's sad that someone local hasn't done it, really – someone who knows the community and their needs. I'm not saying you shouldn't be doing it, Eden,' she added quickly.

'You're probably right, though,' said Eden. 'I wonder if people will think I'm interfering where I'm not wanted because I'm an outsider.'

'We don't have that daft village mentality round here,' Livia said.

'Younger ones don't,' Julia put in. 'I wouldn't say that about everyone.'

'I suppose all we can do is get it up and running and see who comes,' Eden said. 'If people don't want to, then that's that. At least I'll have tried.'

'I think people will come,' Livia said.

Julia poured some gravy over her food. 'So you're here from London?'

Eden nodded. 'Yes.'

'Is that home for you?'

'Just outside. Essex, actually, but, you know, it was only a Tube ride away, so I spent a lot of time there growing up.'

'Essex? Did you like it there?'

'I suppose so. You take where you live for granted, don't you? I'm not sure I ever thought about it that much. I was used to it; it was home.'

'So you don't live there anymore? Where will you go back to when you give up Four Winds?'

'I was in London proper for a while. I don't know... I gave up my flat, so I don't actually have a place to go back to.'

'But you could go to your father's house if you needed to? I know Livia would always have a home here if she—'

'Mum...' Livia interrupted with an uneasy look Eden's way. 'I'm sure Eden doesn't want to think about all that. We were going to talk about the community café, weren't we?'

'I was only making conversation. Eden doesn't mind me asking, I'm sure.'

Livia turned to Eden, who had the feeling her friend was trying to change the subject. If so, it was a bit clumsy, but Eden appreciated the effort. 'Don't let us forget to give you your sewing before you go tonight. Mum's done a lovely job, and your fabric is so pretty.'

'Nice to work with too,' Julia said. 'You chose a good quality one.'

'I only went with the lady's recommendation.' Eden dug her fork into a mound of mashed potato. 'I don't know the first thing about fabric or sewing.'

'My mum taught me to sew,' Julia said. 'One of the first things she taught me, actually, and it's been so useful over the years, I wouldn't be able to thank her enough.'

'Is she...?' Eden hesitated.

'Oh, she's still with us,' Julia replied, anticipating the question. 'But she's not well, and we had no choice but to get her professional care. Alzheimer's – barely remembers me, and no recollection of Livia or the twins.'

'That must be devastating. I'm so sorry.'

'It's life, isn't it?' Julia said with a stoicism that convinced Eden that if she wasn't entertaining a relative stranger, she'd be sobbing now.

The more Eden learned about Livia's family, the more she marvelled at how they managed to stay so positive when they'd endured such terrible loss and sadness. Not only had they lost Livia's dad and sister, but there was Julia's mum suffering this horrible illness – the worst, Eden had often heard people say, where the loved one was gone long before they died. She'd never encountered it, and she hoped she never would. Though Eden had her own pain, the more she heard about Livia and her family, the more perspective she got. What she'd gone through was bad, but there were others going through worse, others who were entirely good and entirely blameless and who didn't deserve it at all.

'Still,' Eden said, 'doesn't seem fair when it happens to such lovely people.'

'We're not all that lovely,' Livia said with a smile that was as stoic as Julia's. 'You should hear us argue on a good day, and you'd realise we can be just as bad as anyone else.'

'Levi threw my doll in the apple tree,' Nancy said as she concentrated on cutting a sausage.

'When was this?' Eden asked.

'Last week,' Julia said. 'Goodness only knows what they were fighting about – neither of them can remember. And he must have a heck of a throwing arm on him. I said he ought to take up cricket, could be a fast bowler for England. There'd be money in that, I bet.'

'We're definitely counting on one of them making our family rich in the future,' Livia said, her smile growing into something more certain.

'I bet they'll both do amazing things in the future,' Eden said. 'With some people, you can just tell, can't you?'

Julia and Livia both looked so proud that Eden wondered which one would burst into tears first. But it was lovely to see. Had her parents ever looked like that about her? They'd doted on her, spoiled her and loved her, but had she ever made them proud? There was a feeling of deep shame at the answer, a truth she couldn't deny to herself. No, she didn't think she had.

'Right...' Julia gave Eden her full attention. 'Tell me about your community café idea.'

'There's not all that much to tell yet. There's quite a bit to work out.'

'I'm sure we could do our best to help with that.'

'I was hoping you might.'

Both Julia and Livia smiled warmly at her, and Eden sent them a smile of her own. Things were moving, and she couldn't quite believe how willing people she barely knew were to help. She was learning that Sea Glass Bay was like that. A month ago, she couldn't even imagine being here, but, so quickly she was hardly aware of it, she was beginning to feel as if she never wanted to be anywhere else.

CHAPTER TEN

Two weeks had passed since Eden's first meal with Livia's family. Since then, there had been four more, not to mention shared shifts with Livia at the Dolphin and lunchtime wanders along the beach, and all the while, assisted by Livia's input, her plans for the community café had moved at pace. She was getting used to the expressions of surprise and some suspicion of her motives from locals she met along the way, but the one thing Eden could say she'd brought with her from a career of sales was that she knew how to persuade a person to see things from her point of view.

And so the day had come for the grand opening. Not so much grand, perhaps, but opening nonetheless. Nancy and Levi and some of their schoolfriends, with grown-up assistance, had put posters around the town to publicise it. Eden, with Ralph's help, had devised a menu and a pricing system that meant she could cover the costs of any food she might have to buy – though a lot of it had been donated by Ralph and his contacts in the trade. The pricing was a cursory thing, really, and the cost of a meal was barely anything at all, and they kept the incentive that for anyone who wanted to pitch in and help, there would be free food.

Eden couldn't remember the last time she'd been this nervous. She'd woken early that morning and had trudged down a rain-soaked pathway into the village to the scout hut, where the caretaker was to meet her with a set of spare keys, with a somersaulting tummy and thoughts like wasps in a bag. There was so much to go wrong, so many ways to fail that she wondered what had ever made her think she could pull it off at all, and the level of doubt was so alien to her that she almost felt she'd turned into a different person overnight. The funny thing was, since her arrival in Sea Glass Bay, she was beginning to sense that she was, slowly and surely, turning into a different person and wasn't sure how she felt about that. She wouldn't have been so nervous about something like this before and, if she was being entirely honest, she wasn't sure she'd have cared this much about whether she succeeded or not. There was nothing material in it for her, so why did it matter so desperately?

Despite the plan to cover her overheads with small donations from diners, Eden had still spent a sizeable chunk of her own money on odds and ends like tablecloths, crockery and cutlery and glasses, vases and flowers and bunting to hang around the hall to make it look more inviting. She'd also had to buy cleaning products, because what the scout hut already had in their stores was OK for sweeping up and washing the odd teacup after a jamboree, but it was hardly enough for a whole sitting of diners and their mess. Wonderful Ralph had given her the use of his van to transport all the things she was going to need, and she'd been on site waiting for food deliveries all morning in a vague state of panic in case something didn't turn up.

After many discussions with Ralph, Julia and Livia, she'd decided to make the inaugural day an evening sitting only, so that they could get everything in place and test the waters. If it proved popular and demand was there, she'd think about two sittings a day – one at lunchtime and one in the evening, on the three days a week the hut was available. But if she thought the rest of her time would be spent bored at home, she was going to be disappointed. Eden was quickly discovering that even a three-day week was going to make a lot more work than she'd imagined, and that most of her time – other than doing her paid shifts at the Dolphin – was going to be taken up dealing with the administration of her new venture.

But she didn't mind that. In fact, in view of the – sometimes complicated – reasons she was doing this, any time taken up with its running was time she wouldn't be dwelling on what a mess she'd made of her life so far. She felt useful and needed and good to be doing something for others rather than taking and taking like the woman she'd always been before.

Livia and her mum still had the ice-cream parlour to run and so couldn't help until they'd closed up, but had promised to come as soon as they could. Ralph had given Eden and Livia the night off with pay, which Eden thought was sweet but unnecessary, but when she said this to Livia, she was quickly reminded that her friend didn't take the gesture quite so much for granted. Livia couldn't afford to lose even the few pounds she might earn from one shift at the Dolphin, and though she was tactful in saying so, Eden felt like she'd been chastised, and it wasn't wholly undeserved.

The sun was still strong when Livia and Julia arrived to help. Eden had left the access door open, and as she heard voices, she shouted them through.

'I'm in the kitchen!'

Julia and Livia appeared a moment later, Nancy and Levi with them, bouncing up and down with more excitement than standing in an industrial kitchen ought to cause any child.

'You don't mind...?' Livia asked as Eden glanced down at them.

'Of course not!' She smiled at the children. 'You want to help?'

'Yes!' Nancy cried, and Levi nodded agreement.

'Cool. I've got flowers over there...' Eden nodded at a spot beneath a worktop where a crate full of flowers she'd picked from her garden at Four Winds lay with their stalks wrapped in damp plastic bags – the only way she could think at short notice to keep them fresh. 'And you see those tiny vases in the bag next to them?'

Both children gave a vigorous nod of understanding.

'So I want one of those flowers in each of those vases. Can you do that? They're to decorate the tables, so it's very important they look nice.'

'Yes!' they both said.

Nancy raced over and pulled out a vase. 'It's small.'

'Big enough for a flower, though,' Livia said. She went to take a closer look in the bag.

'Um, yes, I know they don't match,' Eden said with a light laugh as Livia took one or two out. 'I got them in the charity shop. No idea where they got so many from. There were one or two out on the shelf, and when I asked, they had a whole ton more in the back.'

'It's nuts what you find in a charity shop sometimes.' Livia handed the vase she was holding to Levi. 'Lucky for you in this case.'

'I like to think it's a sign,' Eden said. 'Stupid, obviously, but still.'

'I'd agree,' Julia said. 'A good sign for your project.' She went over to the freezer and began to rearrange the shelves to make space. 'I brought some ice cream down for dessert.'

'We're making rice pudding, aren't we?'

'Yes, but I thought for those who don't want rice pudding.' She turned to Livia. It was then that Eden noticed the bags on the floor where Livia was standing. She handed them to Julia, who took out the tubs and put them in the space she'd made in the freezer.

'They're from the parlour?' Eden asked.

'Yes.'

'You can't... Let me pay you for those—'

'Absolutely not,' Julia said. She slammed the door on the freezer shut. 'It's our donation, and I don't want to hear another thing about it.'

'Thank you.' Eden smiled and resolved to somehow surreptitiously get the money to them at some point, whether they liked it or not.

Half an hour later, the children had completed their task and the tables were dressed in cloths, also scavenged from various places, and the vases set on top, and there was a certain homely charm to the chaos.

'It looks lovely,' Julia said as Eden went through to look.

'It does,' Eden agreed. She smiled down at Nancy, who seemed to be waiting for her approval, while Levi had gone back to the kitchen saying he wanted a drink. 'Thank you for helping.'

'What else shall I do?' Nancy asked.

'How about washing the vegetables?' Julia glanced at Eden as she said it. Perhaps she didn't want to give the impression she was taking over, though Eden wouldn't mind her taking over a bit. She was far better at this sort of thing.

Eden had to reflect that almost everyone here was better at this sort of thing than her. If only she'd taken more notice when her mum had been baking for charity or cooking at the old folks' home at Christmas or any of the other good deeds she'd done over the years. All the times she'd asked for Eden's help and

Eden had refused. Only now did it dawn on her how much it would have enriched her life to get involved, and how much it would have meant to her mum, who'd been desperate for any opportunity for them to spend time together as mother and daughter.

'Washing the vegetables sounds like a good plan,' Eden said. 'There are a lot. Think you and Levi can handle it, Nancy? It's a big responsibility – they have to be super clean. Don't want to serve any allotment bugs up with our dinners, do we?'

'We'll be careful,' Nancy said, racing off to the kitchen to brief Levi on their new job.

'Thank you,' Julia said.

Eden frowned slightly. 'For what?'

'For letting them be involved. They love this sort of thing, and I think it's good for them.'

'I ought to be thanking you all for being here. I love that they want to be involved.'

When they went back through, Nancy and Levi were already sitting cross-legged on the floor, elbow deep in bowls of water, scrubbing so meticulously at a pile of carrots that it was all Eden could do not to stop and watch them with a daft smile on her face, because it was about the most adorable thing she'd ever seen.

Julia was on head chef duty because everyone agreed she was the best cook. Although it made sense for Livia to assist because she knew how Julia operated, at an impromptu supper-cum-planning meeting the day before, they'd decided that Eden ought to help. Eventually she'd have to take on a lot of the cooking, particularly on days when help was scarce. She'd freely admitted that her talents in the kitchen were lacking, and she relished the idea of learning from Julia, who was a great cook.

Every meal Eden had shared with them at Sea Glass Parade had been as good as anything she'd been served in a restaurant.

'Right then...' Julia pulled out a notebook. 'I've written down these recipes as best I can. Most of them I do from memory – it's one of those things where you can do it with your eyes shut when you're not thinking about it, but as soon as someone asks you what the steps are, you can't for the life of you remember. But I think they'll do the job for you.'

'This is all brilliant,' Eden said as Julia handed her the book. 'Perfect. I'm sure they'll be fine, though I can't promise my skill in the kitchen will do them justice.'

'They're foolproof, honestly,' Julia said. 'Things I make all the time and mostly because they're so hard to get wrong. Hopefully, everyone will enjoy them.' Julia peered over her shoulder. 'The most important thing with a lot of these dishes is just getting the timings right. If I were you, I'd make myself a little timescale on a bit of paper somewhere so you know when things have to be added or put into the oven so it all comes out at the same time – if you see what I mean. Then all you have to do is keep an eye on the clock.'

'Good idea.' Eden turned the page to the next recipe. 'See, that's why it's so good to have you here. I need practical suggestions like that. I'd have been all over the place if I'd been doing this on my own.'

'You'd never have been doing it on your own,' Livia said as she pulled Nancy's sleeves further up to stop them getting wet. 'We're excited to help.'

Eden took a moment to recall how keen her own mum had been for Eden to take an interest like this. It was just another one of those moments of torment, because she hadn't been interested, even though her mum was a great cook and loved to create new things. She'd have given anything to have just one of those occasions back, where she could have stood at the stove in their kitchen with her and helped, if only to make Mum smile. But there was no going back, and it didn't matter how big her regrets were – that wouldn't change. All she could do now was move forward and try to imagine how proud her mum would be if only she could see it.

'Without your help,' Eden replied, 'I don't know what I would have done.'

'Seems to me you're the sort of person who would have found a way,' Julia said. 'Shall we make a start?' She looked at her watch. 'If we don't get the stew in soon, we're going to be running behind. Livia... would you rinse the lentils for the vegan chilli while I get started on the stew?'

Like a well-rehearsed military operation, Livia and Julia went to their tasks. They were so in tune with each other, so efficient, it was obvious they'd cooked together many times. For the briefest moment, Eden felt like a spare part and wondered if she ought to just slope off and leave them to it. She couldn't help feeling she'd be more hinderance than help; even the children were doing a better job than she was.

As Julia turned on the stove, she called her over. 'Could you brown the beef for me while I cut the onions?'

Glad to be off the starting blocks and feeling better already, Eden went to get the meat from the fridge where she'd stored it on her arrival. 'Totally. What about the chicken?'

'It won't take so long to cook – we can probably get to that last, after everything else is in.'

Eden nodded as she rinsed the meat. 'Timings... right. I must remember that.'

With Ralph's advice in mind, they would be serving uncomplicated, virtually one-pot meals. It might have been the briefest of menus but, based on Julia's recommendations, they'd opted for a hearty beef stew, a chicken and pasta bake, and a vegan chilli. While the guests were enjoying that, a rice pudding would be blipping away in the oven, ready for the second course. And now there was also a choice of ice cream from Julia's own parlour for those who preferred it.

As they got stuck in, their volunteers began to arrive, starting with Debs, who'd come to the Darling Dolphin for a food parcel during Eden's first shift. Livia and Julia greeted her warmly, and her appearance drew excited smiles and welcomes from the twins. Eden realised that the family knew her well, and she was glad to see that because it meant they already had an understanding that would help in the running of things. As Julia told Debs what needed doing, two more arrived: young Liam, who had also come to the Dolphin that first night for a parcel, and a much older man he introduced as his great-grand-father, Bilbo.

Eden stared at the old man, realising almost as soon as she found herself doing so that it was quite rude.

'Sorry, what's your name again?'

'Bilbo,' the old man said. 'Bilbo Jones. Reporting for duty.'

'Oh... Right... that's brilliant, thank you. Julia, do you know where you want Liam and Bilbo?'

As Julia went to instruct them, Eden leaned in and lowered her voice to Livia. 'Is that his actual name?'

'Yes.' Livia grinned. 'And don't make a fuss about it because he gets really precious if you do.'

'Who calls their kid Bilbo?'

'Mr and Mrs Jones, apparently. I suppose they'd just read the book or something – I don't like to ask. Anyway, it might be that I'm used to it, but I think it sort of suits him. Can't imagine him with a normal name. And you have to admit, he's a bit hobbity.'

Eden tried to keep a straight face as she glanced across at Liam's great-grandfather. He'd have been a very old hobbit, but he was small and slight, and he had a surprisingly thick shock of grey hair, and she could see exactly what Livia meant. But despite the fact that he must have been in his eighties, he was quick and sharp, and as he started to work to Julia's instructions, Eden could already see he knew his way around a paring knife. She was also grateful for any help, no matter how it came.

She decided they'd got off on the wrong foot and went over. 'Don't let me disturb you. I just wanted to come and say thank you for your help.'

'Glad to,' he replied cheerfully. 'Gets me out of the house and it's for a good cause.'

'You'll be eating with us when it's done, won't you?'

'Oh yes, looking forward to it. I don't often cook at home – doesn't seem much point for one, to be honest.'

'What do you do instead?'

'I get invited here and there, or I put a ready dinner in. I eat well enough, but there's nothing like a good home-cooked meal. I used to enjoy doing a bit in the kitchen when my Kathleen was alive. She loved my roast chicken, said it was better than any restaurant.' He tapped the side of his nose. 'The secret's in the basting, you know.'

'I do love a bit of roast chicken myself – my mum's was amazing.'

'You lost her,' he said. 'Julia told me. Must be hard, a young 'un like you with no mammy.'

'I miss her a lot.'

'Well, my love, she'd be proud to see you doing all this.'

Eden's eyes misted. Annoyed, she sniffed hard and swallowed her tears. This wasn't the time for them.

'I hope so,' she said. 'I never did much to make her proud when she was alive.'

'Oh... I can't believe that for a minute.' He swept a knotted hand around the room. 'You don't suddenly become this person. Goodness like this has always been in you – must have been. Don't be so hard on yourself.'

Eden tried to smile.

'I'll let you get on,' she said. 'I think Julia might need me.

And by the way, I'm sorry if I offended... I think your name is very cool. Did it come from the books?'

He looked up in some confusion. 'Books?'

'Yes, you know, the hobbit books?'

'I expect so,' he said with a vague shrug. 'But if it did, my mammy never said so, and my dad wasn't around – died when I was a baby – so he wasn't saying much about it either.'

Eden left him to his work and then went to speak to Liam and Debs, just to make certain they were aware of how grateful she was, and then she went back to Julia, who set her on making a simple pasta sauce for their bake while she saw to the stew. Bilbo began to whistle loudly, causing Nancy and Levi to start giggling and attempt to join in – though neither of them could do anything except make rasping sounds. So Bilbo started to teach them how to purse their lips and eventually a sound came from Levi, and then from Nancy, both children with looks of absolute delight on their faces once they realised they could do it. If Eden had thought them cute before, this was close to over-whelming. She had to force herself not to watch, because she might just spend the afternoon doing that and nothing else.

'Oh... fudge it!'

Eden turned to see Julia frown at the dials on the oven. 'What's wrong?'

'It's been on the wrong temperature... see, the numbers are worn off and I thought it was lower. The meat will be tough as Livia's old Doc Martens.'

'I'm sure it will be fine,' Livia said from across the kitchen. 'Just turn it down.'

'But it's been on... well...' Julia let out a sigh that Eden sensed was full of contained impatience. She could understand where it had come from. The old kitchen of the hut was far from perfect, but they were making the best use of it they could and working out systems as they went for getting around and using the less than ideal equipment. In a few weeks, they'd have it figured out, she supposed, but for now, it wasn't causing tension exactly but making conditions less than ideal for their purposes.

'It'll be fine, Mum,' Livia insisted.

'I know, but I want it to be better than fine. It's Eden's first dinner, and we want people to enjoy it so they come back again next time.'

'Your cooking is amazing,' Eden said. 'Of course they're going to enjoy it.'

'Yes, I'm sure it will be all right, but it's just not going to be my best.' Julia peered at the temperature dial as she twisted it to adjust. 'It's never the same using a kitchen that's not your own because you're used to your own, but I want it to be at least close.'

'It will be.'

'It smells wonderful,' Bilbo said, shuffling over to pat Julia on the arm. She looked up at him, and he offered her a warm smile. 'I'm sure I'll be coming for seconds.'

'Me too,' Eden agreed. But she wished she felt as confident as she sounded. Not for a second did she doubt everyone's efforts in the kitchen, but she did worry that this was doomed to spectacular failure no matter how the food turned out. What if nobody came? What if nobody enjoyed it? What if they all thought it was a waste of time? What if…?

There seemed to Eden so many things that could go wrong here, but she tried to put them out of her mind. She had to remember why they were all here, and that the most important thing in the end was intent. They could only try to give the community of Sea Glass Bay something good and important, something that would nurture those in need and bring people together, and as long as they concentrated on that, everything else would either fall into place or it wouldn't. But at the end of the day, Eden had no more control about that than she did the tide rolling in and out on the beach. People would come or they wouldn't, and they could do their best, but if people didn't enjoy it, there wasn't a lot she could do to change that.

'Ouch!'

Liam held up a finger oozing with blood, and Bilbo dashed over with a tea cloth.

'What happened, lad?'

'Knife slipped... It's going everywhere.'

'Come here...' Bilbo wrapped the cloth around his grandson's hand and led him outside. Eden tried not to see it as an omen. As if she wasn't already on edge.

'I'll take the first aid kit out to them,' Julia said, hurrying to fetch the box from a shelf.

'I hope it's not bad,' Eden said.

'Didn't look it. A good sticking plaster and I'm sure it will be fine.'

Eden glanced across the room at Livia. 'Why do I feel like that's a bad sign?'

'Take a breath,' Livia said with a reassuring smile. 'Affirmation time – right? Say it after me: this will be a success.'

'But—'

'Say it!' Livia insisted, pretending to grit her teeth.

Eden had to grin, the tension draining from her. She closed her eyes, the grin still fixed to her face, repeating the affirmation in a sing-song voice.

'*Ohm... this will be a success.*'

'There you go. You've sent it out into the universe and so it has to manifest. It will be a total success.'

If only it was that easy.

A couple of hours later, as people started to arrive at the hut, Eden realised she needn't have worried. There was such enthusiasm, groups of friends and entire families arriving in good spirits. Eden had expected perhaps a dozen at most, but once she'd greeted everyone and had time to take stock, she noted a full house and was then hit by a sense of panic that they'd underestimated how much food they'd need. But she trusted that the friends she had around her had steered her right and that somehow they'd make what they had stretch. In the end, she needn't have worried about that either – there was plenty to go around, and there would probably be leftovers for people to take home.

Eden hadn't planned to sit and eat with her guests. There were still things to do behind the scenes, and someone had to keep it all ticking over. Besides, she was too wired to be hungry. She flitted here and there, fussing about things that didn't need to be fussed over, which wasn't like her at all but perhaps an indicator – if she'd ever needed one – of just what this project was beginning to mean to her. From time to time, she'd stand at the doorway that led from the kitchen to the main hall and watch the room. Everyone had taken a seat at the table, including her little band of volunteers, and were laughing and tucking in with everyone else. Eden was happy with that. When she'd imagined this night, the scene before her was all she'd wanted to see.

Livia glanced up from her meal and beckoned her. 'What are you doing there? Come and eat!'

Eden shook her head. 'I'll eat later. I have things to—'

'No you don't! Julia cut in, noticing the exchange. 'There's nothing to be done in there that can't wait. Come and sit with us!'

'Honestly,' Eden began, but then Bilbo looked up from his dinner and said the same thing, and eventually Eden gave in and joined them – if only for a quiet life. She helped herself to some of the pasta bake and was almost shocked to find that a dish she'd had a lot of input in was really quite good.

Not for the first time that evening, the strangely melancholy mood washed over her. While she was happy to see others happy and increasingly confident that her first night had been a success, she wished her mum could be here to see it. She could

only imagine the look that would have crossed her mum's face –
bemusement and surprise and perhaps some pride. She had to
wonder what her sister might have made of it. Would she take it
at face value, or would she see some ulterior motive? Eden liked
to think Caitlin would be pleased for her, but she couldn't be
sure of that.

CHAPTER ELEVEN

Eden was tired but happy. As she locked the doors of the scout hut, having seen the last of her volunteers off, in a novel turn of events, she didn't worry about who may or may not be proud of her but allowed some pride in herself. With the recollections of happy faces fresh in her mind, she knew her first night had been a bigger success than she could have hoped for. They hadn't taken a huge amount of money, but she was confident that people had also paid what they could and that everyone had been fair and honest. The money didn't matter – she'd foreseen all along that she might have to find ways to make up the inevitable shortfall, and she was fully prepared for that. She had ideas about how she might do it too, and as time passed, she'd get those plans into action. After cleaning down, she'd gone back with Livia and Julia for tea and long discussions about what had worked and what hadn't, and before she'd realised it, the skies had darkened.

The moon was rising as she made her way up the cliffs to Four Winds, a dove-grey disc scattering its light onto the brisk waves in the bay. It lit the path to some extent, but to be certain,

Eden switched on the torch function on her phone so she wouldn't trip on any uneven ground.

Back at the hut, Nancy had fallen asleep, and Livia had carried her home. It was likely that Levi was exhausted too – both children had been up way past their bedtimes, but Livia and Julia hadn't seemed too worried, acknowledging that this was a one-off in exceptional circumstances. Eden's mind went back to the sight of the little girl, her head resting on Livia's shoulder, and the tender look on Livia's face as she'd scooped her up. She marvelled at how her friend could be so utterly good in the face of the hardships and responsibilities that had been the gift of her life so far.

Four Winds was silent and shadowed as Eden approached the gate. She reminded herself that she ought to contact the owners and ask about getting some more lanterns in the garden, because whenever she went back after sunset, it always seemed too dark to be safe. The torch on her phone was some help but didn't give off nearly enough light. Perhaps she ought to pick up something a bit more heavy duty in that regard. There was no danger from people – Eden felt secure there – but she did envisage a tipsy night out ending in a turned ankle at some point during her stay.

Mission accomplished and safely inside, she was about to get herself a drink when her phone rang. Since she'd left London, casual calls from old acquaintances had all but stopped. The only ones she got now were from Livia or Ralph or Caitlin. The calls from her sister she hadn't yet dared to pick up. But this was a number she didn't recognise.

Wondering if it might be one of her new suppliers with something urgent to discuss, she went to the kitchen and took the call.

'Finally!'

Eden was suddenly hyperalert, any traces of her good mood instantly gone. 'Caitlin, what's this—'

'Number? I borrowed my friend's phone, as you clearly weren't picking up whenever you saw my number. What the hell is going on? Where are you? We've been worried sick here! I've called every one of your friends I could get hold of and nobody knows anything.'

'Caitlin...' Eden let out a sigh. 'I didn't mean to make anyone worry; I'm fine. I'm...' She stopped short of saying where she was. She didn't even want to continue this conversation, let alone get a visit from anyone right now. She'd left because she'd found it so hard to face her family, because every moment in their presence reminded her of what she'd done. She could see their disappointment and the blame in their faces whenever she looked at them, and she couldn't deal with that. In the weeks that had passed since she'd left, nothing had changed. Her dad's sadness was still vivid in her memory, and she knew she was the cause. The same was true of Caitlin's anger; that was because of her too. 'I'm fine.'

'When are you coming home?'

'I don't know.'

'What's that supposed to mean? I phoned your office – they said you'd quit your job weeks ago. And you gave up your flat.

'Is this all because of what happened? You're moping, is that it? You're turning it all into a scenario where you're the victim? Is that what's going on here?'

'Of course not!'

'Because you need to snap out of it. Mum died, and Dad needs you.'

'Don't you think I know that?'

'Then I don't see what this charade is in aid of. Come home and help him grieve like a daughter should.'

'How can I? After what happened, how can I come home?

How can I even look Dad in the eye, let alone comfort him when I'm the reason she's gone?'

'Ever the drama queen. It's always about you, isn't it? You're never going to grow up, are you?'

'Yep,' Eden fired back. 'That's me – the petty, spoiled little drama queen. There, I admitted it – is that what you wanted? Will you leave me alone now that I said it?'

'If you know what you are,' Caitlin said coldly, 'why not do something about it?'

'What do you want me to do? A leopard can't change its spots! I'm good for nothing and selfish and self-absorbed, and I always will be! I can't be what I'm not!'

'Yes, you are selfish! Selfish for not letting us know where you are! Selfish for piling worry on top of everything else!'

'I didn't mean to make anyone worry; I just thought it would be better for everyone if I was out of the way.'

'Living up to the hype. Promises to be selfish and delivers, even while thinking she's doing us all a favour. Congratulations, Eden. You might just be the stupidest person I've ever met.'

'Caitlin...' Eden sighed. She was tired, and she didn't want to have this discussion, not now, not ever. Part of her might have known on some level that she needed to, but that didn't change her reluctance. 'I don't know what you want me to say. I screwed up, I get that you're still angry, but I don't think this is getting us anywhere. Surely it's better if I disappear and let you all get on with your lives? If I'm there, it's only going to keep reminding everyone of what happened that day.'

'Spoken like someone who doesn't have the emotional maturity to own their mistakes and face up to them. Easier to run away than try to fix what you've done, eh? Just when I thought you couldn't get any lower in my estimation, little sis, you've outdone yourself.'

'I'm trying to spare everyone more pain.'

'You're trying to spare yourself pain is more like it. Quite frankly, if you were in front of me at this moment, I'd struggle not to slap you, but I'd keep a lid on it for Dad's sake. And that's what you should be doing. You should be here for his sake. He's the person who's suffering the most here, losing out on all sides and none of it his fault. If you can't see that, then you really are more selfish than even I gave you credit for.'

'I'm not coming back – not yet – and you can say what you like about it because I know it's for the best.'

There was a pause. Eden could almost hear the impatience in it. Then Caitlin spoke again, and it was a tone made of serrated edges designed to hurt. 'Whatever. At least message Dad.'

'I have messaged him.'

'Message him again and tell him where you are. He won't settle until he knows.'

'I'm not...' It was Eden's turn to pause. Perhaps Caitlin had a point – where their dad was concerned, at any rate. But she didn't want to tell him where she was because she knew he'd be in his car and there as fast as he could. It wasn't what Eden needed right now, and she was sure it wasn't what he needed either, despite what Caitlin had to say on the subject. 'I'll call him.'

'Tonight?'

'It's late. I—'

'Call him tonight, Eden. Don't give him another sleepless night worrying about you.'

'Has he...?'

Had it been that bad? Eden wasn't stupid enough to suppose she'd be forgotten, but she hadn't imagined any worries about her would last.

'I wish you'd come home,' Caitlin said into the gap. 'This is all ridiculous.'

'Is it? Would you want me there? Honestly?'

'Dad does. Isn't that good enough?'

'I'll phone him.'

'Let him know where you are; put his mind at rest.'

'I'm not going to do that, but I will do my best to stop him worrying.'

'I don't know what you're doing for money or where you're living, and I don't understand why you're doing any of it, but we do care, no matter what you think. If you're trying to prove some kind of point, then I'm sorry to tell you it's a waste of time. All you're proving to me is that you've learned nothing from the past couple of months. You're as selfish as you've ever been.'

'I'm trying to be better.'

'By disappearing without a word?'

'I thought it was for the best.'

'It's not. It's a stupid thing to do.'

'Caitlin, I'm—'

Whether they'd been cut off or whether Caitlin had simply had enough of the conversation Eden didn't know, but she never got to finish her apology. She could tell that the call was over.

Even though Eden was feeling resentful at Caitlin's tone, she couldn't help but admit that her sister might have a point. Difficult as it was going to be, she'd have to contact her dad sooner or later. Eden had imagined she was doing him a favour by being out of his sight, but perhaps she was mistaken. What if she was making it worse for him, not better? And she wanted to hear his voice desperately, and she hadn't realised how much until Caitlin had put the idea into her head. She missed him. She missed home and her life there, and she even missed her spiky sister.

But that life was in her past, and even if she contacted her dad, it wasn't going to change. She didn't think she could go back to it as if nothing had ever happened, and the fact was she didn't want to. She liked it here in Sea Glass Bay, where nobody knew what sort of woman she really was, where she could pretend to be someone good and where people believed it. Her reinvention was already underway, and she wasn't about to give that up. Maybe she'd go back home one day, but not until she'd done something she could be proud of, something that her family could be proud of too.

She glanced at her phone, left sitting on the table as she placed her mug down. She'd promised to call her dad tonight, but now that Caitlin's voice had faded, the idea seemed daunting.

She took a deep breath and dialled the number. A few words of reassurance was all it needed, right?

It rang and she waited, but when there was no answer and she had to cut the call, she couldn't decide whether she was disappointed or relieved. She decided to send him a text, just to let him know there was no emergency and made plans to try and catch him again over the next couple of days.

CHAPTER TWELVE

The following day, Eden decided to make some calls to see if she could get any donations for the kitchen – either food or money or anything else that could be spared – and then she'd go into town to get some of her own essentials. Perhaps Livia would be free for half an hour at lunch – although Eden was becoming conscious of the fact that she was beginning to rely on Livia's company a lot and wondered whether she ought to give her new friend some breathing space. The thing was, Livia was such brilliant company, and she had such a way of making Eden feel instantly better, just by being there, that it was an easy thing to say but far less easy to do.

What was strange as she walked the high street was how she was suddenly noticed. A few people had started to recognise her in the past week simply because they'd perhaps got used to seeing her around – after all, this was her third week in Sea Glass Bay and most holidaymakers would have been gone by now, and she'd been hanging around the ice-cream parlour a lot, not to mention her job at the Dolphin, of course. But that had been quite low-key, where today it seemed as if she got stared at wherever she went, and she didn't quite know what to make of it. One or two people who'd been at the dinner the previous night stopped her to say hello and tell her how much they'd enjoyed it, which was lovely. But many people she'd never seen before seemed to know who she was – at least, they paid her a lot more attention than she'd expect from a stranger.

'Morning!'

She smiled in acknowledgement as the fourth person she didn't know spoke to her in the space of half an hour.

At the mini market, which was as close to a proper supermarket as the bay had, Eden was picking up some teabags when someone tapped her on the shoulder.

She turned to see Ralph smiling at her.

'How did it go yesterday?'

'Brilliant! All the things you told us to do worked like a dream. I think everyone really enjoyed it too.'

'I think you might be right about that – I've been stopped three times today by people saying how nice it was. Not just because they got fed, but because they got the chance to chew the fat with neighbours they don't usually have time to talk to. It was quite an event, by all accounts. In fact, I might have to come down to the next one myself.'

'You're always welcome,' Eden said, feeling a bit bemused by the praise. She hadn't done anything special, though she was glad to hear her event had created such a buzz.

'So you're ploughing ahead with more of them?'

'Yes. I wasn't sure people would want more, but it seems that they do. I've been stopped a few times today too. And... well, it's probably my imagination, but I feel like' – she lowered her voice, feeling silly for saying it – 'I'm getting *noticed*...'

Ralph laughed. 'Of course you are! Everyone's talking about it.'

'But how do they know...? Well, how do they know who I am?'

'Just because they never said anything before doesn't mean they haven't noticed you. And now they've got even more cause to pay attention. I wouldn't be surprised,' Ralph continued, 'if you don't have more people than you can handle at the next one.'

Eden looked at him in vague panic. 'Do you think so? What should I do? I didn't want the booking system because I didn't want to put people off, but—'

'Don't worry! If you've got a few extra, then I'm sure you could squeeze a few more chairs in for them somewhere. And if you're really packed out, then you'd just have to say first come first served and send them away.'

'I wouldn't want to do that – it kind of defeats the point of opening it in the first place if I have to turn people away.'

Ralph shrugged. 'If I were you, I'd get some idea of numbers in advance. You've got a Facebook page?'

Eden nodded.

'Use that to ask people to let you know if they plan to come. If it's looking a bit hairy, you might need to rethink some things.'

'Like what?'

'How many sittings you do, or your venue, that sort of thing? But I'm sure a smart girl like you will have something up her sleeve, right? You'll have planned for something like this.'

While she'd been hopeful for a good response, Eden hadn't really expected one – at least not this quickly. Lovely as it would be to be packed out, she hoped it wouldn't happen so soon after she'd got her kitchen off the ground. She needed time to refine her plans and systems, having decided early on that she'd play it by ear and develop those as she went along according to how it went. One thing it did do was cement in her mind that this place was needed and that she was doing a good thing, and that she had to find a way to keep it going no matter what obstacles might appear in her path.

'Um...'

'Of course you have.' Ralph gave her a cheerful nod. 'Well played to you. I have to admit I had my doubts about it all when you first mentioned it, but I'm glad to be proved wrong. And if you need anything, you know where I am. By the way, I have a couple of extra shifts going at the weekend if you're interested.'

'Yes – I don't have any other plans. For the time being, I think I'll be keeping the dinners to week nights, because I can't have the scout hut at weekends.'

'Good, good... so I'll send your hours over later when I've worked out the rota. Cheerio then.'

Ralph reached past her to get a box of teabags of his own and then strode to the checkout. Eden paused for a moment but then began to smile. No matter how worried she might be about her ability to manage the community café project, if what Ralph had told her wasn't exaggerated – and he wasn't the sort of man to exaggerate – then she had to love the response. All she'd wanted was for it to do some good, and it sounded as if it already had. The notion was encouraging. She could do this – she had to do this. It mattered. Something she was doing mattered, and that was brilliant.

Ralph had put Livia on the same Saturday evening shift as Eden. He seemed to do that most of the time, which suited Eden just fine because she loved working alongside her. As the last customers left the pub and they started to clean up, Ralph came through and poured himself a brandy at the bar.

'It's been a busy one, girls, hasn't it?'

Livia tipped a full drip tray into the sink. 'You can say that again!'

'Not that I'm complaining,' Ralph added. He nodded at the bottle. 'You're both staying for a drink before we turn out the lights?'

Eden was putting some freshly washed glasses away. She glanced at Livia.

'I don't see why not,' Livia said. 'Are you staying, Eden?'

Eden paused as she considered the walk home. There were moments, now that she was here and living like a local, where the romantic clifftop retreat that had seemed so appealing when she'd booked it felt like a very impractical folly. It was lovely to wake up with those views in the morning but not so much fun to grope her way up the precarious path in the dark, no matter how stunning the moonlight might look on the sea as she went. But she did want to stay, and in the end, the temptation was too much.

'I suppose one wouldn't hurt,' she said. 'If I break my ankle going home, I've got another one, right?'

Ralph chuckled. 'You know I could get one of the kitchen lads to run you up there. Wouldn't take them a minute.'

'It's fine – don't ask anyone to do that. People want to get home; they don't want to be messing around driving up to Four Winds at this time of night. Besides, that path is as much a nightmare for a car as it is to walk. Just ask my delivery drivers.'

'Well, the offer's there. I'm sure one of them wouldn't mind.'

Livia slotted her tray back and lifted a second one out. 'Have you thought about swapping your accommodation?' she asked Eden. 'Maybe get somewhere closer to town?'

'I've already committed to it,' Eden said. 'And I do really like it up there. It's just sometimes it makes life a bit difficult. It's not forever, though, so I'm happy to manage.'

'It is a lovely spot,' Ralph agreed. He handed Livia a pint of lager. He hadn't asked what she wanted, but she seemed content with his choice. 'Spent many a happy hour up there with your uncle.'

'Did you know each other well?' Eden asked him.

'Oh, I was a youngster, but I used to go up with my mum to get eggs and honey – like a lot did round here – and he always had time for me. He'd spend hours showing me how he looked after the bees. Let me take the honeycombs out a few times too. And, of course, what young lad doesn't want to pet the chickens?'

Eden could think of a lot of boys she'd grown up with who wouldn't be remotely interested in bees or chickens, but then, she supposed growing up in a place like Sea Glass Bay was very different. Plus, Ralph was from a different generation too. Perhaps there wasn't all that much to do here back then. It might have been that messing around with chickens was about as exciting as it got. Either way, although she couldn't imagine it, there was something that sounded idyllic about the whole thing, and she wondered whether – had she grown up back then instead of now – she'd have been a better, happier person.

'You know,' Ralph continued as he mixed an orange gin and lemonade for Eden, making her smile that he already knew her favourite drink. 'I'll be sorry to see you go when it's time, Eden. I reckon a few round here will feel the same.'

'I'm going to do my best to hand over the kitchen to someone so they can keep it going,' Eden said, and Ralph chuckled.

'That's not all anyone will miss you for, you daft thing. Speaking for myself, I'm already fond of you.'

'Me too,' Livia said, catching Eden and her precarious emotions quite by surprise. 'You'd better not lose touch when you do go.'

'I won't,' Eden replied, her voice cracking so that she had to turn away and concentrate really hard on rubbing out an invisible smudge on one of her glasses.

'I bet your folks are missing you back home,' Ralph said. 'Are they going to come over and see you soon? Six months is a long time. You'll have to bring them up here when they do.'

Eden nodded shortly, her gaze still on that invisible smudge.

When she collected herself enough to look up, she saw

Ralph leaving the bar with a fresh drink and heading to the kitchens.

Eden turned to Livia. 'Ralph has been so lovely to me; I'm sure I don't know what I did to deserve it.'

Livia stopped to take a sip from her glass. 'He meant what he said – he likes you. I think he will miss you when you go home. He's like that, gets attached to people. And not just because they're staff.'

'Maybe I won't even go home.'

Eden had said it before the thought had fully formed in her mind. Livia stared at her. But as soon as it was out, Eden wondered whether it might be the truth of her feelings, forcing their way to the surface before she'd had time to process them.

'I don't know,' Eden said. 'I like it here, and I feel as if I'm settling in. Maybe I'll stay.'

'Just like that? What about your family? And you had a great job in London, didn't you?'

'It was well paid, but it wasn't that great. And my family...' Eden shrugged.

Livia regarded her for a moment. 'What's going on with you? I mean, really? You don't have to tell me, but if you need to get something off your chest... Like this community café thing. Don't get me wrong, it's brilliant and everything, but what does it matter to you?'

'I want to do something good.'

'But why? What for?'

'Does there have to be a reason?'

'Maybe not a reason, but there has to be something that motivated you.'

Eden gave her a small smile. She didn't doubt Livia's astuteness, but she hadn't realised just how keen it actually was. 'I'm motivated by wanting to be better, that's all. I don't think I've been a great person so far, and I want to change that.'

'So stick a tenner in the odd charity box. That's what everyone else does.'

'You don't think I ought to bother with the kitchen?'

'That's not what I meant. Of course I think you should bother with it, but going that extra mile isn't what most people do to make themselves feel better. So why? Why are you really doing it? What made you feel like such a bad person that this is what you did to make amends? And for the record, whatever it was can't have been that bad. I don't believe for a minute all this stuff about you being a terrible human.'

For the briefest moment, Eden thought about coming clean. About how her selfish behaviour was responsible for her mum's death, about how she'd run away saying that it was to make things easier for everyone else when really, deep down, she knew that running away had been just one more selfish act on top of all the others. She was running away from what she'd done because she couldn't face it.

Another unwanted flashback filled her mind, and try as she might to shake it, there was no letting go...

Caitlin glared at Eden from across the dinner table. Eden pretended not to notice and instead poured herself some water from the jug that sat between them.

'Here we are then – just another fun family Sunday lunch. Honestly, I don't know why I come. I suppose I'd miss the insults if I didn't get my weekly dose.'

'Nobody wants lunch to be like this. You could choose to behave like a decent human being and then it wouldn't be.'

'Jesus, Caitlin, get off your high horse! Nobody died!'

'You wouldn't say that to Uncle Terry, though, would you? No – because you know it would be out of order.'

'I forgot the dog for, like, a couple of hours.'

'You forgot him for a whole day! Uncle Terry trusted you to

go and check on him and take him for a walk because you promised you could do it! The poor thing was dying of thirst when Terry got home.'

'Don't exaggerate – he wasn't dying of thirst. He had a bowl of water when Terry was back and he was OK.'

'No consequences. There never is for you, is there? It's like the community centre all over again.'

'God, not this again! That was months ago!'

'For you, yes. Mum's church group are still dealing with the fallout from that grotty little backroom deal.'

'I didn't make the deal!'

'No, but you had a pretty big hand in setting it up so you could get your employee of the month sticker, didn't you? Get a nice fat bonus you didn't tell us about? A promise of promotion for passing on the information – information that was for family discussion only and you were asked not to pass on.'

'The church couldn't afford to keep it on – everyone knew that.'

'Your bosses didn't, until you told them. They swooped in and got the place cut price because they knew the church couldn't afford to do anything else, and now there's nowhere for community events around here, and that's thanks to you.'

'You have no clue what you're talking about. They'd have bought it anyway – they'd been looking at that plot for ages; it's in a great location for those apartments.'

'Yes, but they might have given enough money to pay for a new place somewhere else. As it was they paid peanuts.'

Eden sighed with impatience as she reached for the salt. 'I don't know why you keep going on about it; it doesn't make any difference to you.'

'It makes a difference to Mum! Or have you forgotten the charity coffee mornings and bake sales that she's been doing there all these years?'

'Caitlin, please... Don't drag me into this. I never said—'

Eden's mum started to protest, but Caitlin held up a hand to stop her.

'Why do you always do this, Mum? Why do you defend her when you know she's done wrong?'

'She was only doing her job.'

'It was more than her job! She could have kept her mouth shut and she'd still have been doing her job! She didn't have to blab to her bosses about the church's finances!'

'Most churches are in the same position,' Eden's mum said wearily, rubbing her temples. 'They'd have worked it out.'

'Stop it!' Caitlin demanded. 'Stop pretending it doesn't matter! You're upset – we all know it – say so! Tell your favourite child you're upset! I'm sick of being the messenger!'

'Nobody asked you to be anyone's messenger,' Eden's dad cut in. 'And we don't have favourites.'

'You're just as bad!' Caitlin replied, her voice rising. 'Eden did a shitty thing, but neither of you will say so. It's so obvious she's your favourite – I wouldn't have got away with a thing like that. I would never have done a thing like that, but to listen to you now, you still think I'm the one in the wrong for bringing it up? What's the matter with this family?'

'What's the matter with you?' Eden slammed down her cutlery.

'You – that's what!'

'Girls!' Eden's dad stood up, arms outstretched like a referee in a boxing ring. 'Do we have to do this at the dinner table?'

'Where would you suggest we do it?' Caitlin asked him coldly.

'Perhaps nowhere?' Eden's mum cut in. Eden frowned, but then her rising irritation was stopped in its tracks. If she hadn't been so lost in the heat of the argument, she might have taken the signs more seriously. Her mum suddenly looked pale – grey almost. 'I'd really rather we didn't do it at all.'

'Then tell Caitlin that!' Eden fired back because she couldn't leave it. She and Caitlin had always been as bad as each other in that respect – they both had to have the last word. Whenever Eden would reflect on it in the months after this final family dinner, she would see that she and Caitlin were more alike than she'd ever been happy to admit. One would launch an attack, the other would dig their heels in and neither would ever say they were wrong even when they could plainly see it.

'She takes and takes,' Caitlin said, rounding on her mum and dad. 'She never stops, and you never do anything. She borrows some money' – Caitlin crooked her fingers into speech marks – 'and doesn't give it back. She takes your things. She promises to do stuff and then forgets and thinks that's OK. And maybe I do overreact to some of that stuff, but it's because it never ends and nobody ever says anything. But I can't let this one go. The community centre – that was a massive deal for you, Mum. Those coffee mornings and those bake sales and the Christmas dinners for the old people and all that other stuff – that was a huge part of your life, and it's gone, and all you can say is you'd rather not talk about it? It's gone because Eden did another selfish thing, and you're just going to ignore that? The buck has to stop eventually!'

'There'll be other charities—' Mum began, but Caitlin cut her off.

'They were your friends! They'd been your friends for years!'

'She can still see them!' Eden protested. 'They can just go to the pub or something like everyone does!'

Caitlin whipped round. 'You don't get it, do you? Maybe because you don't have friends, only shallow colleagues and acquaintances who like you because you wear the right clothes and go to the right restaurants, but they don't know a thing about you. You have no idea what real friends are. You'll never under-stand what it is to have passion for a cause, to work with people you like to help others and not yourself. Everyone at that group loved what they did; they'd spent years doing it, looked forward to

*the meetings – like some had literally nothing else in their lives –
and you took that from them!'*

'I didn't!' *Eden's eyes filled with tears, but they weren't hurt
or sadness or even rage. They were indignant and they were frustrated because she was losing this moral argument and she didn't
want to admit it. Yes, she'd repeated something they'd discussed
at dinner one day about the church being broke and desperate for
money and how they might have to sell some of their land, and
yes, she'd been asked at the time not to tell anyone, and perhaps
she'd done that hoping for some kind of gold star from her bosses.
But she hadn't meant this to happen. Could she have foreseen it?
Perhaps, she had to admit, but admitting it only added guilt to the
mix. Of course she'd seen it coming because how else was it
going to end? The company she worked for were known for
swooping in and grabbing land and for making huge profits on it.
There was no other way it was going to end.*

*Her mum got up from the table. Going over the scene again
and again after the event, Eden would hate herself for not taking
more notice. For not seeing how pale her mum had become, how
vague, how laboured her movements were. None of them noticed,
but that didn't make it any better.*

'I'm going to get some air...'

*Eden had heard her say it, but nothing had registered. Only
Caitlin, for a split second, voiced any concern, but their mum
shook her head as she made for the door.*

'I'm OK. I'll be back in a minute.'

*But then came the sickening thud, a sound that would stay
with Eden for the rest of her life. Her mum had collapsed,
straight down, hitting the floor like a deadweight. And then
everyone leaped up and the rest was a blur. Even as they turned
her over, Caitlin searching for a pulse while their dad tapped at
her face and called for her to wake up, the awful truth was
staring them in the face. In the time it had taken for Eden to draw
one breath, her mum had taken her last. She pulled out her phone*

and stumbled over every word as she called for the ambulance, but in her heart, she already knew it was too late.

Eden shook off the memory, tears squeezing her throat. She had to keep it together. If she started to cry now, Livia would want to know why.

And despite what she'd promised Caitlin, she hadn't yet spoken to her dad. Even as she was trying to be better, she was still being selfish. She'd picked her battles but, in a way, perhaps she'd picked the ones that didn't really count. But then she looked around at the pub where she already felt settled and happy, and at Livia, who meant so much to her after only a few short weeks, who'd taught her more about being a decent human than anyone else had in her twenty-seven years on the planet, and she knew that if she said those things out loud, it would be the end of all this.

'You don't have to tell me,' Livia said, seemingly able to sense Eden's reluctance.

Eden let out a sigh. 'I'm just not... I don't want to talk about it if that's OK. Sorry.'

'No need to be sorry. Consider it forgotten. So what's the plan for the next dinner?'

'More of the same. I mean, I think it went quite well. What do think?'

'I think so too. We'll do our best to be there again.'

'I know you have a lot going on, so—'

'But until you get off the ground properly, Mum and I want to offer our help. I'm sure in a few weeks you'll have more volunteers and donations than you can cope with—'

'And diners,' Eden cut in, thinking about what Ralph had told her.

'And diners,' Livia agreed. 'But you'll have plenty of help, and you won't need us. Until then, we'll do what we can.'

Eden gave her a grateful smile. 'I never expected to make such a good friend when I came here. Especially this quickly. Thank you.'

'Did you expect to spend the six months alone?'

'Honestly, yes. I was OK with that, but I like this outcome better.'

'Good. Anyway, let's get this bar cleaned up so we can go home!'

'OK,' Eden said, her mind going back to all the things she'd wanted to tell Livia but couldn't. Maybe she was overthinking it. Maybe, if she explained it, expressed her remorse, accepted the blame and tried to make Livia understand how she'd learned from the trauma she'd caused, her friend would be able to see past it. Maybe nothing would change, apart from a new comprehension of Eden's motives.

Then again, what if everything changed? What if Livia didn't understand? If Caitlin had been right about one thing, it was that Eden's behaviour in the past had been pretty shitty.

So she went back to the cleaning and decided to say nothing more about it.

Two days later, Eden and her little team were back at the scout hut getting ready for another community dinner sitting. Except that her team had grown by two more members – Bilbo's 'lady friend' Mavis, who went dancing with him on Saturday nights, and who everyone knew was secretly his girlfriend, and her neighbour Val.

While Eden was thrilled with the extra help, she did start to wonder whether she might have to put a cap on the number of volunteers. Firstly because the kitchen simply wouldn't be big enough for them all to work safely, but also because if she wasn't careful, she'd have more volunteers than actual dinner guests. As much as she'd love to bankroll the entire project, those little donations from her diners – however small – made a huge difference to her ability to shop for decent food. She'd rather not if she could help it, because she didn't want to put people off, but when Julia said exactly the same to her, she wondered whether she'd simply have to get tougher about the whole thing. It was funny, because being tough and pragmatic had never been a problem in her previous career in property, but things had changed.

'Where would you like me, dear?' Mavis asked Eden.

'I'm not really sure,' Eden said. 'You probably know better than me what needs doing – I'm new to all this cooking business.'

'You must have cooked before,' Bilbo said, laughing an old, husky laugh.

'Well, yes, but not like this. It's always been oven chips and microwave pasta. My mum was a brilliant cook, but I never took any notice when she tried to show me how to do things. Too busy on my phone or wanting to go out to meet friends.'

'That's all youngsters,' Bilbo said. 'Things haven't changed. My dad used to try to teach me woodworking, but all I wanted to do was be out chasing skirt.'

Eden giggled. 'Chasing skirt? I can't imagine you being that naughty, Bilbo. You seem like such a gent!'

'Looks can be deceiving,' Mavis said drily, making Eden laugh again. 'He's a rogue, this one. Terror of the tea dance. Scourge of the scone table. When we were youngsters, all the girls around here were sweet on him – and he knew it.'

'Including you?' Bilbo put his arm around her and grinned.

'I kept my distance. Too big for your boots by far, you were.'

'And am I too big for my boots now?'

She pushed him off but with a grin of her own. 'I'm still trying to decide about that.'

'What if I sing you a song?'

Bilbo launched into something that Eden vaguely recognised, some old swing classic she'd probably heard on an advert. He was surprisingly good. In fact, he was very good. Everyone in the kitchen turned to see who was singing and smiled, and when he finished, there was a spontaneous round of applause.

'It's a long time since I heard you sing, but you've still got it,' Julia called over. 'I remember you doing turns at the Dolphin all the time when I was young. You ought to see Ralph about doing some more.'

'Oh no,' Bilbo said, trying to sound modest but clearly loving the attention. 'Those days are over.'

'Thank God,' Eden heard a small voice say and turned to see Bilbo's great-grandson, Liam, shaking his head with some humour.

Everyone who heard him started to laugh, and the usually shy Liam grinned.

'Cheeky pup!' Bilbo replied, though with some humour. 'You didn't used to say that. It was all, "Great-Grandpa, sing a song" or do a magic trick or some other thing.'

'You do magic too?' Eden asked.

'I like to call it sleight of hand,' Bilbo said. He went over to her, lifted a hand to her ear and then appeared to produce a coin from it.

Eden had seen it done on TV over the years a million times, but there was something about it being done right here with her that sent her into a giddy, childish spiral of glee. The reaction caught her by surprise. She'd spent the last few years of her adult life being cynical and grown-up and surrounded by people as jaded as her. She giggled again.

'That's so cool! How do you do it? Can you show me?'

'Absolutely not. I'd be kicked out of the Magic Circle if I started to show every Tom, Dick and Harriet.' He reached behind her other ear and produced another coin, and she grinned again as he gave it to her.

'Better take it steady, Bilbo,' Julia called over. 'You'll be bankrupt if you keep giving all that money away.'

Eden smiled as she handed it back to him.

'Keep it towards the kitty,' Bilbo said.

'Thanks.' Eden went to drop it into the slot of a money box Livia had brought in for donations.

'So.' Bilbo rubbed his hands together. 'Where would you like me to start?'

Eden glanced at Julia. Livia's mum had already become an unofficial foreman. She knew how to run a kitchen well, and two of the recipes they were going with tonight – honey and mustard chicken with potatoes, and a lentil ragu – were hers, so it seemed sensible to Eden to let her take control over the way they were prepared and cooked. The other dish they were putting out was fish and chips. Ralph had managed to send some prepared catering bags of chips and breaded fish that he'd got cheap from a supplier, so all it needed was to be put in the oven close to service. Eden was perfectly capable of that much, at least. She had to reflect with some humour that it was about all she was capable of, but that was OK. It was early days, and she'd learn on the job, so when the time came for her to cook without Julia's guidance, she was sure she'd be able to manage, though she doubted it would be as good as Julia's.

'I need some chicken boning,' Julia said. 'Do you think you and your magician fingers can do that for me?'

'I'll do that with him, shall I?' Mavis said, going to the fridge without further prompting.

'That would be great, thanks,' Julia said. She then set about directing everyone else while Eden went out into the main hall with Liam to start setting the tables and dressing the room to make it as welcoming as it had been on their first night. Because the hut was used by other groups and clubs, they had to take everything down once they'd finished with it, but that wasn't a huge problem, and it meant Eden could keep an eye on all their stuff to make sure none of it went missing.

With the extra hands, everything was ready far earlier than it needed to be. Julia gave instructions for things to be kept warm, apart from the food they wouldn't need to put in the oven until the last minute, and they all stopped for tea and biscuits. The scout hut was equipped with an enormous teapot and plenty of mugs, and Eden helped Livia to make sure everyone got a drink.

The kitchen was warm and fragrant from the food they'd cooked and full of good-natured chatter. Eden looked around and couldn't help a swell of pride. All this was down to her. She'd gathered these amazing people together. It was only the second evening, but already she felt certain she'd never want to give this up. It was a million miles away from anything she'd have been a part of in her old life back in London, let alone founded, and yet she was beginning to feel as if this was what she'd been put on the earth to do – it had simply taken a bit of time for her to figure it out. Perhaps recent mistakes and tragedies had played their part too, but she didn't want to dwell on any of that now, not when she was so happy.

After tea and biscuits, they started to make the final preparations, and not long after that, the first guests arrived. Eden was pleased to see some faces from the previous dinner, happy they'd enjoyed it enough to come again. There were plenty of new ones too, and for a scary moment, Eden was concerned her predictions that she might not find everyone a space would come true. But they shuffled around and found extra chairs, and with a few of the volunteers – including Eden, Livia and Bilbo – eating in the kitchen, they managed. Eden would have liked to have been in the main dining hall, but she didn't mind being in the kitchen with such good company, especially when Bilbo started to show her some more of his tricks with knots and napkins and playing cards. She needed to eat on the go anyway if she wanted to keep tabs on how everything was running, so she soon realised sitting in the dining room with everyone else would have been pointless.

At the end of the meal, as everyone started to shuffle out, the compliments on the food and expressions of gratitude were even more heartfelt than they'd been on the first evening. Eden could see how people were already starting to accept her and how they felt more able to be open with her. More people than she could remember told her how she'd saved them from some miserable night on their own with nothing but a slice of toast or a bowl of cornflakes. She'd never have looked at somewhere like Sea Glass Bay and thought there might be want, but it went to show that looks could be deceiving. Perhaps there was want everywhere if you looked hard enough, even in a place as picture-postcard perfect as this.

'I've had a lovely evening,' Mavis said, grabbing both Eden's hands.

Eden couldn't help but stare at her. 'You've worked like mad!'

'Oh but I had fun! It's been wonderful to spend time here with you all. A change from being at home in front of the telly. I hope you'll want me again for the next one.'

'I'll never say no to help.' Eden smiled. 'I'm just shocked you want to come and do it again.'

'Of course I do!' Mavis gave her a peck on the cheek. 'Goodnight, my love. You'll let Bilbo know if you want me, won't you?'

'I can let you know myself that I definitely want you.'

Bilbo appeared at Mavis's side and took her arm. 'Come on

– let's get you home. Goodnight, Eden. Thanks for the lovely dinner.'

'Thank you, Bilbo – you've been brilliant. I don't know what I would have done without you. In fact, I might hire you for entertainment next time!'

Eden's smile was stuck to her face as she watched them leave together, Liam trailing after them like a sheepish spare wheel, and she was still smiling as she watched the rest of her helpers follow, until it was just her and Livia, Julia and the children.

'I think this was better than the first one,' Julia said. 'I can't remember when I enjoyed myself so much grafting. And I've spent more time with people I know from the town than I have in years – and some of them I'd forgotten what lovely company they are. I think this could become a real social event, you know. It's almost like a party in there once we get going.'

'I can't believe I was so nervous at the start,' Eden said.

'Me neither,' Julia replied. 'At least you know now you needn't have been. Have you told your dad about it? I hope so. I expect he'll want to come and see what you're up to at some point? I'd love to meet him if he does, so don't forget.'

Eden's smile slipped at the mention of her dad, but she was too happy to let it unsettle her for long. 'I expect I will, but we've got a lot to do yet. Maybe in a few weeks.'

'Let me know. I'll cook for him.'

'He can eat here,' Livia said. 'At the hut.'

Julia laughed lightly. 'He's going to want more than one meal! I'd love to have him over for dinner, Eden,' she added. 'I've got to meet the man who raised such a wonderful woman, haven't I?'

Eden wanted to curl up and die. Wonderful woman? It was hardly the description any of her family would use. If only Julia knew the truth.

CHAPTER THIRTEEN

Eden might have known her new life in the bay was going too well. Ralph had asked her to do a last-minute extra shift, and the irony was that she wasn't even meant to be working that night. Afterwards, she couldn't decide whether she was being cut a break or given a bad hand by being there, but when a face from her past – one she never imagined she'd see again – walked into the Darling Dolphin that night, Eden couldn't have been more horrified.

The night had been quiet so far, and Eden had taken the opportunity of many gaps between customers to grill anyone who'd listen on new ideas for her community café.

'I'm thinking about a lunch club,' she said to Livia on one such occasion. 'For the old people. I think Bilbo and Mavis might host it. They could do dancing and stuff, and we could do an afternoon tea type thing with sandwiches and cakes.'

'There's already a tea dance in town.'

'Well, OK then, there doesn't have to be dancing. Something else? Bingo? Old people love bingo!'

'You have to give out prizes for bingo. Have you got the

money for prizes?' Livia leaned on the counter, and Eden felt as if she was trying not to laugh. But she didn't let it faze her.

'Can't they play just for fun?

'Bingo is a serious business, you know. Nobody plays for fun.'

Eden frowned. 'You think it's a terrible idea.'

'I think you might be getting carried away. I think what we've got is just right. Remember what Ralph said: you don't want to take too much on; you need downtime for yourself, or you'll burn out and be no good to anyone.'

'I know, but I just...'

How could Eden explain it? The feeling she was getting from her success was like a high, and she couldn't get enough of it. Being so needed, doing so much good, feeling as if she mattered, it was almost addictive to her. The more she did, the more she wanted to do.

'Why don't we talk to Ralph some more later when we've got time? And maybe Bilbo will have some thoughts. After all, you did just say you wanted him to play a big part in your lunch thing. He might come in later, and we can grab him then. If not, pop over to his house tomorrow.'

'I don't know where he lives.'

'That's easily fixed – I do.'

Eden was about to reply when her attention was drawn to the entrance. 'What...?'

Livia followed her gaze. 'What's the matter?'

Eden would have told her, but the fact was she couldn't quite believe what she was seeing. One of the partners in the company she'd worked for in London had just walked in. But... surely it couldn't be? 'What's he doing here?' she murmured.

It had to have been him she'd noticed over the past few weeks. Only a couple of times from a distance on the beach, and she hadn't been certain – in fact, she'd dismissed it, certain she was wrong. She wished now she had been wrong because this could only be bad news. She didn't know what he was doing in Sea Glass Bay, but her brain worked quickly to figure it out. And she came to one awful conclusion. The land the scout hut stood on was up for sale, and he was in the business of buying land like that to build on. Unless he was on holiday, but she doubted that. The coincidence was too big – he had to be here after the land.

He gave the pub a cursory once-over, but he didn't seem to have noticed Eden behind the bar.

'Who's that?' Livia asked.

'Cam bloody Faulkner,' she whispered. 'Balls of stone and a heart of steel.'

Livia started to laugh. 'Shouldn't that be balls of steel and a heart of stone?'

'Either way it's bad news. If he's got his sights set on our bit of land, we're going to have a fight on our hands.' Eden grimaced. She knew this because, to her shame, she'd helped him get what he wanted in the past. It was Cam she'd gone to with the information that had led to him picking up the community centre her mum volunteered at for a knock-down price. That brief conversation with him in his office had seemed so innocuous at the time but had come back to haunt her in the most tragic way. She'd spent many hours wishing she could take back her words.

'It's not our land—'

'You know what I mean.' Eden stiffened. 'He always gets what he wants, but not this time. He's never had to get it from me before.'

Livia stared at her, and Eden glanced to her side to catch it. Puzzled, surprised – she could understand why. Cam's appearance had set off alarm bells, and Eden had come out fighting already. She didn't even know for certain he was here about the land. For all she knew, he could have been on a lovely little jolly. Except for the fact that she knew him of old, and he didn't do lovely little jollies in sweet, unspoiled British resorts. He worked hard and played hard. He was more about swish hotels in Dubai or luxury yachts on the Med than quaint seaside towns.

'Sounds like you've had run-ins with him before,' Livia said.

'No. Before we were on the same side. I worked for his company in London. Back then I'd have been selling the places we built on the land he acquired. I'd have loved him when my commission came in. But I know how he operates, and that's what worries me.'

'You don't even know—'

Eden didn't get to hear the rest of Livia's sentence. As Cam turned her way, she was gripped by a sudden panic. Before he could see her, she dashed through the doorway at the side of the bar and into the tiny storeroom where they kept their cleaning supplies. She didn't know why she'd reacted that way; she only knew that she didn't want him to see her. Not here, doing this job.

What did it matter? Her rational response would have been that it didn't. What did she care if he saw her working in a pub? He was nothing to her. He might have gone back to his company and perhaps had a laugh about seeing her, and there might have been a few days of gossip, but it would have been forgotten soon enough. And it wasn't like she'd be seeing any of her old colleagues any time soon – if ever again.

Then there was the matter of what had brought him to Sea Glass Bay – it had to be something to do with the land where the scout hut stood. Presumably he'd come to check it out. If that was the case, then she ought to find out all she could about his plans, and that would mean facing him whether she wanted to or not. Unless... she could get Livia to find out. Could she? Was there a way Livia could start up a conversation and drop it in? Cam was the sort of guy who'd love showing off to a pretty girl. So if he was up to something like that, he'd probably want to boast about it.

Putting her head around the door she hissed out, 'Livia!'

Her friend turned to her with a confused look. 'What?'

'Come here!'

Livia went over, and Eden ducked back inside the cupboard. 'What's...? You're not hiding from him, are you?'

'I bloody am! You don't know him.'

'He can't be that bad.'

'I just...' Eden grimaced. 'I just can't face him right now. I know it's weird and childish, and I can't explain it, but I can't. I'm sorry.'

'You can't stay here all shift.'

'I know. I'm going to go in the kitchens and see if they need me – if I can get past without being noticed. Can you serve him? And try to get him talking – see if you can find out why he's here.'

Livia looked unconvinced but nodded. 'I'll see what I can do. But you're going to have to be quick because he's at the bar checking out the whiskies. That'll keep him busy for all of thirty seconds.'

'Don't worry, I can do it in ten. Just go and serve him... please!'

Livia went out, and Eden could hear her make quite a fuss of Cam. Clearly she was doing her best to keep him distracted to allow Eden's getaway.

But as she emerged from the cupboard, she glanced up to see him looking her way. There was instant recognition – she could see it in his reaction, the way he paused, a faint look of confusion on his face, but he didn't say anything. She wondered if he'd recognised her on the beach and dismissed it, as she'd done with him. She supposed, as she hadn't told anyone at the company where she was intending to go when she'd left London, he might have been confused to find her here and perhaps doubted the accuracy of his recognition. She'd done exactly the same, after all. Context – or lack of it – was a weird thing that could play tricks on someone. That was fine by her – he could be as confused as he liked; she wasn't about to put him straight.

In the kitchen, she made a pretence of needing to check something on a food order, hoping to mess around long enough for Cam to leave the bar area and sit down. But even as she did, it soon became depressingly obvious that her spontaneous escape had been silly and pointless. What if he decided to enjoy his drink at the bar? She'd have to go back out there sooner or later. And who was to say he'd only have one drink and then leave? Even if he went to sit down, he might well come to the bar for another round, and Eden might have to serve him.

As she turned to go back in, Livia met her at the kitchen doors.

'You've been rumbled,' she said. 'Sorry, I did my best, but he asked your name, and then he said he knows you. I mean, I had to tell him... I didn't know what else to do because he seemed as if he knew anyway.'

'As soon as I got in here, I knew you were right about me doing a runner. I couldn't have hidden in here all night, could I? It's all right. I suppose I ought to go and say something to him.'

'Like what?'

Eden shrugged. 'Bog off back to London?' She shook her head. 'I don't want to get into any kind of proper conversation with him because I just don't like him. He's all smiles and charm, but he's not a very nice guy underneath it.'

'Hmm... well he just bought us both a drink. In fact, he gave me forty quid. A bit flash, I'll admit, but I'm not going to complain. I put your half behind the bar for when you're ready.'

'He can have it back – I don't want his drink or his money.'

Livia raised her eyebrows. 'Wow... you really don't like him, do you? What's he done to you?'

'Nothing. It's what I know he's capable of that bothers me.'

'I think you should probably just accept the drink and try to be nice to him. He's a customer, after all. Or if you don't want the drink, put it in the kitty for the next community dinner or something.'

Eden nodded. 'I'll do that. Twenty quid will buy a lot of pasta from the wholesalers.'

They both spun round before Livia could reply to see Ralph staring at them from the kitchen doorway.

'What's going on here? Mother's meeting? Has the bar gone self-service?'

'Sorry, Ralph,' Livia said, hurrying past him. 'I'm on it.'

'Sorry...' Eden made to follow. 'It was my fault – I messed up an order and Livia was helping me to put it right.'

'I don't see why it takes two of you, but OK. Please don't leave the bar unattended like that again.'

As she walked across to the bar, Eden could see Cam leaning against it with his whisky, talking carelessly to Livia. He turned and grinned at her approach.

'This is a turn-up for the books. Of all the places I might have expected to run into you. What are you doing here? And you work here? The fast-paced world of property development not exciting enough for you?'

'Something like that,' Eden replied stiffly. 'I'm spending the summer here. This is a temporary job to give me something to do.'

He nodded slowly as he sipped his drink. 'I can't say it makes much sense to me, but whatever floats your boat.'

'So...' she continued, trying to keep her tone neutral, 'you're here on holiday?'

He shook his head. 'No. Business.'

'Oh?' Eden's heart sank. She had the most awful feeling she already knew what the business was. She had to ask, but she wondered if she really wanted to hear the answer. 'So you're after acquiring somewhere local? In the bay? Because I'm not sure I know of anywhere...'

'Some small parcel of land. I think there's a scout hut or something on it now. I've been looking around here for a while, and it seems like the best bet.'

'This is a very quiet resort – wouldn't you be better off in one of the bigger holiday towns?'

'You know how this works. We buy the land cheap, and we make the town a desirable destination, and our investment becomes a stroke of genius. We could make a killing in a place like this – there's a lot of untapped potential. If we can push prices up, our bit of land—' He stopped and fixed her with a look of humour. 'I don't know why I'm explaining it to you – I'm sure that has already occurred to you. When your sabbatical is over, you might even want to get involved in the deal – after all, you'd have a working knowledge of the town, wouldn't you? Perfectly placed, I'd say. That's assuming this' – he swept a hand, taking in the interior of the pub – 'isn't your new career, of course. In which case, I will assume you have even less interest in what I'm doing here.'

'I asked, didn't I? Of course I'm interested, or I wouldn't have said so. And if you recall, I'm not on sabbatical. I left. For good.'

'So you did. I assumed you'd change your mind...'

He studied her for a moment, careless humour in his expression. 'So you decided to come on holiday and get a job in a bar when you already had a very good job in London? Fancy that. I heard you'd gone weird, but I didn't believe it.'

'You couldn't have heard anything because I haven't been in contact with anyone from the company since I left,' Eden replied with a coolness she didn't feel.

'Right. In that case, I must have heard that before you left.'

'I heard you'd turned into a heartless bastard... Oh no, hang on, you didn't turn into one because you were always one.'

'You can't talk to me like that.'

'Yes I can – you're not my boss any longer.'

'I'm your customer.'

'A customer we can do without.'

'Harsh,' he said, grinning as he sipped at his whisky. This was amusing him, and the idea only riled Eden further. 'Is there a reason for this sum-up of my personal worth or...?'

'Do you have any idea what your plan will do to this community?'

'Of course I do. I know it as well as you do. It didn't seem to bother you quite so much before, back when you were making all that money selling all those lovely properties that did things to communities.'

'Before it wasn't... Before it wasn't *here*. London suburbs – people there expect prices and land values to go up; it's the deal when you live in London.' Eden wondered vaguely whether Cam even remembered the community centre deal, the one she'd tipped him off about. To him, she supposed it had been nothing, just one of a string of deals he made every week. She'd never made it clear how significant it had been to her mum, and she doubted he'd have cared even if she had.

'We've never just operated in London.'

'I know—'

'And you were never bothered when it was Newcastle or Liverpool or Manchester or some other city or town. So you're what? A NIMBY now? You're suddenly a community warrior because it happens to be a place where you are? Is that it? Would you have quite such a conscience if you'd never heard of this place?'

'I don't know. Maybe not. But I do know this place, and it's brilliant and special, and I don't want to see the community here destroyed. Life is hard enough without you working to push up property prices.'

'Hard for who? You? For everyone else who doesn't have the drive to get themselves a decently paid job? If people can't afford to live here, that's their problem. If they can't afford to live here, they'll have to find a way to afford it or leave. Isn't that how it always works? You never had a problem with it before.'

'I do now.'

'Why?' He studied her for a moment. 'What does it matter to you? You said you were only here for the summer.'

'Why do you care? It's got nothing to do with you.'

'Tell me anyway; I'm intrigued. You're only here for the summer; it's not your home.'

'I know, but... well, I've got something going on... actually...' Eden took a breath and smoothed her expression. Perhaps if she came clean, she could appeal to his better nature. Even Cam Faulkner must have one of those. If she told him why she wanted him to leave that plot alone, he might understand, maybe do it as a favour to her? After all, they'd been on the same side once. Not close, admittedly, but surely the fact she'd worked for him had to be worth something? 'We use the scout hut every week for community dinners.'

He frowned. 'What's a community dinner?'

'It's a dinner for the community.'

'Yes, I'm not stupid. What I'm asking is, why would anyone run such a thing? Surely if the community wants dinner, they eat at home or they go to a restaurant. So what's that about?'

'It's for people who struggle. Either because they're down

on their luck financially or because they're lonely or isolated in some way.'

'And you run that?'

'Yes. Sort of. With help, of course.'

'Why?'

'What do you mean, why? Does there have to be a reason?'

'Of course. What do you get out of it?'

'Nothing.'

'Rubbish!'

'OK, I get... It makes me happy.'

He shrugged. 'Well, there's no accounting for taste. A rare steak and a decent red would be more my thing, but whatever.'

'Listen, Cam, I'm asking you...' She lowered her voice and glanced uneasily around the pub before turning back to him. 'I know we were never close and you don't owe me any favours, but please... could you see your way to leaving this one be? Set your sights on something in a town that won't be quite so affected? Surely Sea Glass Bay isn't all that? And I've seen the plot – its tiny, hardly worth bothering with.'

'I'm perfectly aware of how big it is; I wouldn't have come here if I hadn't thought it worthwhile.'

'No. Come on, Cam. Please. There must be a dozen places on this coast that would be better. Surely the other partners would be pleased if you got somewhere already established. It's just one lousy little plot in a tiny seaside town. Just leave and forget about it. Let us have our thing.'

He shook his head. 'All you've done now is intrigue me.'

'Look, I'm telling you it won't be suitable. I'm trying to save you a wasted trip.'

'Of course you are. So you don't need to run your thing from there?'

'Why do you think I'm asking for this? What do you want? You want to make me beg?'

'Not really... All right, maybe just a bit.'

She shook her head slowly. 'You haven't changed. This is all just a game for you, isn't it?'

'I'd be lying if I said I didn't enjoy a challenge, but no, it's not a game. At the end of the day, I'm doing my job.'

'You don't have to enjoy it quite so much.'

'What's wrong with enjoying my job?'

'Depends on what it is, doesn't it? When it involves ruining people's lives—'

'How is this ruining anyone's life? Just find somewhere else to do your supper club or whatever it is.'

'There is nowhere else.'

'There must be.'

'Nowhere we can afford.'

'Not my problem. Put your prices up so you can afford... Who even uses it anyway? A handful of scroungers?'

'Loads of people! They come every week, and they love it – and they're not scroungers!'

'OK, OK, they're not scroungers. There's no need to get angry. You do realise I'm a customer here and you're supposed to be nice to me?'

'I ought to have you barred.'

He shook his head slowly, regarding her with amusement. 'Entertaining as I'm finding this, I don't have time for it. I'm going to acquire the land. Where you go or what you do is not my problem.'

'What about the scout hut then? Could you see a way to—'

'If you're about to ask if we can leave it there, then you're more deluded than I thought. You know that's not going to happen. The land will be cleared, and something far more profitable will be built there. Sorry, Eden. You've lost this one already. If I were you, I'd accept defeat with some grace and find somewhere else to do your suppers.'

'You realise I'll fight you. And you know I can be a pain in the arse, so I hope you're ready to spend a lot of time and money trying to get that land. And if that's the case, maybe you go and tell your partners that it won't be worth it. After all, it's a tiny plot in a small, insignificant seaside town – how much money can you make out of it?'

'If it's so insignificant, then why are you so bothered about it? And don't give me that – you know as well as I do the land in places like this is gold dust. Up and coming, as yet unspoiled, beautiful location – if you like that sort of thing, of course. We can make a lot of money from it. You're going to have to do a lot better than that to put me off. Frankly, I'm insulted that you don't consider me a more worthy adversary.'

Eden was riled. It was true she'd never spoken to Cam in this way before, despite the fact he'd always made her a bit nervous when she'd worked for him and they'd never had what anyone would call a friendship. But she didn't work for him any longer, and now he was here threatening everything that was giving her life meaning. She couldn't help but speak to him this way. 'You think you're a worthy adversary?'

'I know I am. I'll win; I always do.'

'That's because you play with rules fixed in your favour.' Eden regarded him for a moment, processing what she knew of him, her thoughts a melee that she was working hard to form into some kind of useful strategy. 'I wonder how good you'd be if someone else set the rules. I think you'd be in for a shock.'

'Yeah? You keep dreaming. I can win by any rules.'

'Care to put that to the test?'

He finished his drink. 'I think it's time I left.'

He turned to the doorway, but Eden wasn't done.

'Scared, are we?'

'What?' He spun back to face her. 'Scared of what? You and your old folks' army?'

Eden folded her arms and fixed him with a challenging stare. 'Yeah, I think you are. You might not want to admit it, but we both know local opposition can be a pain in the arse.

And take it from me, I can rally some serious local opposition. We might not win, but it would make your life very difficult for the next few months. Then again, we might win. Sometimes – not often – but sometimes local opposition does win. Is it worth the risk? Wouldn't it be easier to move on and try for a plot that doesn't matter quite so much to the people who use it?'

'I don't think so. I'll look forward to coming down here and laughing at your home-made, misspelled placards.'

'There'd be more than that.'

'Oh, like chaining yourself to trees? Please, you and I both know I've seen it all before, and it's never made a bit of difference to the outcome. So you all go ahead and stage your little sit-ins and enjoy them, because you won't be able to sit there for long.'

'Hmmm. So you think you can win by any rules?'

'I'm a born winner. I can win no matter what.'

'Then come and volunteer for me.'

The words were out before Eden had even thought about them. They'd come from nowhere, and instantly she regretted it. But that regret turned into intrigue as she noticed the shock on his face. She'd achieved that much at least – something she'd never have expected to see on Cam Faulkner. How far could she push this? Was she on to something?

'Don't be ridiculous,' he said.

'What's ridiculous about it? Come and volunteer for me. Two weeks in my kitchen. If your conscience is still clear about what you're doing after two weeks there, then I'll hold up my hands in surrender.'

'I'm not volunteering in your ridiculous kitchen.'

'Scared it might get to you?'

'Of course not. It's insane, that's all.'

'You're scared. You don't want to do it because you know it will make you feel guilty.'

'It won't make me feel anything. It would be a complete waste of time.'

'Well, if you think you're so immune to persuasion, then surely two weeks of chopping the odd vegetable is a far easier battle than months of local action to stop you demolishing the scout hut? Two weeks and it would be over, and you'd have your land.'

His frown turned into a mocking smile. 'You really think you can win by making me spend two weeks in your stupid kitchen?'

'With people you'll grow to love, yes.'

'I highly doubt that.'

'We'll see.'

'I'm not doing it.'

'Aren't you?' Eden raised her eyebrows.

'Absolutely not.'

'Surely it's a no-brainer. Two weeks. If you're not convinced, you'll get no opposition and you've won. It's that simple.'

'I'd have your word on that? This isn't some stalling tactic that you'll stretch out when I tell you it hasn't convinced me at all?'

'You have my word. If you're not convinced, then we'll leave quietly.'

He was thoughtful for a moment. Eden could see she'd hit a nerve, but would he take the bait? She knew he was smarter than that, but she also knew his competitive nature would make it hard for him to resist a challenge, especially one he'd think he could so easily win.

Eden had other ideas, of course. She knew how easy those people in her kitchen were to love, even for someone with a heart of stone like Cam Faulkner. She might not have bet her entire life savings on it, but she'd certainly put a considerable sum out there. After all, they'd won her over, and hadn't she once been as hard and cynical as Cam? True, she'd had reasons for wanting to change, and so perhaps she'd been a bit more open to it, but who was to say similar things weren't going on in Cam's life right now? For all she knew, he could be harbouring a secret longing to change, just as she'd been. At the end of the day, she was increasingly convinced this was the only way to win this battle, and she had to give it a try. All that other stuff she'd talked of – it rarely worked, even if it postponed things. This might not work, but she had more control over it than anything else, and she had faith in her new friends.

'Come on,' she pressed. 'Why the hesitation? Is it because you think I might win the bet?'

'A bet? Is that what this is?'

'Of course it is. I'm betting the future of the community café. You're betting the deal. And the odds are massively in your favour – at least, you think they are. Surely it's a dead cert as far as you're concerned? And if it is, what's the problem with saying yes?'

'All right,' he said slowly, mockingly, supremely confident that this would be a walk in the park. That's what he thought, Eden could tell, but she was going to prove him wrong, and then she'd enjoy seeing that smile wiped off his smug face. 'Two weeks. But I come in, I stir your soup or whatever other shit you have lined up for me, and I don't do anything else. No talking to me, no trying to win me round, no socialising of any sort.'

'You're going to have to talk to someone at some point, if only to communicate tasks.'

'Then the minimum – that's all. Don't think you can try to be my friend. Don't tell anyone else to try to be my friend—'

'As if anyone would want to. We're not desperate, you know.'

'Good. So long as we're clear. I'm not going to fall for your emotional blackmail, if that's what you think. I'm only doing this because I have to admit you're right about one thing – it's a speedy and easy solution, and why wouldn't I take it?'

'Good, well that's one thing we can agree on then. It's a speedy and easy solution.'

He let out a laugh that was unexpectedly genuine. 'I can't fault your tenacity, though. Let's also agree that we both think we're going to win and that the other one is sadly misguided.'

'True enough. So when can you start?'

'You're really not going to let go of this, are you?'

'No. When can you start? What are you doing this Wednesday?'

'Um...' He got out his phone and opened the diary app. 'What time?'

'About three.'

He looked up at her. 'Three in the afternoon? What time do you eat? I thought it was dinner.'

'It is, but there's a lot to do.'

'I can't make three. Some of us still have a proper job, you know.'

'When can you make?' Eden asked, ignoring the jibe.

'I suppose I could make four thirty. Maybe four at a push.'

'Right, so get there when you can. Four, four thirty, it doesn't matter – we'll find some way to make use of you. And don't try to be crap at everything so we stop asking because that's not going to wash. While you're there, think of me as your boss and treat me with the respect you'd give your boss, which means doing things to the best of your ability. If you're doing this thing, you're going to commit.'

'Yes, boss,' he said, and that mocking tone was back.

'Good. Just as long as we're clear. If you don't play by the rules, then I won't either – remember that.'

'OK, OK, I got it. Wednesday then.'

'Are you staying close by?'

'Hotel. Close enough, don't worry.'

'I wasn't. I just wondered...'

'If I'd use it as an excuse not to come?'

'No. I only meant... forget it.'

He gave a dismissive wave as he turned to leave. As soon as he was gone, Livia came across from the other side of the bar where she'd been polishing glasses, probably in a bid to look as if she wasn't listening when, in reality, she could hardly do anything else. Eden didn't blame her – she'd have been eavesdropping too.

'What was all that about?'

'Well, I hope it's a stroke of genius on my part, but I'm already worried I've dropped a massive clanger. Then again, sometimes in life, you have to take a risk, right?'

'Well, that's not cryptic at all...'

Eden gave a rueful smile. 'I laid down a challenge to try and save the kitchen. Mr Faulkner is going to come and work for us for two weeks—'

'*What?*'

'And then,' Eden continued, acknowledging Livia's incredulity but not addressing it, 'if he hasn't been convinced of its value, I said I'd give up the fight for the hut and let him have it without a fuss.'

'You can't do that!'

'It was the only way, trust me. I realise it sounds like madness, but I know what that man is capable of. Normal weapons won't work – we have to go nuclear or not at all. You can petition and stage sit-ins and get the local papers in and all that, but it won't matter to him. I needed something outside of the box... I only hope this is good enough.'

'So do I – for your sake.'

Eden sighed. 'I suppose there would be other venues. Not nearly as suitable. Not suitable at all, in fact, but...' She shook herself. 'I don't need to worry about that because I have a plan.'

'You do?'

'Yes. We're all going to go on a major charm offensive. He's going to have so much fun he won't want to leave once his two weeks are up.'

'How does that help us keep the hut?'

'Well, he'll like us all so much he won't want to be such a Scrooge McDuck.'

Livia slowly shook her head. 'I hope you know what you're doing.'

'Me too,' Eden said, not entirely sure that she did. Had she just signed the death warrant for her community café?

CHAPTER FOURTEEN

Eden fully expected a no-show from Cam. If it had been the other way round, she didn't think she would have turned up either, so it was a jolt to be peeling potatoes and staring out of the window of the scout hut kitchen to see a car pull up in one of the parking spaces at the back and him get out. But then she gave the matter a second thought and decided that she ought to have seen it coming. He'd have come just to prove a point, to prove her wrong, to win the bet, or simply to be as contradictory as he could – perhaps all of those things. He'd have come because he'd have known she'd suspected he wouldn't, just to irritate her.

Her eyes followed him across the car park. He was wearing well-fitted jeans and a soft sweatshirt. She'd never seen him in what she assumed were his scruffs. Some of her colleagues at the property company had fancied him like mad, but though she'd appreciated his chiselled good looks, she'd made a point of taking no notice. He wasn't someone who made himself easy to like. Today, though, away from that environment, now that he was no longer her boss... If these were his scruffs he ought to dress that way more often because he wore them well. In fact, very well. He looked...

Annoyed at the train of thought, she scowled, and then he looked up at the window and caught it. Good. He wasn't here to make friends, and she couldn't allow him to see any weakness.

Livia appeared at her side. 'Hmm...' she said, following Eden's gaze. 'There's a turn-up for the books. Didn't think he'd actually come.'

'Me neither.'

'So that's a win for us straight off.'

Eden turned to her. 'Is it?'

'Of course. He's intrigued enough to be here and, let's face it, we couldn't very well win him over if he hadn't even been here to win over, could we?'

'Well, there's a logic in there somewhere,' Eden said with a smile. 'I certainly can't fault it.'

'Shall I go and meet him at the door? He's going to have his defences up as soon as he sees you, but I might be able to disarm him – he'll have to be on his best behaviour for me, after all, because I'm a stranger.'

'You're not, because he met you at the pub, and I don't think he does best behaviour for anyone. He doesn't think he owes people the basic courtesies the rest of us do.'

'That sounds a bit harsh,' Livia said, and Eden could see the doubt in her expression.

'Trust me, I know it does, but I also know him. The world owes him a living, and he owes it nothing. He takes what he wants and doesn't care who goes without so he can have it, and the only people worth his time are those he wants to sweet-talk because they can do something for him.'

'Must be why he's come then,' Livia said, laughing lightly. 'Because he knows we have something he wants. Don't forget, that's another advantage we have.'

'It's not much of one,' Eden said ruefully. 'I'm under no illusions that this is a long shot and it'll be a miracle if we actually manage to change his mind. It's just the only shot we've got as far as I can tell. But if he wanted to, he could have this place off us tomorrow. He's probably only here because he finds it funny that I'd even challenge him at all.'

'Well then,' Livia said, turning to leave the kitchen, 'like a giant-killing FA Cup upset, we'll just have to give him the shock of his life, won't we?'

A couple of minutes later, Livia returned with Cam in tow. Nobody else in the kitchen had taken much notice of Livia and Eden discussing him at the window, but now that he was here, every eye turned to see. If he felt their scrutiny, he didn't show it. He was as cool and nonchalant as always, a fact that riled Eden before they'd even spoken a word of greeting. She was going to have to get a hold of this dislike otherwise she was going to lose this battle in no time at all.

'Afternoon,' he said, sweeping his gaze over the assembled volunteers. 'I'm Cameron – though my friends call me Cam.'

'Hello, Cam!' everyone else said.

Julia wiped her hands on a dishcloth and went over to shake his. 'I'm Livia's mum, Julia.'

He smiled as he took her hand. 'Livia's mum? No way! You couldn't be old enough!'

Julia laughed, but she gave him a look that said she knew how this game was played too. 'I think you might be telling me a little white lie, but I'll take the compliment.'

Cam's hand went to his chest in a dramatic gesture of inno-cence. 'I would never!'

'Right...' Julia nodded to Eden. 'I believe you two are well acquainted.'

'Hi,' Eden said. 'It's good to see you.'

He raised an eyebrow in disbelief.

'Yes,' Eden said, 'despite what you think, it really is. We're always grateful for extra hands, and tonight is going to be a busy one.'

Everyone introduced themselves and greeted him in turn while Eden shared a significant look with Livia. Battle had already commenced.

'Right,' Julia said, turning back to Eden once the formalities were over. 'Where do you want Cam?'

'Um... what do you think?' Eden asked her. 'Something straightforward?' She looked at Cam. 'What are your culinary skills like?'

'Well, I know the right way to open an oyster, and I can sear a tuna steak to perfection. What level of skill does that suggest to you?'

'There won't be much call for searing tuna steaks,' Eden said, wryly acknowledging his sarcasm. 'But we do need some tins opening and seasoning and some peppers and onions dicing for the tuna pasta bake. In fact, we need some cheese grating for that too. Think I can leave you with those tasks?'

'I'm sure I can manage.'

Eden looked at Julia.

'I'll show him where everything is,' Julia said.

Liam and Bilbo, who'd messaged ahead to say they were running late, arrived at that moment. As they did, the room was suddenly alive with far warmer greetings than they'd had for Cam. Nancy and Levi, who'd been colouring on a table at the far end of the kitchen to keep them out of the way until there were tasks they could do, looked up at the old man's arrival and broke into broad grins.

'Bilbo!' Nancy cried, running to throw her arms around his legs.

'Steady!' Bilbo chuckled. 'You'll have me over – it doesn't take much these days!'

'Can you do a trick?' she asked breathlessly.

'Yes!' Levi agreed. 'Do a trick, Bilbo! Do the coin one!'

'You mean this one?'

Bilbo produced a shiny fifty-pence piece from behind Levi's ear and held it out to him. Levi's mouth opened into a delighted circle of surprise.

'That's yours,' Bilbo said. 'After all, I found it behind your ear. Don't spend it all at once.'

'Me now!' Nancy almost yelled with the force of her impatient enthusiasm.

Bilbo did the same and handed her the coin.

'You two will have poor Bilbo in the workhouse,' Livia said with a fond smile at all three of them.

'Mustn't leave you out,' Bilbo said, going over to Livia and taking another coin from behind her ear too. She burst out laughing.

'You keep it,' she said, handing it back.

'No,' Bilbo said firmly. 'This is yours – I found it behind your ear, not mine.'

'I'll have it!' Levi said, and Livia frowned at him.

'I'll have it if nobody else wants it,' Cam cut in with such wry amusement that the entire kitchen went as silent as the bar room of a western film as the gunslinger walks in.

'Bilbo,' Eden said, sensing the tension. 'This is Cam, our new volunteer.'

'Only for two weeks,' Cam said, extending his hand for Bilbo to shake. 'Pleased to meet you. Unusual name. My great-uncle knew a man called Bilbo. Served with him in the navy, I believe.'

'I was in the navy,' Bilbo said, puffing out his chest. 'What ship was he on?'

'I know he was on more than one... hang on a minute...' He pulled out his phone and sent a quick text. 'Just asking my dad,' he said.

Less than thirty seconds later, it bleeped a reply.

'Wow, he's quicker than usual,' Cam said, opening up the

message. 'He says there was HMS *Victorious* and HMS *Vanguard*.'

'That was mine!' Bilbo said. 'The *Vanguard*! What's your uncle's name?'

'It was William Faulkner, though everyone called him Razor because he was so sharp – apparently. That's the way he always told it anyway. He died when I was quite young, so I might have that wrong.'

Bilbo's eyes were like the dinner plates Liam was fetching from the cupboards. 'Never! Old Razor! I knew him! Good lad he was. Older than me; looked out for me when I first joined the ship. What a small world!'

'It would seem so,' Cam said, and Eden could tell that the smile on his face this time was genuine.

As far as she was concerned, this was brilliant. Of all the goals she could have scored, she never imagined it would be such a blinder. And so early in the game too. She thought quickly and perhaps a little ruthlessly. She needed to make sure Bilbo had lots of contact with Cam. Some might have said she was exploiting the connection, but it was only what Cam would have been doing, and if it got her closer to keeping the scout hut, then she'd do whatever it took. There was no way she could look such a handsome gift horse in the mouth.

'Bilbo,' she began sweetly, 'could you give Cam a hand with the ingredients for the pasta bake? He'll need help finding things in the kitchen, so if you team up with him, it will speed all that up a bit.'

Bilbo gave a smart salute. 'Ma'am!'

'Eden...' Liam called over, and she nodded.

'That's fine – I know you're already way ahead of me. You start setting up in the dining room, and I'll be in to help you shortly.'

When she looked back, Bilbo was questioning Cam about his great-uncle, and Cam was being about as pleasant in his replies as Eden had ever seen him. She glanced away to catch Livia flashing her a grin. Eden returned it. So Livia had worked it out just as she'd done. It was going to take more than a chance family connection, of course, but perhaps winning Cam over wasn't going to be such an impossible task after all.

As everyone went back to their work, Eden tried to keep tabs on how Bilbo was getting on with Cam without making it too obvious. She realised Cam might not be so easy to hoodwink, but as Bilbo was entirely innocent of any ulterior motives, she trusted that his good humour and easy-going nature, coupled with the instant connection, would go a long way to softening Cam without it being contrived.

She listened as Bilbo launched into anecdotes involving Cam's uncle, and she could hear Cam laughing easily from time to time. He even asked questions, so he was clearly engaged. Eden couldn't believe her luck and wondered when Cam was going to turn back into the man she knew and loathed. She didn't dare look for fear that Cam would catch her and read her expression. If he did that, the jig would most definitely be up. And she had to admit that it seemed as if Cam was getting stuck in. She'd expected him to be reluctant to get his hands dirty, perhaps mess around in a corner of the kitchen and stay out of proceedings as far as he could, but she was pleasantly surprised to see that wasn't the case. Perhaps it was because he'd clearly warmed to Bilbo, but whatever the reason, Eden wasn't going to complain about that either.

She'd worried that him being there might be disruptive for everyone else, especially if he made his disdain for what they were doing known, so it was a relief to see that nothing of the sort was happening. In fact, Eden heard one or two occasions where he'd taken a job from Bilbo and told him to take it easy. Bilbo only laughed and said he would do nothing of the sort, but it was a kindness that Eden struggled to equate with the Cam she knew.

. . .

'Would you like a cup of tea, Cam?' Julia called over from the giant teapot that she was filling with freshly boiled water. Julia filling the kettle had become the unofficial signal for a quick break over the past few weeks. Everyone would down tools for ten minutes or so, and catch up on how the work was progressing and what still needed to be done, as well as catch up on the odd bit of gossip or news.

'Thanks, Julia,' he said gallantly. 'I'd love one.'

Julia smiled and nodded. She didn't need to ask anyone else because none of the regular volunteers ever refused her tea. Eden looked around the room at her team – as she'd come to think of them – and wondered how much longer this would last. It seemed she'd only just got used to them all and started to think of them as not only essential help but as friends too, and already that was in danger. Julia and Livia weren't going to be doing this forever, for a start. They couldn't spare the time long term – they'd begun with that understanding, and Eden respected it. But what about the others? Would her kitchen even survive past the next two weeks and Cam's influence? She supposed they could keep going for a while until the land was sold and the hut demolished, but having that fate hanging over them would change the way people viewed the project and perhaps make them decide it wasn't worth investing their time. She hoped not, but she wouldn't blame them.

As Julia handed out the drinks, Eden edged closer to Cam with hers, wondering if he'd say anything about how he was getting on.

'This is a good cup of tea, Julia,' was all he said, though he threw Eden a sideways look that said he was fully aware of what she was hoping for and he wasn't going to oblige. As far as he was concerned, she could carry on guessing.

'We've got some biscuits in the tin over there if you want

one,' Julia said, angling her head at a shelf. 'Technically they're the scouts' biscuits, but I know they won't mind too much if we have the odd one.'

Cam went to look inside the tin and pulled out a chocolate digestive. 'I can't remember the last time I had an old-school biscuit.'

'I'm surprised you've ever eaten one,' Eden said. 'Did they eat pov food at Eton?'

Cam grinned, seemingly unfazed by Eden's taunt. 'I didn't go to Eton. It was a good old state school for me.'

'Really?' Eden frowned. Not that she'd ever known much about his past, but to her mind, he'd always had the air of someone privately educated: he was well spoken and eloquent, had immense confidence and assurance of his place in the world. He'd always seemed like a man brought up in the belief that he was superior. She supposed it just went to show how wrong someone could be. But if his self-belief didn't come from school, she quickly decided his parents must have done a real number on him.

'Really,' he said. 'My parents are working class, just like...' He paused. 'Well, I don't know. I don't suppose any of us knows all that much about each other's past, do we?'

'People do make assumptions,' Julia cut in. 'It's when we make an effort to set them aside that we learn about each other. What did your parents do for a living, Cam?'

'Dad is a painter and decorator, and Mum was a teaching assistant – she took early retirement when Dad started his own business and was bringing enough money in.'

'So actually, they're not so working class now,' Eden said.

He turned to her as he bit into his digestive. 'How do you come to that conclusion?'

'Well, your dad owns his own business. That must make him middle class, right?'

Cam shrugged in a way that Eden found instantly irritating,

like he was mocking her. 'Can't say I'm all that interested in class wars like you are.'

'I'm not! I'm not interested in anything of the sort! I'm just saying—'

'And I'm just saying I don't think it matters what class you're from. It's what you do. You make your own fortune – at least, that's what I took from my dad's example. You do what you have to do. The only person who can lift your status or sink it is you, nobody else.'

'That's rubbish!' Eden said. 'That's assuming we're all on a level playing field to start! Some people are born into such poverty that they don't stand—'

'Like you?' Cam said in such a wry tone that Eden was all at once incensed and ashamed. 'Do you think you speak for all those people? Do you think you know what it's like? I thought your family had always been well off.'

'I think...' Julia cut in then glanced around the room. Eden followed her gaze and saw some awkward looks. She realised instantly that Cam was doing his best to wind her up, and it was working like a charm. 'That this might not be a conversation for this evening. I think it might need more attention than we have time to give it.'

This was Julia's tactful way of defusing an almighty argument, and Eden had to admit that her assessment of where the discussion with Cam had been going was bang on the nose. Eden had been losing her temper, fired by his sardonic tone and, perhaps, a little bit of shame because he'd made a valid point about her own upbringing. If what he said about his own family was true, then she'd had the more privileged upbringing.

Considering what she was asking people to do here, she felt an odd kind of imposter syndrome. Not the sort that people usually got when they felt unqualified to be in a position of authority but exactly the opposite, where she felt unworthy to speak for people who were struggling because she'd never struggled. Perhaps everyone saw her as a rich girl playing at social warrior. She hated the thought so much she could almost have burst into tears. Did they feel insulted by her efforts? Did it look like a game to them? That wasn't her intention at all. She had to somehow make everyone see that.

'Eden...' Julia waved her over. 'Could you just...?'

Eden went over, and Julia leaned in close, dropping her voice to almost a whisper. 'Are you all right?'

'Of course,' Eden whispered back.

'Don't let him get to you. He said it himself: it doesn't matter where you come from; it's what you do that counts. You've started something amazing here, and none of us cares what the motivation was. We only care that you want to make it work as much as we do. Hold on to that, my love.'

Eden gave her a grateful smile. 'Thank you; I needed to hear that.'

'I thought as much. Now...' she added in her normal tone, 'would you mind taking a cup out to Liam? I don't think he heard me shout up.'

Eden picked up a mug and headed for the doorway to the main room, conscious of Cam's eyes following her. She could just imagine the smug look on his face. She was angry, but more with herself than with him because she'd let him get to her just as Julia had said. So much for this being an easy battle.

Cam had turned out to be a surprisingly hard-working team player. Not that Eden was under any illusions about his intentions, but help was help, and at least he did that well. And once the combative nature of their interactions had calmed down, she was also surprised to find that they got along well – certainly better than they'd ever done during their time working together. Admittedly they had never worked closely on anything back in London, and it was perhaps because of that she'd never really taken the time to get to know him as a person at all. He'd always just been Cam Faulkner, the best and brightest of the partners, the man who'd do anything to close the deal.

'He's either a brilliant actor, or I think he might have had a good time here tonight,' Livia said quietly to Eden as they finished wiping down the kitchen, having sent Cam on his way.

'I wouldn't like to put much money on either right now,' Eden said. 'I must admit I can't read him. I thought it would be easy, but...'

'You don't know him quite as well as you thought you did?'

'Something like that. How do you think it went? Do you think we made any headway?'

'Tonight?' Livia paused, a damp rag in her hand resting on the worktop. 'I suppose it's only the first night. He's here for two weeks, right?'

'So what you're saying is we've got two weeks to really turn the screws?'

'If that's the way you want to put it, yes.'

'Suddenly it doesn't seem like long enough. Two weeks is six dinners and we've already done one. So that leaves five evenings to persuade someone who's doing his best not to be persuaded. I mean, I know he got on with everyone, but I don't think for a minute that he'd even give any of us a second thought once he leaves here. He certainly won't be worrying about whether this place can keep going or not. He might do his two weeks and even have a good time, but once he's gone and the land is sold, I'm sure he won't ever think of it again.'

'Then why are you even doing any of this? I thought you believed it would work? If you don't think—'

Eden took up a sweeping brush that had been leaning against the wall. 'I thought at first... but now I'm not so sure.'

'Give yourself more credit. I still think it could work, but even if it doesn't, we've tried. At least we're doing something, and we can't do much more than that.'

Eden began to sweep. 'You're right – ignore me. Livia...' It was her turn to pause, a question on her lips and fear in her heart for what the answer might be. 'When Cam said I was well off... that my family were well off – not rich, you understand, but OK for money – you don't think... well, you don't think people feel insulted by me wanting to help?'

Livia smiled. 'Why would they? Anyway, nobody really knows what your family background is. It's certainly not the first question anyone asks me: "Hello, can I have the shepherd's pie? And by the way, is Eden loaded? Because if she is, I don't want the shepherd's pie after all.'

'I'm not loaded—'

'You know what I'm saying. Stop stressing. Everyone understands what you're trying to do and that your intentions are good, wherever they began. Cam's playing mind games with you – you must see that.'

'No more than I've been doing with him, trying to guilt him into leaving us be.'

'Exactly!' Livia said brightly. 'You're a good person; your background doesn't change that.'

'That's just it...' Eden was suddenly nervous as she stopped sweeping and looked around. Julia was outside putting the recycling into the correct bins. The children were with her, ostensibly helping but in reality making the job twice as complicated. Everyone else had left. There was only her and Livia here, and Eden wondered whether this was the moment. She wanted so desperately to tell Livia everything, to explain why she was in Sea Glass Bay and why she was doing this, and she hoped she knew her friend well enough to know that she'd get an understanding response. But Eden couldn't be sure, and she was terrified of losing the woman who'd done so much to help her turn her life around, even if that woman wasn't aware of just how important a part she'd played. Livia was her best friend – perhaps her only friend right now.

She pulled in a long breath. 'I don't think I'm all that good. I let Cam get to me because he knows me from a time when I was far from good. I suppose I'm scared that he'll tell you all the truth and you won't want to know me anymore. I've made mistakes, Livia. I want to put those right, and I want to be better.'

Livia smiled. 'Eden... you don't need to tell me any of this. I don't care what you might have been like before – and for what it's worth, I can't believe for a minute you were a bad person, even though you keep trying to tell me you were. I know who you are now, and I like you. You're doing a thing that nobody else in the bay wanted to do, and you're helping a lot of people. I see how hard it is for you and how much it means to you. No matter how this all ends, even if we lose the hut, that's good enough for me. You've given it your all, and you should be proud.'

'But I still feel as if I ought to tell you the truth.'

'About what?' Livia's smile slipped, and the sight unnerved Eden. Would what she was about to say change things, despite what Livia had just told her?

'About what happened before I left London. Why I... I suppose I ought to be more honest about that too. I didn't just leave London; I ran away. From something I did.'

'Something you did?' Livia was frowning. 'Not something... illegal?'

'God, no! Not that, but... well, it was...'

Why had she started this conversation? Why couldn't she have kept her mouth shut? This wasn't going to end well. Just as Eden had feared, Livia would see her in a whole new light, and any friendship they'd had would be over.

'Listen, Eden, I don't know if I want to hear—'

At that moment, Julia came in, wiping her hands down her apron.

'The bloomin' bin bag just burst all over the place! Stupid

cheap muck! Eden, I think we're going to have to get better quality ones next time. Is there something I can use to clean the back yard? A spare brush or something?'

'Oh...' Eden glanced at Livia. While part of her was thankful for Julia's interruption, she was also tired of keeping her past away from everyone. But it would have to wait. She wanted to share it with Livia but not with Julia, and, besides, it felt as if the perfect moment had gone.

Livia went to the supply cupboard. 'I think I've seen a yard brush here somewhere... ah!' She pulled out a wooden broom and handed it to her mum. 'That do?'

'Perfect,' Julia said.

Livia turned to Eden, and before anything else could be said, she shook her head with a smile. 'I know you feel like you have some big reveal and that it might make everyone hate you, but I don't see how that could possibly happen. If you want to tell me, then you can tell me, but let's wait until we've got the proper time, eh?'

Eden nodded. 'Thanks, Livia.'

'No problem. Let's get finished here. I don't know about you, but I'm gagging for a drink!'

CHAPTER FIFTEEN

Cam had come back for the next volunteer dinner, and the one after that too. He arrived at the beginning of the second week not long after Eden herself. This was the first time she'd be here without Livia and Julia, who had important things to take care of at the ice-cream parlour, things they'd put off until they could do so no longer, and then Livia had a shift at the pub. Eden had expected this day to come – they'd always been open about their ability to commit long term – but knowing that didn't make her feel any less cut adrift. Julia especially had become her right-hand man – or perhaps the reality was that Julia had actually taken charge, leaving Eden to be her right-hand man.

With two members of the team down and Eden running the ship, she'd gladly taken advice from Ralph about the best menu to go with, one that would cut work down to a minimum while still offering three wholesome and nutritious options. They'd settled on a Moroccan-style one-pot chicken stew with bulgar wheat; simple fish and chips that could be oven-baked; and a vegetable lasagne, prepared by one of Ralph's chefs as a favour earlier that day so it would be ready to go into the oven with the fish and chips. Eden had been grateful to Ralph; while she still felt nervous about running the kitchen, she was hopeful it would be enough to ensure things ran smoothly. All she really needed to do was to prepare the ingredients for the stew – something that she could do herself if she allowed enough time. She'd arranged for the rest of her volunteers to arrive later once she'd prepped everything and put it into the crockpot to simmer, and so was surprised to look up from dicing peppers to see Cam's car pull up in his usual spot. Wiping her hands, she went to open the door.

'You're early,' she called as he got out of his car. 'I don't need anyone for another couple of hours. I thought I'd said last time—'

'You did,' he said, locking up and striding over anyway. 'I was just at the ice-cream place, and Livia said you were here on your own.'

'Oh,' she said with a wry smile. 'And you thought it was a good opportunity to do me in and get your competition out of the way?'

'If only it were that easy,' he replied with a wry smile of his own. 'Livia said she and Julia couldn't make it tonight and you had to start early to make up for it. I had a spare half hour, and I thought you might want help.'

Eden frowned. 'That's noble of you.'

'You think there's an ulterior motive?' he asked, his smile widening.

'Of course I do. You're trying to tell me there isn't?'

'I wouldn't dream of it. Regardless of any motive, are you saying you don't want my help? If you're accepting it with your eyes wide open, then you have nothing to lose by accepting it, do you?'

'So there is a motive?'

His hands went to his pockets, and something in the way he looked at her now was so unexpected, she hadn't a clue what to make of it. His smile faded, and he simply nodded slowly, all the while holding her in that strange, unfathomable gaze. 'I suppose there might be.'

'What?'

Whatever had been going on in his head, he seemed to shake himself free of it and the wry smile returned. 'I didn't think you needed reminding. Don't we both have the same motive? To win the bet?'

'You think coming to help me will win you the bet? If anything I'd say it's a sign I'm winning.'

'Ah, but maybe that's what I want you to think. So shall I stay, or do you want me to go?'

Eden sniffed. 'You might not come back if I let you go, so you'd better come in.'

She moved from the doorway to let him through and went back to her chopping while he pulled an apron from a peg and put it on. Then she looked up at the sound of his voice.

'Where do you want me to start?'

Eden waved her knife at some sacks in the corner of the room. 'There's a ton of veg to peel and chop over there. Take your pick which you do first. I also need some garlic mincing.'

'I can do that.'

Cam went to the sacks and opened the first one. 'Carrots?' He looked up. 'Want me to peel them?'

'Yes, please.'

She went back to her peppers, the sounds of him tipping the carrots into the sink and then turning on the tap a soundtrack to her thoughts. Why was he here? What was he up to? He had to be up to something, didn't he?

'You know,' he began as he turned off the tap, 'it's a shame we didn't get to know each other better when we worked together.'

Eden looked round. 'Is it? You said I was weird.'

'I did. I suppose that was uncalled for.'

Eden raised her eyebrows. 'Thank you? I'm assuming there was an apology of sorts in there.'

'I suppose there is. I don't think I'm the only one who made judgements, though, am I?'

'I haven't decided yet. If you think this is going to get me to drop my guard, you can think again.'

'I'm trying to pay you a compliment. I won't bother again.'

'And there was no ulterior motive for that? Just like there's no ulterior motive for coming in early to help me when you have no reason to and you know I'll be alone?'

'Don't worry – I'm not going to jump you, if that's what you think.'

Eden stared at him. The shock she felt wasn't because of his statement – it was because suddenly, from nowhere, the image of them pressed against each other, right there at that moment in the kitchen, invaded her brain. The harder she tried to banish it, the more insistent it was, until she had to turn away for fear he'd be able to tell what was going on in her head.

He's the enemy, he's the enemy...

She had to remind herself of that. She had to remember why he was here and what his intentions for her precious community café were. He was up to no good, and no good could come from getting involved. It was probably what he was after: seduce her and soften her will. She couldn't allow it to happen. She couldn't even allow herself to fancy him – though that got harder with every hour she was in his company. She'd never told him she fancied him, had she? Or anyone else for that matter. But he was assuming that she did? How arrogant did that make him? Or was she giving off signs so obvious he couldn't fail to notice? If she was, that would have to be wrestled under some kind of control because she couldn't have him thinking that sort of thing.

'It's quiet in here,' he said, tying his apron and rolling up his sleeves to wash. 'It's weird; I'm not used to it. Usually it's all noise and chaos.'

'It's a busy kitchen, that's for sure. I quite like it that way.'

'I didn't say it was bad, just that this is weird.'

'Put the radio on if you like.'

'I could. Or we could just talk.'

Eden burst into laughter. 'Us? What would we talk about?'

'I don't know.'

'There you are then...' She paused. 'And don't even think of drawing me into a discussion about this plot of land thinking you might be able to twist me round to your way of thinking because that is not going to happen.'

'I wouldn't dream of it. I don't need to anyway because we both know how it's going to end. I don't think that means there has to be animosity between us while this thing plays out, though.'

Eden rested her hands on her hips and turned to him with a frank gaze. 'You really think it's going to be easy, don't you? You think you're just going through the motions?' She retrieved her knife and started to slice her pepper again. 'Think that if you want to, if it makes you feel as if you're winning, but don't imagine for a minute that it's going to be as simple as that.'

'I never thought it would be simple – you're involved.'

'Thank you.'

'I'm serious. I always thought you were capable... more than capable. I was sorry to hear you'd left the company – you had a great future there ahead of you. Why did you leave?'

'My mum died.'

'Yes,' he said slowly, 'I heard that, and, for the record, I'm sorry for your loss. That doesn't really explain it, though.'

Eden paused. 'Do you remember,' she said after a moment, 'I came to you at the back end of last year, and I told you about some land with a community centre on it that you could get for a knock-down price?'

He was thoughtful for a second but then shook his head. 'Can't say that I do. Does it have a bearing on any of this?'

'In a way. But if you can't remember it, then...' She shook her head. He'd think her silly if she told him the truth and, as she'd suspected, the deal had meant nothing to him anyway. 'Never mind. I left because it wasn't where I wanted to be, and it wasn't where I wanted my life to go. That's all.'

'It's a shame – you'd have done all right. You'd have made more money than you're going to do here too.'

'Maybe I decided money wasn't as important as I used to think it was.'

'Whenever anyone says that to me, I always think how naive they are. It sounds laudable and idealistic, but life isn't like that.'

'Sometimes it is. I'm starting to see you can make a choice that makes it so.'

He gave a wry smile. 'OK, you do you. I still think this will go my way in the end. You and I know it's bigger than you and you won't be able to fight it.'

'I can fight. I might not win – I know that, but I can still fight.'

He picked up a bulb of garlic and tossed it into the air, catching it nimbly as it came back down. 'Whatever. We have that sorted, so let's talk about something else. Aren't you sick of arguing about this scout hut every time we see one another?'

'OK,' Eden said slowly. 'What else do you want to talk about?'

'I don't know. What are you into?'

'Nothing really.'

'Nothing?' He chuckled. 'You must be into something! You don't watch films, go swimming, cook? You must do something.'

'Nothing that would interest you, I'm sure.'

'Try me.'

'I like foreign films.'

'There you go then. I like foreign films too. What kind?

French? German? Or do you like a bit of South Korean cinema?'

She shrugged. 'All sorts. What's your favourite?'

'I like all sorts too.'

She threw him a sideways look. 'Are you taking the piss?'

'No!' He held his hands up in a gesture of surrender. 'Of course I'm not! What else? So you like films. You like wine? Hiking? Something more unusual... macramé? Extreme knitting? You're learning to play the saxophone?'

'Now I know you're taking the piss.'

'Then laugh with me. I'm teasing, but only a little. I can't help it when you're taking everything so seriously. I'm trying to get to know you here.'

'Why?'

'Why wouldn't I? We worked together and I don't know a single thing about you. So then I find myself here and you're here – seems like a weird coincidence we've been pulled together like this, don't you think? So I feel as if there must be a reason – maybe it's because I'm meant to get to know you better.'

'It's a funny way to make friends – trying to destroy my project.'

He was silent for a moment, and his smile faded. 'I didn't come here for that – I came here because the land was going up for sale. I certainly didn't arrive with the intention of destroying anyone's project. Come on, Eden – you know that. It's not personal.'

As much as she wanted to refute his point, she couldn't.

'It's just bad luck,' he continued into the gap her non-reply had left. 'Is there really no other venue in this whole town you could use?'

'Maybe, but I don't see why I should have to. And it wouldn't be as perfect as this one is.'

'Are you maybe just being stubborn for the sake of it? Have you looked?'

'Yes,' she said, though something in those words rang a little too close for comfort too. She hadn't made much of an effort to look for alternatives because she'd been so determined she was going to keep hold of the scout hut, whatever it took.

'And you realise,' he added, 'that even if you chase me away, the owners of the land are still looking to sell it. Sooner or later, someone will buy it. You'll lose, whether it's to me or someone else.' He paused again. 'Let me find somewhere else for you to go. What do you say?'

'Clearing the way for you to swoop in and get your offer in on this place?'

'Yes. But you'd be all right. We'd both be all right.'

She shook her head.

There was building exasperation in his reply. 'Why are you being so awkward? Is it so hard to see sense?'

'We won't both be all right. You'll be significantly better off.'

'It's my...' Cam let out an impatient breath. 'Forget it. It's like headbutting a wall over and over, talking to you.'

'Sorry. I'm not going to change even though I know you're right. I suppose it must be infuriating.'

'Weirdly, I wish I could say it is, but I can't. I sort of respect it. I almost like it. I don't know what that says about me, or what you might be doing to my brain, but I almost feel as if I'd be disappointed if you did back down because...'

'What?'

'I'm going to regret saying this, I just know it. But I think it makes you a bit cool.'

Eden couldn't hold off the smile that spread across her face, but she didn't let him see it. 'I'll do my best not to disappoint you then.'

'The game is afoot, eh?'

'It's properly on. I've only been warming up till now.'

'I look forward to things getting heavy then.'

Eden's grin was fixed in place as she went back to her work. A moment later, he started to whistle. She snuck a glance to his workstation to see him peeling the garlic with a smile of his own. Was it her imagination or had the room suddenly got a lot hotter?

When there was a knock at the back door a few minutes later, Eden couldn't help but be thankful. Her thoughts were taking her to strange places, all of them involving Cam and various steamy scenarios, so the arrival of someone else would at least distract her from them. She went to the door to find Bilbo, Mavis and Liam there.

'Hello, you lot! You're a bit early.'

'Julia said you were on your own...' Mavis peered round the door and then fixed Eden with a strangely knowing look. 'But I see you're not. Hello, Cam,' she called in.

'Ah, reinforcements!' Cam gave her a cheeky wink. 'Just as well. Eden's no use at all – I'm practically carrying service today.'

'Very funny.' Eden frowned at him. She moved back from the doorway to let her volunteers in. 'It's good of you to charge down here, but we would have managed.'

'We're here now,' Bilbo said cheerily. 'Might as well make use of us.'

Eden began to assign tasks, though she was aware that they probably knew what needed to be done better than she did.

Bilbo sidled up to Cam as she was explaining to Liam where the spare chairs were kept. Eden was distracted by their conversation, doing her best to stay with Liam but unable to stop herself from eavesdropping.

'I found this...'

Eden glanced at them to see Bilbo hand Cam a photograph.

'Thought you might like to see it,' he continued.

Cam took the photo and broke into a broad smile. 'That's you! And is that...?'

'Razor, yes, your great-uncle. That's us onboard the *Vanguard* off the coast of Gibraltar. I can't exactly remember what year, but it must have been about 1953. I was only a runt of a boy. There's Tommo... he was your uncle's best friend.'

'I think he might have mentioned him once, but it's so long ago I can't recall,' Cam said. 'This is brilliant! Can I take a copy to show my parents?'

'Well...' Bilbo looked doubtful. 'It's the only one I have, so I wouldn't like to let it out of my sight...'

'I'll just scan it with my phone; I won't have to take it anywhere.'

'Oh, in that case, of course! I'm glad you like it.'

'I do,' Cam said, gazing at the black-and-white snap. 'Thanks so much for digging it out.'

'Thank you for reminding me about old Razor. Was good to me, he was, always looked out for me. I was right fond of him.' Bilbo looked up at Cam through old eyes and smiled fondly. 'When I look at you, I can see something of him.'

'Ah, I think he was a much better man than I am.'

'Different times make different people, but it doesn't change the heart,' Bilbo said.

'I don't know about that.' Cam put the photo on the table and got out his phone. 'But I appreciate the sentiment.' He snapped a copy and then handed the original back to Bilbo, who put it carefully into an envelope and went over to Mavis, who put it in her handbag.

By this time, Liam had gone off to find the extra chairs and Eden wandered over to Cam. She didn't want to give him the impression she was interested in him, but she was mad with curiosity over the photo. 'Let's see,' she said, trying to get a glimpse as he looked at his phone.

He held it out. 'There's my uncle,' he said, pointing to a man who was far taller than Bilbo, suntanned and slim in a naval uniform. It was hard to make out his features, but from what Eden could see, there was some family resemblance. Her eyes went along the row of men on the deck of the ship. It was easy to pick out Bilbo, and she smiled at the sight of him as a youth. This day must have felt like a lifetime ago to the old man standing in her kitchen today. In the background were the rocks that must have been Gibraltar, a moment of a day that would never be that exact moment on that exact day again, captured and frozen in a grainy, dog-eared photograph. Eden was suddenly struck by how transient life was, how moments and events blew through it like leaves in the wind, and her smile faded. It was so short and so fleeting – she knew that only too well.

She turned away, afraid she might start to cry if she gave it any more thought.

'That's lovely,' she said. 'But I'd better get on.'

Taking a second to collect herself, she went to the sink and pretended to wash her hands. When she turned back, Cam was watching her with a strange expression on his face.

'I'll make a cup of tea, shall I?' Mavis announced, and Eden had never been so glad of a distraction before.

'Who's up for a drink after we finish here?' Cam called as the team started to clear down. Eden had just seen off the last diners. It had been another successful and cheery affair, and while she was happy that people seemed to love their dinners, that fact was bittersweet. Wouldn't it be typical that she'd finally got something wonderful going, something that people wanted and needed, something she could be proud of, only to have it snatched away? Perhaps it was a bit spoiled to see it that way, but Eden had grown up spoiled, and even though she recognised it, she cut herself some slack. She couldn't change who she was overnight, but at least she was trying.

'At the Dolphin?' Mavis asked.

'I thought so,' Cam replied. 'Unless you know a better pub nearby?'

'Nowhere better than the Dolphin,' Bilbo said.

'I don't think I will...' Liam came in from the main room, presumably having heard the conversation from in there.

'I don't suppose you want to be supping with us oldies, eh?' Bilbo said to him.

'Hey.' Eden laughed. 'Less of the oldies! I might look haggard from a night frying chips, but I'm not old!'

'Don't be daft,' Mavis said. 'You're still as pretty as a clifftop buttercup.'

Eden flushed.

'Honest!' Mavis insisted. 'As soon as I clapped eyes on you, I said to Bilbo, "Oh, isn't she lovely!" And Bilbo says, "Yes, she is. Inside and out."'

Eden blushed harder still and turned her concentration to the dishwasher. When she looked up again, she caught Cam grinning her way. What was up with him? For a moment, she considered throwing a cup at his head to wipe the smile off his face, but was thankfully distracted from the idea by Liam asking whether she needed anything else because if she didn't, then could he leave because he wasn't planning on going to the pub.

'Of course!' Eden said. 'You don't need to ask, Liam! You're doing us the favour; I'm not your boss, you know!'

Liam gave an awkward smile and then went to have a quick word with Bilbo before grabbing his jacket and heading off.

'I don't know if my old legs will take a walk up to the pub tonight,' Bilbo said. 'I might have to let you down.'

'You say that' – Mavis wagged a finger at him – 'but then you'll get home and wish you'd gone. Afraid of missing out – that's always been your trouble.'

'There comes an age where your body won't let you do anything but miss out,' Bilbo said, though his tone was playful. 'And I have to save myself for the afternoon dancing tomorrow, don't I? Don't want to let you down – I'd never hear the end of it.'

'Aww, come on, Bilbo,' Cam said. 'You've got to come. I want to hear more stories about Razor in the navy. How about I give you a lift up in my car? And if your legs are still tired later, I'll pay for your cab home.'

Bilbo broke into a smile, and Mavis simply shook her head.

'Didn't I say so? He couldn't miss a party if his life depended on it.'

'It's not a party,' Bilbo said.

'That's what you think,' Cam replied. 'It all depends on how the night goes, but there's every chance it could turn into one!'

At this, Bilbo looked about as excited as an old man could look, and he suddenly seemed forty years younger. Eden thought – not for the first time since she'd met him – that he might well have been an absolute menace as a youngster, but in the best possible way. No wonder he'd needed Cam's great-uncle to look out for him in the navy.

Eden walked up to the Dolphin later than everyone else, having seen them all off so she could check around and lock up. Some had wanted to wait, but she'd insisted they go on and start their socialising, and she'd be there soon enough.

When she arrived, she could hear laughter from outside the pub. She walked inside to find Bilbo and Cam giggling together like children, and broke into a broad smile. It was funny, however, that she was pleased to see it, but this time it had nothing to do with her wanting to win the bet with Cam. She was genuinely pleased to see them get along and to see them becoming such good friends. Then again, it was impossible not to love Bilbo, even if you were Cam Faulkner.

'Here she is!' Bilbo threw his arms in the air, cheering like a football fan as he spied her coming through the doors.

Cam turned to Ralph, who was manning the bar alongside Livia. 'Orange gin and lemonade. Better make it a double, Ralph.'

Eden frowned slightly as she approached the bar. 'How did you know?'

Cam grinned. 'I pay attention.'

'There you go.' Ralph put her drink down. 'It went all right today?' he asked Eden. 'As you didn't have Livia or Julia? Bilbo says you did a great job.'

'I have to admit to being impressed myself,' Cam said.

Now Eden knew he was drunk for sure.

'It was all right, I think,' Eden said. 'Not as bad as I'd worked myself up to think it might be. Definitely helped that you gave us all that food ready to go – the lasagne went down really well.'

'Glad to help.'

Eden looked to see that, while the pub wasn't packed out, it was busier than it would be on most weeknights, and her volunteers had probably swelled the numbers. Livia gave her a vague wave from the other side of the bar as she served someone.

Eden turned back to Ralph. 'You seem busy. You need me to hop round to the other side and lend a hand?'

'We've got it all under control.' Ralph patted her hand as it rested on the bar top. 'You've worked hard – you deserve a drink.'

'I really don't mind. I'm not tired at all—'

'Wouldn't hear of it, my love. Come on – drink up and think no more about it.'

Eden smiled up at him. She felt certain he needed an extra pair of hands but realised no argument would persuade him to let her help out. In which case, there was no point in worrying about it. Cam lifted his glass in a toast to her. He was smiling, and it seemed so genuine, so full of admiration and affection, that for a moment she almost believed it.

'Cheers!' he said.

'Here's to being halfway through the bet,' she said, reminding herself that this was still part of the game and she couldn't fall into the trap of thinking otherwise.

'Halfway through the bet,' he agreed. 'It's far more fun than I ever imagined it would be.'

How many gins was that she'd got through? More than she'd kept track of, and she hadn't paid for a single one. She couldn't be sure of who'd kept topping her up at this point but had a feeling it was Cam. If this was all part of his strategy, then the joke was on him. He could spend his entire yearly bonus on gin for her, get her drunk enough to need a stomach pump, but he'd never get her to give up the scout hut. So let him embark on his own charm offensive, and then he could watch as she took it and turned it back on him. It was already working because he was laughing and joking and enjoying himself like he was one of them. A few more evenings like this and there was no way he could turn against these people by selling them down the river.

Cam spun round from a joke he'd just shared with Ralph and leaned in close. Eden could feel his breath on her cheek, a sudden thrill running through her. She tried to banish the kick of excitement, but she couldn't. She reminded herself, once again, that this was a game they were both playing, a game she had to win. How could she win if all she wanted to do was surrender to the enemy?

'What?' she asked stubbornly.

'Ever had a Ramos Gin Fizz?'

'I don't think so. What's in it?'

'Gin.'

'Yes, I got that much. What else?'

'Some other stuff. Want one?'

Eden shook her head. 'Ralph doesn't do fancy drinks like that. Not much call for it here, so I don't suppose he'd know how to make it to your exacting standards.'

'Who said anything about Ralph making it?' He grinned, leaping away from her. He went to the bar and rapped on the wood. 'Landlord! Might I be indulged for one moment behind your bar?'

Ralph came shuffling over with a frown. 'Eh?'

'I want to make a Ramos Gin Fizz for Eden. Unless you know—'

Ralph sniffed and gave a vague shrug. 'Put the money in the till and you can make whatever you like.'

'Thank you!' With a grin back at Eden, he waited for a second while Ralph opened up and then slipped round to the other side of the bar. He began to scoot back and forth, collecting up bottles and laying them out. 'The secret's in the mixing,' he said as he went along.

Eden got up to take a closer look. 'This should be good. I suppose you're some kind of whizz. Went on one of those naff cocktail-making experience days for your birthday, did you?'

'No,' he replied carelessly. 'I worked in a bar in the West End.'

'You worked in a bar?'

'Isn't that what I said?'

'It's just... when did you work in a bar?'

'In my early twenties. I learned to make everything. We had wall-to-wall celebrities and millionaires in there – we had to learn to make everything. I don't think there's a drink in existence I didn't get asked to make at some point.'

Eden watched him get to work and tried not to look impressed, though she was finding it difficult. Try as she might to deny it, there was something sexy about him behind there with shirtsleeves rolled back and his hair dishevelled in the most delicious way. She was certain he was as drunk as her, but it didn't seem to be hampering his efforts. In fact, he made it look all too easy, and that was even sexier.

After a minute or so, he slid a glass across to her. 'Try it. Then tell me it isn't the most delicious thing you've ever tasted.'

Eden grinned as she took a sip. It was pretty good. In fact, it was spectacular. She tossed her hair back and grimaced. 'It's all right if you like that sort of thing.'

'I'll have it back then.' He began to reach for it, but she moved it from his grasp.

'I might as well drink it now you've made it.'

'Shall I make another?' he asked with a mischievous look in those dark eyes. 'To be going on with when you've done with that?'

'I don't suppose it would be the worst thing I've ever had to endure if I have to drink another,' Eden said, holding tight to a grin that threatened to give the game away.

'High praise indeed,' he said, starting to measure out again. He looked up at the rest of the volunteers. 'Can I get anyone else a lovely cocktail?'

Eden glanced down the bar to see Livia smiling as she watched and Ralph simply shaking his head in disbelief. It seemed they'd well and truly taken over his bar. Eden hoped he wouldn't be too annoyed about it, but he didn't seem to be, and she had to admit that he'd probably take more money tonight than any other regular weeknight for a long time.

At the tables where everyone was sitting with pints and shots, there was a chorus of agreement. Hands shot up.

'I'll take that as a yes then,' Cam said. He threw another grin at Eden. He was enjoying this, but she was suddenly struck by a lightning bolt of suspicion. What else was he up to here?

Surely he wasn't just throwing his money around like this from the goodness of his heart?

She decided not to let it worry her. As long as she kept that cynicism firmly in her head, he could play all the games he liked. It would be a cold day in hell when he caught her out.

Her thoughts were interrupted by the appearance of another glass in front of her.

'Get that down you,' Cam said, looking mightily pleased with himself. 'I've a mind to run up a decent tab on here tonight before we leave.'

Cam did run up a sizeable tab. Eden swayed on her feet as she got on her coat and he went to settle it. Most of the other volunteers had gone home. Many of them were older and tired more quickly, or had jobs to go to in the morning. The ones who'd clung on to the bitter end said their goodbyes, leaving Eden to hang back, feeling it rude to leave before she'd done the same with Cam.

Against her better judgement – or rather, what would have been better judgement had she been sober – she'd had the most brilliant evening. Cam had proved to be more agreeable company than she could ever have imagined. He was witty, interesting, gregarious and really rather lovable – and somewhere in the back of her mind, it annoyed the hell out of her. In the morning, when sense had returned, she'd realise it was all part of a charm offensive designed to combat the one she herself had embarked on, but for now, she found herself more attracted to him than ever.

'If I'd known how much fun this place could be, I'd have come here years ago,' Cam said as he fetched his jacket from the booth where he'd left it.

'I told you it was more than just a poky little seaside town.'

'Oh, it's that. Still, it's one I could get to like.'

Eden watched as he fastened his coat. 'Do you actually mean that?'

'Of course I do.'

'Can you repeat it? Only I'm having trouble with the idea that you might be admitting you got us wrong.'

He gave her the soppiest grin. 'Don't get ideas, Eden. I never admit to being wrong. Usually because I never need to.'

'You just said...'

'Well, maybe I did. But let's forget it happened and never speak of it again.' He paused, a little uncertain.

Eden wasn't used to him looking uncertain, and it threw her. 'What?'

'You've got a long way to go for home?'

'It's a bit of a walk, but I can manage.'

'Let me see you back to your place before I go on.'

'I don't need—'

'Please. I know I don't do an awful lot of chivalry but let me do it this once. I'd feel guilty going back to my hotel and knowing I hadn't seen you home safely.'

'I've walked it dozens of times since I came here – honestly, it's fine.'

'I'm sure you have. Think of it as a favour to me.'

'Will it win me points?'

He grinned. 'It might. I tell you what, you try some more to persuade me you're right about this community kitchen business while we walk and I'll pretend to be listening. At least you'll feel like you're doing something useful.'

It was Eden's turn to smile, bigger and wider than she would have allowed in different circumstances. 'OK,' she said.

After saying goodnight to Ralph and Livia – who seemed surprised to watch them leave together – they stepped out into the night.

The sky was clear with a full moon, and as they made their way up to the cliffs where Four Winds Cottage stood, the heavens began to emerge. No longer obscured by the lights in the town, great swathes of sparkling stars filled the sky. The wind had picked up, but it wasn't cold enough to bother Eden; it only helped to clear her head. Their conversation was easy and good-natured, and despite Cam's promise that Eden could talk about her community kitchen, they barely mentioned it.

'Seriously,' he said as they began the path that led to the cliff top, 'do you climb this every day?'

'Yep.'

'Jesus, what possessed you to rent a place up here? Did you know it would be like this?'

'More or less. I used to visit this place as a kid. I remembered liking it up here, but I'll admit that my memory of the walk must have been a bit hazy. And I'd never had to do it with more than enough cocktails in me, on a dark night, as a kid.'

'I should hope not,' he said with a laugh. 'I can't imagine you as a kid.'

'Can't you?'

'I can imagine you as a smaller human, but not what you might have been like.'

'I could say the same for you. I bet you were born in a pinstripe suit holding an iPhone.'

He turned to her. It was dark, and she couldn't see his expression, and she wondered suddenly if she'd offended him. The tone of his reply seemed to suggest that it wasn't offence she'd caused but some consternation. 'Is that really how I seem?'

'You are very focused on your job. I don't think I've ever met anyone quite as focused as you.'

'Even tonight? I thought it had been a relaxed evening. We didn't talk about business once.'

'We did. Earlier on when you came to help me at the scout hut. See, it's such a part of your DNA, you don't even know when you're doing it.'

'But that was— No, you're right. I suppose I did.'

'In fairness to you, I don't remember which of us actually started it.'

'Hmm...'

They were silent for a few minutes. Both needed their breath as the path steepened, but as it levelled out again, he resumed the conversation.

'You've never said what brought you here. It's quite a random decision, isn't it? You just woke up one morning and thought, *I'm going to give up my job and move to the seaside and do good deeds*?'

'It didn't happen quite like that. I needed to leave London.'

'Needed? Sounds heavy.'

Eden tucked her wind-tangled hair behind her ears. Had she been more sober she'd have decided she'd already said more than she'd wanted to. Drink had lowered her guard, and though she recognised it, her thinking was too hazy to do anything about it. Part of her didn't want to bring it up because doing so would mean acknowledging his part in it, however unaware he'd been, and she didn't want him to feel he was being blamed. The blame for what had happened, for what she'd done, lay with her. She'd chosen to tell him about the financial troubles at her mum's community centre, and she'd tipped him off that he'd be able to get it at a rock-bottom price. What he'd done with that information was a natural response, given that it was his business to make money out of property and land. It had been her job too once, and it was funny how different it all seemed now that she was on the other end of it.

'Things were... things were happening that I needed to get away from. Family stuff, that's all. I needed some space.'

'You could have taken a few weeks out. A sabbatical even.'

'I needed a lot of space, and I didn't know how much would be enough, so I figured... It wasn't really even a plan; I suppose you could say it was a knee-jerk thing. Something happened and this was what I did.'

'Now I have to know.'

'You really don't want to.'

'I do. I don't know why, but I want to understand what's going on here, why you're doing all of this.'

'Would it make any difference? Would it change your mind about the land and the scout hut?'

'I don't know. I suppose not. It's not really in my gift to change it. I keep telling you that, and you don't want to listen. I'm not the one selling it, after all, and if not me, someone else would buy it eventually.'

'So what's the point in knowing my story?'

'Because... because I couldn't imagine any circumstances in which I'd do the same.'

'I think we've established we're not the same at all.'

'Aren't we? Don't you think we're a little bit the same? Look at us here: neither of us are backing down over your little hut. I know for a fact that neither of us would ever back down. I think we're a lot more alike than you realise. But this' – he waved a hand, encompassing the clifftop – 'this I couldn't imagine doing. And all the community stuff. I'll admit I still don't see what anyone gets out of that. But I also have to admit...'

He paused.

Eden searched her bag for her keys as Four Winds Cottage reared out of the gloom. 'Admit what?'

'I'm kind of impressed. More than impressed. I'm... maybe ashamed that I'd never have it in me to do the same. Maybe a bit in awe too. You've been here for a few weeks and yet you've set up that place, and you'd fight to the end for it. People here love you already, I can tell that much. And I think to myself, well, if everyone here loves you like they so obviously do, there must be something I haven't seen yet, something about you, something... well, amazing.'

Eden shook her head. 'You've definitely had too much to drink.'

He laughed. 'I'm sure I have.'

'I think you ought to sober up a bit before you head back down the cliff. After all, you don't know the path at all and it's dark. I don't want you to fall.'

'Those things don't change if I sober up.'

'No, but it will be one less worry if you can walk in a straight line.'

'I'm perfectly capable.'

'Even so. Come in and have a coffee, if only to make me feel happier.' Eden pushed open her front door and reached for the light switch to illuminate the hallway. 'And it's just coffee, not *coffee*... so you can wipe that grin off your face.'

Cam's grin broadened as he followed her inside, taking in the low-beamed ceilings with the dried flowers hanging from them, the tiled floors and unevenly plastered walls.

'This is... quaint,' he said. 'Remind me... it's not yours, is it? You haven't bought it?'

'God, no, I couldn't afford this! I've got a six-month lease.'

He frowned. 'Only... so you're doing all this community stuff and you're not even staying? I got the impression you'd made this place your new home. The way everyone talks about it at the kitchen makes it sound like you're here to stay.'

'I've thought about it a lot,' Eden replied with a sudden candour that surprised even her. She'd toyed with the notion but not seriously. Much as she would love to stay, the idea had no shape. It didn't seem practical, for a start. She couldn't afford Four Winds, even if it was for sale, and the task of finding an affordable alternative seemed overwhelming. Sea Glass Bay was hardly the glitterati of seaside resorts, but it was still a desirable location. And if Cam got his way, prices would go up even further with the new development on the scout hut land. If it was a decision she needed to make, then she would have to reach a decision soon. One thing she knew for sure was that, perhaps for the first time in her life, she was somewhere she belonged, somewhere she was accepted. Whoever she'd been before Sea Glass Bay, she didn't want to be that person any longer. She wanted to forget that woman. Though there was always the memory of what she'd done to remind her that she'd never fully shake that person, maybe there was a way to consign her to history.

'What would you do?' At her behest, he took a seat at the table while she filled the kettle.

Eden turned off the tap. 'What would I do? I haven't thought that far ahead. I'd keep the community kitchen going, if I could. Maybe I'd even grow it.'

'But you'd need a job. Surely you're not going to stay at the pub?'

She turned to see him look vaguely incredulous. 'Why not?'

'You're far too capable and qualified to work at a pub.'

'What if I want to work at a pub? Capable and qualified is all very well if that's what you want. I like the pub. It's friendly, and I don't get stressed, and I get to spend time with people who actually care about me and not just whether I can hit a target or not.'

He shrugged. 'The more I know about you, the more I realise I never knew you at all.'

Eden smiled. 'We weren't exactly close colleagues. Why would you?'

'You knew me.'

'Did I?'

'According to Livia, you knew exactly what to expect when I arrived in town that day.'

Eden's mouth fell open. 'That little... Consorting with the enemy, eh? I'll have to have words with Livia!'

He grinned.

'What else have you and Livia been whispering about?'

'Oh, this and that. Don't worry, she hasn't committed any serious espionage for me. It was only a bit of idle gossip. I had plied her with a couple of glasses of rum by this point, so I don't think she was entirely to blame for any secrets she might have given away.'

Eden pulled two cups from a cupboard and spooned coffee into them. 'Maybe I did. You have to admit you're a bit of a poster boy at the company. Most people have the measure of you – when it comes to work, in any case.'

'Poster boy, eh? I quite like that. And when it's not work? How well do you think you know me out of work?'

'I don't know. I'm still figuring you out.'

'Instinct. Give me your gut feeling at this moment.'

Eden turned to watch the kettle boil. What was her gut telling her? She turned back.

'I think,' she began slowly, 'that you're not quite as ruthless as you want everyone to think.'

'Guilty. Anything else?'

The kettle switched itself off, and she poured some water into the mugs. 'You're moderately funny. You can tell an entertaining story, and you make good cocktails. I think you'd like to be liked.'

'Wouldn't we all? Surely you want people to like you. Isn't that really what your community kitchen is about?'

'No!'

He raised his eyebrows, and she had to smile.

'OK, maybe a bit.'

'It's not your fault. Every kind act is done with some selfish intent – it's human nature. It's why we do kind things because, ultimately, we hope to get something out of it.'

'That's bull.'

'No, it's not; it's a proven fact. You can google altruism in psychology and it's there in black and white. It's evolution, and you can't fight it. Humans started out doing things for other humans because they realised they might need the favour returned one day. It's a way to survive.'

Eden put her hands on her hips. 'OK, so that could be true of giving someone in need a fiver to get some food, but how do you explain bigger things? Like'– she clicked her fingers – 'like laying down your life for someone? Explain that, Freud. What does the person laying down their life get out of it, apart from being dead?'

'Humans got so good at the altruism thing we didn't know when to stop.'

'That's mental.'

'I never said the theory was perfect.'

Eden brought the coffees to the table and sat next to him. 'So that's how you defend refusing to be kind, is it? It's an inbuilt instinct that you – because you're so much cleverer than everyone else – can choose to ignore?'

'I never said I could. I'm volunteering for you, aren't I?'

'To win a bet.'

'At first, yes. But now... do you really think I refuse to be kind? You think I'm never kind?'

'I don't know you well enough to say either way. But you just told me the theory yourself. If you're occasionally kind, it's because there's something in it for you. So if you – Cam Faulkner – buy a load of drinks for a load of villagers, presumably you thought you'd somehow benefit somewhere down the line.'

Cam winced. 'I asked for that.' He reached for his coffee, taking a moment to consider his response. 'All right, I suppose I did. But then I kept going because I was enjoying myself and I didn't want to go back to my hotel alone. I wanted everyone to stay, so I kept buying the drinks.' He put down his cup and looked up at her. 'Is that so bad? And I'm sorry but there's more. Maybe I didn't want to keep everyone at the pub. Maybe I wanted to keep some people there more than others.'

Suddenly, she was adrift. He held her fast in his gaze. She'd sobered, she felt sure of it, so if that were true, why did she suddenly have the maddest urge to kiss him? Surely that was alcohol thinking for her? She couldn't...

It all happened so fast, afterwards she couldn't truly say who had moved first. But in the next instant they were kissing. Her hands were all over him, full of fire and need, and he responded in a way that left her feeling she'd never been kissed properly before, as if all the men in her past had been practice, and she'd been built to kiss him and him alone.

He was breathless as he pulled away. 'I'm sorry, I don't know what—'

Eden tugged at his shirt, his sudden humility and doubt only causing her to ache for him in a way that might see her lose her mind. She pressed her lips to his again, volcanic and urgent, and knew what she wanted. He wanted it too – every response in his body told her so.

'Upstairs,' she murmured. 'Now.'

CHAPTER SIXTEEN

What was that weight across her chest? Something warm, something... Eden ran a hand along the arm. She opened her eyes, instantly awake, and then groaned as the previous night came back to her in sharp and mortifying detail. What the hell had she been thinking?

Cam slept peacefully beside her. She'd never seen him look like that before. Breathing steadily, the glow from the sun outside the curtains lighting his face, he looked younger, somehow almost vulnerable. She was so used to seeing the alpha side of him, the confident, swaggering career man, that it came as something of a shock.

But then she recalled how he'd been in bed. For a while, that man had been there, but as they'd become more intimate, he'd become gentler, considerate and... Eden might almost have called it loving. But they didn't love each other. She still wasn't sure she even liked him, despite the fact they were currently in bed together. But the night had been amazing. Whatever else she felt, she couldn't deny there had been some deep connection that had been so much more than sex. Had she imagined that? Perhaps. She'd been drunk, after all. Sort of. When she really thought about it, could she honestly say she'd been drunk enough to blame what she'd instigated on the alcohol? Hadn't she already wanted it, way before the first glass in the Dolphin? On some level she knew that to be true too, and she couldn't quite decide whether the fact angered her or scared her. This wasn't supposed to happen, and now that it had, things were about to get a whole lot more complicated.

He stirred and smiled in his sleep, and something stirred in Eden. She frowned.

Absolutely not. We're not doing that again, ever, no matter how sexy he looks.

Moving his arm, she tried to get out of bed without waking him, not really sure if she ought to anyway. He couldn't stay there; she had to get him out of the house as soon as she could.

Despite her efforts, he opened his eyes this time, and as he focused on her, he began to smile.

'Good morning.'

'Good morning. I'm just going to make coffee – want one?'

'I seem to recall it was you making coffee that got us here. What was that you said about not getting ideas?'

'I'll take that as a yes. Come downstairs when you're ready.'

'You're not bringing them back up here?'

'I thought you'd want to get up. Don't you have work today?'

'At some point, yes, but there's no rush. Bring them back to bed; we could talk.'

'We can talk in the kitchen.'

'But it's nicer here. Warmer, more comfortable.' He reached out to pull her back, but she swiped her hand out of his way and grabbed the dressing gown from a hook on the back of the bedroom door.

'I'm sure, but neither of us will get much done today if we spend it in bed.'

He looked faintly disappointed but said nothing else.

Eden left him and headed down to the kitchen, but the image of him lying in bed looking so damn seductive wouldn't leave her. Truthfully, she wanted to climb back in bed with him as much as he wanted it. Talk about muddying the waters. She'd just about stirred up the whole ocean bed with her little lapse.

Down in the kitchen, her phone lay on the table where she'd left it the night before. She noted a couple of unread text messages that must have come in overnight or this morning. One from Ralph asking about an extra shift and one from Livia wanting to know if she'd got home OK. Eden couldn't help a wry smile. Livia didn't really want to know if Eden had got home OK; more likely she was hoping to find out what had happened during the walk back with Cam. Eden was quite sure she'd never have guessed exactly what had happened, because she could hardly believe that herself, but she might assume that some discussion of the community kitchen would have taken place, and she perhaps hoped to hear that Eden had made some headway. She was typing a brief reply when Cam came into the kitchen.

'Oh.' Eden looked up from her phone. 'I didn't think you'd be down so quick.'

'I thought I'd better do as I was told. Seemed like you meant business.'

'Do you want some breakfast? I don't have loads in, but I'm sure I can offer you something before you leave.'

He frowned slightly as he sat down at the table. 'Whatever you have... Have I done something wrong? If it's about last night, I'm sorry but—'

'Of course not. I wanted that too.'

'And you had a good time? Because I did, and not just because...'

'Yes.'

'Then why are we here again?'

'Where?' Eden paused from searching her fridge for something she could put on toast.

'Like two people who are at war? Why so formal again? I thought we might have got past that.'

'I'm sure you'd like that, wouldn't you? It would make your job easier.'

'I'm actually offended you still think so little of me you'd say that.'

She pulled out an egg box and opened it up to find there would probably be enough to scramble and share. 'Do you eat eggs?'

'What? Yes, of course... You haven't answered my question.'

'You didn't exactly ask one. You just said you were offended.'

'So why are you being like this? I thought you wanted last night too.'

'I did...' Eden paused, softened by his expression. He seemed regretful. Was he wishing they hadn't slept together? Part of her wished it too, but part of her had loved being with him so much that she couldn't imagine undoing it. Without understanding why, it made her sad to think he might wish it hadn't happened in the same way. 'I did want to, and it was great... more than great. It was lovely.'

'But...? I sense a but.'

'There isn't one.'

She put the eggs on the worktop then opened the dishwasher to fetch the saucepan she hadn't yet had time to put away.

'Oh,' he said. 'That's OK then. Want me to make the coffee while you do that?'

Eden nodded as she cracked the eggs. 'I'm going to scramble them because we only have three. It should stretch.'

He brushed past her, close enough that she could feel his

breath on her neck as he went to the kettle. She almost melted from the sense of his proximity, and it was all she could do not to drop the eggs and turn to grab him. It would be all too easy to take him back up to her bedroom for another taste of what had been so delicious the night before, but she steeled herself and killed the desire. What good would it do? If things were complicated now, doing such a stupid thing would send it to a whole other level.

'Sounds good,' he said.

They were silent for a moment as he filled the kettle and she mixed the eggs with some milk and seasoning.

'Because,' he said into the gap, 'if you had a good time, then I wondered if you fancied doing it again. Not the sex, I mean. But a drink. With intent this time.'

'Intent?' Eden dropped the fork into the sink. 'Like a date?'

'Why not? You look shocked. Is it such an awful idea?'

'Ordinarily I'd say no, but you can't be serious? With everything going on between us you think it's a good idea to go on a date?'

'Why not? We can keep it separate, surely? That's business and this is... well, pleasure. At least I thought it might be.'

Eden shook her head, staring at him.

'Ah,' he said. 'I see. In that case, perhaps I ought to go.'

'Have your breakfast first.'

'Thanks, but I'm sure I can catch the last half hour of breakfast at the hotel so I won't trouble you.' He began towards the doorway. 'I don't suppose you've seen my shoes...?'

'I'm sorry,' Eden said lamely. 'I... You must understand? It's easier for both of us if we don't get any more involved than...'

'I understand. I think it's an oversimple way of looking at things, but if that's what you want...'

It wasn't what she wanted. She liked him. She more than liked him, and she wanted nothing more than what he wanted. But how could she? It would be madness to make this situation more difficult than she already had. As she watched him leave the room, she wanted to call him back. She wanted to say to hell with it, let's go for that drink.

But she didn't. His intentions seemed genuine, and perhaps they were – and if they were, then the mistake was on her. But how could she trust him? She couldn't separate the fight for her community café from her personal feelings for him, even if he could. And if he said that, it still wouldn't mean anything. If she lost herself – as she feared she might – if she strayed too far, she might find herself faced with an impossible choice: Cam or her community. If that were to happen, there really was no contest, and all she'd get for making the right choice was heartbreak. Better to end this before it went too far.

When he came back to the kitchen, he was dressed. Collecting his jacket from the chair where he'd left it the previous night, he nodded coolly.

'So I'll see you in a couple of days at the hut.'

'You still want to come? I—'

'That was the agreement, wasn't it? Don't worry – I gave my word, and I won't go back on it. I said I'd help for two weeks, and I will.'

'Thank you,' Eden said, wondering why she had the sudden urge to burst into tears.

Without another word, he turned to leave. Eden let out a sigh as she heard the front door close. She looked at the eggs in the pan and decided she wasn't hungry after all.

Perhaps Eden had been feeling particularly vulnerable after Cam's hasty exit, but an hour later, she dialled her dad's phone number. She didn't think a simple phone call had ever made her so anxious, but as soon as she heard his voice, the worry drained from her. Though she'd lost her nerve since the last call when he hadn't picked up, afraid he wouldn't want to speak to her, she realised now she'd needed to hear it, more than she ever imagined she would. His deep tones were like a blanket to wrap around her soul.

'Hello, Eden,' he said, as if there had never been any gulf between them, as if nothing had happened and she'd simply called after a busy week to ask how he was. 'I'm glad you've decided to phone.'

'Me too!' she said, fighting back tears. 'I'm so sorry, Dad.'

'I've told you before, you have nothing to be sorry for.'

'But I do!'

'Is this why you disappeared?'

'No... yes. I suppose so. Caitlin said you were upset.'

'Not upset but worried. You didn't have to go; we could have worked it out. Where are you?'

'I'm...'

'I won't come over if you don't want me to. I only want to know you're all right.'

'I know. I'm in Sea Glass Bay.'

'Really? You mean the Sea Glass Bay where you used to complain about it being the most boring holiday place we could ever take you to?'

Eden gave a watery smile. 'Weird, huh? I thought about where I wanted to be and... I don't know. I know when I was a kid, I used to complain. But I used to complain about everything, didn't I?'

'You weren't that bad—'

'Dad, I was. We both know it, and I don't mind if you say so. But after Mum died, I thought about everything, and I just had the most brilliant memories of this place. I was always happy here, even when I said I wasn't. I thought I could do with some of that.'

'Has it changed much?'

'Not as much as you'd imagine,' she replied, deciding

quickly not to tell him about the land-acquisition drama and how it had more or less taken over her life.

'We had some good holidays there.'

'We did. Dad, I... are you all right?'

'Missing you. We all are.'

Eden doubted he was speaking for all the family. Caitlin, for one, was definitely not missing her. But to her surprise, she suddenly realised that *she* was missing Caitlin. Sour-faced, judgemental, disapproving Caitlin, the sister she could never please... Despite that, she was still Eden's sister, and the thought of how long it had been since they'd last been together provoked a pang of longing that caught her completely off guard.

'Do you think you might come home soon?' he added. 'Caitlin says you quit your job.'

'I'd planned to stay here for a while, until things... well, until things settled.'

'They're settled now.'

'I don't know. Maybe with you, Dad, but I don't think Caitlin is ready to forgive me yet – and I honestly don't blame her. Besides, I have things going on here.'

'You've met someone?'

Eden couldn't help a small smile. If only he knew. 'No, nothing like that. I've got involved in... well, I've got a job.'

'Doing what you did in London? I didn't think there'd be much call for—'

'At a pub, actually. Behind the bar.'

'Oh.'

'You're shocked?'

'I must admit I didn't see you working behind a bar. But if you enjoy it, that's the main thing.'

'I do. I love the people I work with.'

'Good for you then. Is it permanent? Is that why you don't know when you can come back?'

'Just for the summer, I think. I suppose things might change, but so far that's all I've been asked to do. It's not full-time, just shifts as and when. It suits me, gives me time to do other things.'

'And you have enough money?'

'I'm fine – don't worry about that.'

Eden's mind went back to all the times he'd asked that question and she'd taken the cash no matter whether she needed it or not, simply because it had been on offer, or all the times she'd asked for money for something frivolous or unnecessary just because she could. As she recalled that version of Eden Sherwood, she realised she was beginning to hate her. But she knew her dad would always ask and he'd always give what he could. She understood that in many ways he felt it was the only tool he had to stay relevant in her life, and the thought of that made her sad. Her past behaviour had probably made him feel that way. She didn't know how to put it right, but she knew that she'd have to start trying.

'I've got plenty,' she said. 'I have some put by, and I have the wages from my bar job, and I'm really not spending much at all here.'

'But you're not struggling?'

'Not one bit. Dad... are you doing OK?'

'Yes, don't worry about me.'

'Because Caitlin said—'

'You know what your sister is like; take no notice. She worries far too much.'

For the first time, Eden was glad about that. She was glad her sister was fussing over their dad because she wasn't there to do it. But there was guilt too – guilt upon guilt. Eden knew she ought to be there. She could go home today, but now she had things going on here and it wasn't so simple.

'I started this...' She searched for a way to make her dad understand what she was doing. He'd be confused, he would wonder why and she didn't blame him. Most of the time she still didn't understand what was driving her to keep the community café open; she only knew she had to. 'It's sort of a soup kitchen,' she concluded, hating the term that Livia had warned her not to use but knowing her dad would instantly get it.

'A soup kitchen? Like those places you see on the streets around Euston?'

'Not exactly, but that's the gist. Nicer than those. More like a café where people don't have to pay the bill. I mean, they pay if they can afford to, but a lot don't have all that much to give. That's sort of the point.'

'How can you make a profit?'

'I don't. I make enough to keep it going.'

'Oh. That's...'

Surprising? Eden could imagine why he might be grasping for the right reaction. She'd have been grasping too.

'Well done,' is all he managed. 'That's a wonderful thing to do. When you say you started it...?'

'When I began working in the pub, I realised there were a lot of people here who struggle for the basics, and I thought I could help. I get a ton of support from the locals. I started it, but honestly I don't do that much running of it. There are people here way better at that than me.'

'I'm sure you're just being modest. I'd like to come and see it, if I may. Not right away, of course, but perhaps when you're ready for a visit.'

Eden smiled. 'I'd like that, Dad.'

If it was still open after the next few weeks, of course. Eden knew only too well there were no guarantees of that.

'For now,' he continued, 'tell me about it. I'm interested to know how it works.'

Eden's smile grew, despite her misgivings. She began to tell her dad all about her café, so glad she'd finally picked up the phone.

CHAPTER SEVENTEEN

'Here he is!' Bilbo turned to the door, Eden following suit to see Cam walk in. He gave everyone a stiff nod and strode up to Eden.

'Hi,' she said.

'Hi. Where do you want me?'

She didn't know why she'd expected anything different, considering what had happened the last time they'd been together, but his coldness still shocked her. He hadn't even acknowledged Bilbo, and for the last few café sittings, they'd been like some unlikely buddy movie pairing.

'Everything all right there?' Bilbo called over.

Cam turned to him and smiled, but there was courtesy in it and nothing more. 'Yes. Are you all right?'

'I can't grumble,' Bilbo said.

'Good.' Cam turned back to Eden, leaving poor Bilbo looking confused.

Eden would have to talk to him later and try to make him see that it wasn't his fault Cam had reverted to the miserly presence they'd endured the first time he'd come to volunteer. And she'd have to do that without revealing any of the truth – easier said than done.

'Well?' he asked tersely. Or was that just in Eden's imagination? She was oversensitive, given the events of the past couple of days, even she couldn't deny that. Perhaps there was nothing in it at all.

'Could you make a start on washing the potatoes?'

'It would be my pleasure,' he said, spinning round to go to the store cupboard. Oversensitive or not, there was no mistaking the sarcasm in his tone this time. Eden could only be thankful that she had Livia back with her, grateful for that much moral support.

'What's up with him?' Livia asked in a low voice as he strode off.

Eden gave her a pained look. 'I'm not sure you want to know.'

'I absolutely do want to know, even more since you've dangled that carrot in front of me.'

'Later,' Eden said as she saw him return, dragging a sack to the sink.

'A drink up at the Dolphin when we've finished?'

'Just us?'

'If you like,' Livia said. 'But I can't do much about it if anyone else wants to come.'

'I know.'

Eden watched Cam empty the sack into the sink. One thing she was quite sure of, he wasn't going to be entertaining anyone at the Darling Dolphin tonight. She was surprised to see him here at all. A bit of her had to hand it to him – she wasn't sure she'd be able to turn up like this if the tables had been turned. She supposed he was offended and maybe embarrassed about what they'd done and then her refusal to make it more. She supposed he wasn't used to being turned down in that way either. Of course, the irony was she hadn't wanted to turn him down at all and this whole charade could easily have been avoided. But then, wasn't life full of ironies like that?

Before they'd finished clearing down the kitchen at the end of the sitting, Cam pulled on his jacket and headed for the door. The last few times he'd been he'd said goodbye to everyone if he was leaving them, especially Bilbo. He'd even given him a lift home, and then, of course, there had been the riotous night in the Dolphin they'd all enjoyed together. But not tonight. As the door slammed shut with a mumbled goodnight, Bilbo tied up the rubbish bag he'd just pulled from the bin and watched through the window as Cam got into his car. Then he went over to Eden, who was wiping down the oven.

'Is he all right? Doesn't seem himself today.'

'He's exactly himself today,' Eden said with more irritation than she'd meant to. But Cam had been so much his old self this evening that she'd come close on more than one occasion to telling him they didn't need his service and asking could he please bugger off.

'Oh dear,' Bilbo said, presumably because he didn't know what else to say.

Eden grimaced. 'I'm sorry, Bilbo. I didn't mean it like that. I suppose it's sort of my fault. Cam and I fell out. It's nothing to do with anyone else, and I'm sorry you've all been dragged into it.'

'You're not being moody about it,' Livia called over.

'I guess that makes me the grown-up,' Eden said, not feeling very grown up at all. When all was said and done, if she'd controlled her ridiculous urges the night he'd come round, there would be none of this. Cam would have nothing to sulk about, and they'd all be getting on like a house on fire. The bet was almost over, but she already knew she'd lost and it was her mistake that had blown it at the last minute. They'd been doing so well up until then; Eden was certain they'd been winning him over.

Bilbo looked about as sad as Eden had ever seen him look. She wondered if he still thought he'd done something to offend Cam, despite her reassurances. Whatever the reason, she hated to see the gregarious and lovable old man so down.

'Why don't you head home?' she told him. 'We can finish here.'

'You don't want me?'

'Of course we do!' Eden smiled. 'We'll always want you! I only meant it's been a long afternoon and perhaps you might like to put your feet up. Nice half of stout and some telly? Liam always says how much you like your half a stout of an evening.'

Bilbo hesitated but then nodded. 'All right then – if you're sure.'

'I'm sure. Liam will walk back with you?'

'I expect so.'

'We'll be in the pub later if you want to come to us,' Livia called over.

'I might,' Bilbo said. 'Actually, I think I will. What time will you be there?'

'Not for another hour or so,' Eden said. She glanced at Livia, and knew she understood.

Bilbo and Liam went, and then, one by one, as they finished their tasks, the other volunteers went too, leaving just Eden and Livia to lock up.

'How about you tell me this big secret now we're alone?' Livia said.

Eden let the utensil drawer slam shut and turned to her. 'I slept with Cam.'

Livia froze as she stared at her. 'What?'

Eden gave a grim nod. 'I know what you're thinking, and yes, I think it was a stupid thing to do as well.'

'When? Oh, wait, let me guess...'

'It's not hard to work out, is it?'

'You were quite drunk.'

'A bit too drunk, apparently.'

'Well... was he any good?'

'Livia!'

Livia held out her hands. 'I'm just asking! I'm bound to be curious!'

'I don't really think that's the issue here.'

'So what happened?'

Eden raised her eyebrows, and Livia grinned.

'OK,' Livia said, 'I know what happened. What I mean is, what happened after the thing that happened? Did he go straight away? Did he stay the night? I'm presuming it was at your place and not his hotel? You did both walk up there together after you left the pub, didn't you?'

'My place, and he stayed the night.'

'God, I'd have loved to have been a fly on the wall in the morning when you had to face each other. Was it crippling?'

'It was for me. He wanted to do it again.'

'What?'

'He wanted to take me on a date.'

'But that's... wow! So what's his problem today? Don't tell me... oh, Eden. Don't tell me you turned him down!'

'Of course I did!' Eden began to throw the used tea towels into a linen basket for washing.

'Don't you fancy him?'

'Yes, I fancy him. But it's *him*, isn't it? Cam bloody Faulkner! I can't start that sort of nonsense with him.'

'Maybe you should have thought of that before you jumped his bones.'

'Thank you,' Eden said with a withering look. 'That has occurred to me more than once since it happened.'

'So he's got the hump about it? Wounded pride and all that?'

'It looks that way.'

'And you're scared he's going to double down on his plan to get this land now you've pissed him off?'

'I'm going to assume it's a given.' Eden slumped into a chair at the table. Tears were close to the surface, but she was too exhausted to cry. She'd worked so hard, fought for the survival of this place that she loved so much, that she knew her dad was proud of, and for what? To shoot herself in the foot at the final hurdle? Cam had been humouring her all along – to a degree she'd always known that – but she still believed there was a chance she could change his mind. But now there was no chance. He'd get the land because his pride had been wounded and he'd want to teach her a lesson. So that was that. How long did she have left? she wondered.

'I suppose this means we're going to have to find somewhere new whether we like it or not,' Livia said.

'I suppose so.'

Livia went over and rubbed a hand across Eden's back. 'Don't feel bad. It was always an outside chance anyway – we both knew that. You tried and it didn't work out. It'll be all right in the end.'

Eden gave a weary nod. 'You're right. I just got so caught up in this, and I thought... I don't know what I was thinking. Cam said it – everyone was thinking it – we were sunk from the first moment the land went up for sale. I should have realised – it would have saved a lot of pain.'

'Come on,' Livia said briskly, pulling Eden out of the chair by her hand. 'Let's get to the pub and get some booze inside us, and while we're at it, we can pick Ralph's brains for a plan B.'

· · ·

The Dolphin seemed far too quiet when Livia and Eden arrived, but perhaps that was just as well when they found Ralph manning the bar alone.

'You should have phoned me,' Livia said as he informed them the 'new lad' hadn't turned up for his shift.

'Luckily it's not so busy,' Ralph said. 'I won't be paying him, mind,' he added gruffly, 'and I've a good mind not to give him another shift. Not turning up without so much of a whis-per... not on.'

'Don't stress about serving us,' Livia said. 'We can get our own. We'll give you a shout to see we've dropped the money in the till.'

'Don't be daft,' Ralph said. 'Last orders in an hour – how much can you drink by then? Not much – take what you want and we'll say no more about it. How was the dinner sitting tonight?'

'Good,' Eden said in as neutral a tone as she could manage.

'Your Cam was in here not half an hour ago. Took a quick double and then headed straight off. I thought he might have been waiting for the rest of you.'

'Oh, I think he had things to do,' Eden said. *Her Cam?* Was that how everyone had seen them? She scanned the tables in the bar. 'It's dead in here tonight, isn't it?'

'It's been busier. Still, that's how it goes some nights.'

Eden had wondered if some of her volunteers would be here, but even Bilbo, who'd said he'd come, was absent. It was just her and Livia and three random holidaymakers at a table by the window.

Livia went behind the bar to get the drinks for her and Eden. As she put a gin and lemonade in front of Eden, she nodded towards Ralph. 'Do you want to ask him about the hut situation?' she said in a low voice.

Eden took the drink and shook her head slightly. 'I don't think so, not yet. We don't know for sure what's happening, do we? I know it doesn't look good, but I'm choosing to cling on to a last bit of hope that it might still work out in the end. You've got to, haven't you?'

'It was just a thought as we had him here and it was quiet. But I get you.'

'Cam only owes us one more session and then we'll know, won't we.'

'After the way he was tonight, you think he'll even turn up next time? Maybe he's already made up his mind?'

'That's not him. At least I don't think so. He'll want to prove a point, so he'll see it through. He'll also want to be able to say to me he won fair and square because that will shut me up for good.'

'And will it? He doesn't even owe you that really. I mean, he knows he can take that land any time he wants regardless of the bet.'

'I did say I'd give up if I didn't change his mind during the bet, and he said he'd play by the rules too. He knows and I know he could have just arrived and got what he wanted.'

'So why didn't he?'

Eden shrugged. She didn't know. She supposed she'd never know. 'Whatever the reason, something tells me he'd have stuck by his agreement, so I suppose I have to stand by my agreement too.'

Livia took a sip of her drink. 'Seems like an odd way to go about something that means so much to you.'

'I know,' Eden said. 'Looking back, it was a bit stupid. But what was said in the heat of the moment was said and we shook on it, and that's that. There's time yet – let's see what happens.'

'At least you're sounding more optimistic than you did earlier.'

Eden picked up her glass, staring into the depths. 'What else can I do?'

. . .

Eden woke with the community kitchen on her mind. She'd
fallen asleep turning over the problem and it seemed had spent
the night mentally processing it as she slept, opening her eyes to
find it still there, lodged in her brain. There had to be other
venues, of course, but none she'd come across during her initial
search had suited them quite so well. In fact, as far as she could
tell, the others would involve a massive amount of compromise.
The numbers could be accommodated, but the facilities weren't
there, or vice versa, or the location was too far out, or they
wanted an expensive rent or something else that would cause
problems. Eden supposed she would have to keep trying until
she found something that worked because, despite what she'd
told Livia the night before, she was almost certain that the scout
hut would soon be lost.

As she made her first coffee of the day, wondering what to
do to take her mind off things, her phone rang. She pulled it
across the worktop to see it was Livia.

'Hello,' she said. 'This is early, even for you. So what did I
leave in the pub last night because it must be something like
that.'

'I've just heard from Liam...'

Eden's smile disappeared at Livia's tone. 'What's
happened? Is he all right? It's not...'

'Bilbo died last night! Liam called to tell me, but I couldn't
ask much because he was trying to get to all of Bilbo's friends to
let them know.'

Eden shook her head slowly. 'I can't... But we saw him last
night! He was working and he seemed... He even said he'd come
to the pub! Did Liam tell you anything at all?'

'Only that Bilbo got home, said he felt a bit off but told
Liam he'd be OK and he'd phone in the morning. But when
Liam called earlier, he couldn't get any reply. Found him in the

armchair. He must have just passed away right there.'

'Oh...' Eden was numb. She didn't know how to feel because she was struggling to comprehend it. How could it be that Bilbo who had been there, working alongside her, one minute would be dead a few hours later? He'd been quieter than usual, but she'd assumed that was down to the sour atmosphere caused by Cam. Had there been more to it than that? And if she'd missed something she ought to have picked up because she hadn't been paying attention, Eden would never forgive herself. She'd done that once before with equally tragic consequences, and the thought that she somehow could have prevented this would haunt her... but surely not? She thought back to everything that had happened, everything she'd seen the previous evening. Had there been any signs that Bilbo was ill? She couldn't recall anything at all.

'Want me to come over?' Livia's voice brought her back to the room.

'Aren't you supposed to be working at the parlour today?'

'Yes, but I could spare some time. Mum would understand. In fact, we discussed closing for the day because she's cut up too and it didn't feel right to open, but quite honestly, we need the money and, like Mum said, Bilbo wouldn't have wanted that. He wouldn't have wanted a fuss at all.'

'I'm fine; it's not me anyone needs to worry about. Should we go and see his family later? Just to pay our respects? And what about Mavis? We ought to go and check on her.'

'I'd say in a couple of days, not today. It's all still very new, and I expect they'll have enough people knocking on the door today.'

'You're right. You're always right – I don't know what I'd do without you.'

'Mum's here – she says come for tea later if you feel like you need some company. I'm on shift at the Dolphin tonight, but it might be nice for you to come up there too. I would imagine lots of people will go up there to raise a glass to him if you wanted to join in.'

'It's sounds... actually, it sounds nice. Sort of cathartic. It'd be good to hear about him. I will, thank you.'

'There's no better place at times like these than with others who can share the loss.'

Eden thought back to her mother's death. Had she sought anyone out to share her loss with? Now that she considered the question, she realised she'd done the opposite. Would she have coped better if she'd spent time with her loved ones instead of pushing them away, bearing her grief in a self-imposed solitude, feeling as if she'd no right to share it when she'd done so much to cause it in the first place? On reflection, she could see how right Livia was – yet again. Livia was the friend Eden had never known she'd needed – she only wished she could have found her long before this.

Eden had spent the morning moping. She'd felt it might help to cry, but she simply couldn't find her tears, the shock of Bilbo's departure and her struggle to process it too big for her to get past. It was strange considering how much crying she'd done for other things over the past few months that she couldn't do it now, arguably when she really ought to have done.

In the end, unable to settle down to anything, she decided the best idea might be to do something that involved nothing of note, and so she grabbed her keys, left her phone behind and set out over the clifftops.

The day was grey and the clouds low, even though it was warm, the sea like a sheet of steel in the bay and the rocks tumbling down to it black and slick, and she felt it quite suited her mood. She marched for an hour along the path that traced the line of the coast until it took her away from the view, where she then retraced her steps, somehow needing the comforting presence of the grey ocean and the crashing waves, however foreboding it seemed today. She emptied her mind and thought only of her footsteps and the wind on her skin, eyes turned to the horizon where the breeze tried to chase away stubborn clouds, hoping that simply being in the moment might help her process thoughts that seemed too complicated to face head on.

She might have been out for an hour, or she might have been out for three – without her phone to tell her the time, she had no way of being certain. But when Four Winds came into view once more, a squat, stone square in the distance, she did feel lighter and calmer than when she'd left it. She was surprisingly hungry too, running through a mental list of food she thought might still be in her fridge from the last time she'd ordered shopping – which was quite a while ago. Eating so often at the community kitchen with everyone else, sometimes at the pub and on occasion with Livia, Julia and the kids, there hadn't been much call for a huge amount of grocery shopping, so she couldn't be sure what she had available. Whatever it was, she'd find a meal from it somehow. She could have gone into town to buy something there but wasn't sure she was ready to face anyone who might want to talk about Bilbo just yet.

But as she drew closer, she could see a figure making its way up the path that ran perpendicular to the one she was currently on, from the town up to the cottage. He stopped for a moment, as if he'd seen her, and then began to walk again, and there was no mistaking his intended destination. But at the crossroads, he changed direction and began to make his way towards the clifftop where she was.

She frowned as she recognised him. 'Cam?'

'I tried phoning you, but I couldn't get an answer. I was... never mind.'

'Sorry, left my phone in the cottage.'

'Doesn't matter. I heard about Bilbo.'

'Ah...' Eden stopped on the path. 'How?'

'Livia was at the ice-cream place. She took a minute out to tell me, said I ought to know because she thought we got on well.'

'Bilbo liked you. I think you probably reminded him of his younger days in the navy too, because of your great-uncle and everything.'

'It's weird, isn't it? I can't get my head around how sudden. I mean, he was there last night, working like normal and then... gone.'

'Life's like that, isn't it? Are you all right?'

'Me? Why shouldn't I be? I hardly knew him.'

Eden didn't think Cam looked all right despite his reassurances, but she decided not to say so. He looked how she felt – numb and disbelieving. Nobody had seen this coming, and it seemed everyone was struggling. Bilbo was such a force, such a character that it was hardly surprising even people who barely knew him would be affected by his death, especially as it was so sudden.

'I'm heading home,' she said. 'Do you maybe want to come in for a minute?'

He paused, uncertain, but then he nodded. 'Actually, I think I'd like that.'

She began to walk again, and he fell in step beside her. They were quiet as they made their way back, but it was an easy enough silence. Eden wondered why he'd come. Perhaps he was wondering the same thing too. He'd been friendly with Bilbo, but he'd only known him a couple of weeks, yet the way he seemed to have been affected was bigger than that.

At the house, she invited him to sit at the kitchen table while she made drinks with an odd feeling of déjà vu. It wasn't so long ago that they'd been in this same kitchen doing the same thing, only the circumstances had been very different.

'I was so awful to him yesterday,' Cam said into the silence.

Eden turned from stirring the coffees. 'Do you think so?'

'Don't you? I could tell by his face he couldn't understand. Like a bloody puppy being told off and not knowing what for. I just wanted... I didn't want anything to do with any of you. I had a job to do and I'd lost sight of that, and I thought I just needed to get back on track. One more sitting, right? And then I was done and I could forget about this stupid place. Then this morning Livia comes to me and...'

He looked up at her as she came to the table.

'I'm sure Bilbo wasn't offended by you. He only thought...'

'What?'

'He only wondered why you'd been distant.'

'I didn't mean to... It wasn't anything he did.'

'He knew that.'

'I still feel terrible about it. The last he saw of me was me being an absolute dick to him.'

'You can't change any of it now, so there's no point in dwelling on it.'

'You do think I was out of order then?'

'That's not what I meant. If it was anyone's fault, it was mine, wasn't it? I pissed you off, right?'

'Of course you didn't. You had every right to refuse me and... well, I was pissed off at the time, but I realised you were never going to do anything else. How could you? We were on opposite sides, and I'd have done the same in your situation. I didn't reset my boundaries yesterday because I was pissed at you; I did it because I realised I'd got too close to the situation, in every way possible. I'd made friends and I'd fallen— It doesn't matter now. All I'm trying to say is you were doing what I should have done. We never should have... well, you know.'

A strange kind of disappointment washed over Eden. While she agreed with everything he was saying, to hear him say they shouldn't have spent that night together made her feel sad and empty. She'd told herself a dozen times since it had been a mistake, and she'd resolved to keep an emotional distance, just as he had clearly decided to do, but it hadn't stopped her thinking: what if? What if they did give it a try? Could there be anything in it? She'd tried hard to make it otherwise, but he'd been on her mind in one way or another a lot over the past couple of days, and not all of it had been to do with the sale of the land. She'd thought about his smile, his voice, his eyes, the feel of his skin next to hers, the smell of him, the sounds of his quiet breaths as he slept, the way the sun caught his hair to reveal auburn highlights as if revealing a secret treasure, the odd, unexpected look of softness when someone at the kitchen had thanked him for some little assistance or other. He wasn't the ogre he pretended to be, and she wished he'd show more of that hidden side because she felt it was a side she could grow to like, even love.

Silly, of course. That was never going to happen. Circumstances had thrown them into opposition, and there was no bridging this gap. They were working towards very different goals and very different lives. How could there be any common ground, no matter how attracted she might be?

'I suppose so. And, you know, it wasn't completely your fault. I wanted to... Like you say, it doesn't matter now. It happened and we move on.'

'Anyway, I wanted to see if you were OK. I know you were fond of Bilbo.'

'As all right as anyone in the bay is today,' Eden replied. 'But thanks; I appreciate that.'

'I also wanted to tell you I'm not going to be coming back to the kitchen. I'm sorry if that leaves you short of help, but—'

'No, I totally get it. I half expected you to say so – I was quite surprised to see you there yesterday, if I'm honest. Thank you for your help. And for giving us half a chance to show you what we do. I know in the end you were right – there's no stopping progress – but not many people would have bothered to get to know us at all.'

'I had fun.'

Eden sipped at her coffee, giving him a look of faint disbelief from over the rim of her cup.

'Honestly,' he said. 'I'll admit at first I was sceptical, but I couldn't help it. You were right about that – you did all wear me down. I'd love nothing more than to walk away and say hey, keep your hut, but...'

'I know, business.'

'But you have to understand that the land is still for sale. In that respect, it doesn't matter what I do or say because even if I walk away from it, someone else will buy it eventually, and I don't see many buyers wanting to keep that rotting old hut.' He shrugged at Eden's look of offence. 'Sorry, but you have to admit it's seen better days. It's a prefab and it looks old – it's probably already twenty or more years past its use-by date.'

'I suppose you're right. It just suits us so well.'

'What if I...?' He paused, as if working something out before he said it. 'What if I could find a way to get both of us what we want?'

'OK,' Eden said slowly. 'I'm listening.'

'What if the sale goes ahead – to me? And the hut will still have to go – there can't be any movement on that. But what if somewhere in the development we allowed space for some kind of community hub, something comparable in size, something with everything you need. We'd be able to make money renting it out for events and such, but perhaps we'd be able to come to some sort of subsidisation arrangement for you guys. Kind of like a gesture of good faith, to show that we're not coming to destroy the community and as recompense for allowing it all to go through with your cooperation instead of your opposition. What do you think?'

Eden's eyes widened. 'You'd really do that?'

'I'd try. I couldn't absolutely promise, but I feel confident I could swing it with the partners.'

'I feel confident you could – don't forget I've seen you in action.'

'Do you need to discuss it with the others before you give me your answer?'

'Perhaps. I imagine they'll all say the final decision is with me – and of course, it's not my land or my building, so I don't know whether the owners need to be consulted too.'

'Once the land has been signed over, I don't really see what it has to do with them. You might mention it as a courtesy, but I don't think you need to. If you want time to talk to your team, I can give you that.'

'That would be amazing. I don't know what to say.'

'You don't need to say anything. I'm glad we've come to an agreement – of sorts, at least. It will make things easier from here onwards.'

'I hope so.' Eden wondered whether she ought to offer some sort of apology for being such a thorn in his side, but then decided – however softened she'd become by his suggestion – that she owed him no such thing. She'd been fighting for something that mattered – not just to her but to many people. He surely understood that. In his own way, though she felt the cause was far less worthy, he'd been doing exactly the same. If the whole thing was rerun ten times over, neither of them would have done anything differently, even armed with the knowledge of how it would end. 'Thank you. I know you didn't have to do this.'

'I want to help if I can. Don't forget that it's not set in stone. You might still want to look into a plan B.'

'I'm already on it – Livia and I are going to do some research. We're also going to get Ralph's help.'

He looked into his mug for a moment and then up at her again. 'Will you even be here when all this happens? Aren't you supposed to be heading back to London at the end of the year?'

Eden took a deep breath, for the first time about to air a

decision she'd made in her head weeks before. 'I'm not going back to London. I want to stay here. This is where I belong.'

He nodded, holding her in a thoughtful gaze. 'I can see that. It suits you far better than London ever did.'

'I think I'm a better person here.'

'I think everyone is. I think Sea Glass Bay makes you that way.'

Eden chanced a small smile. 'You know that old film, *Brigadoon*?'

'Never heard of it.'

'Oh,' she said, her smile growing. 'It was just... Never mind. There's no point trying to explain it if you don't know.'

He pulled in a long breath. 'Look, thanks for the coffee and everything, but I think I'd better go.'

'You don't have to—'

'I do. A lot of work on, you know? Emails to send, people to call.'

'Oh, yeah, I remember what all that was like.'

'I suppose you look at me now with pity,' he said, and Eden was struck by the sudden melancholy in his expression. Where had that come from? He'd been sad about Bilbo, of course, but even so, this was almost... if she didn't know better, the only word she'd be able to find was *existential*. Like he'd suddenly discovered his whole life had been a lie.

'No,' she said, trying to shake the thought. 'I look at you like someone with a proper career. I mean, look at me now.'

'I am,' he said. 'You look happy. You never looked this happy when we worked together.'

'Cam... are you really all right? Because if you want to talk—'

'I'm fine. Ignore me – weird day, right?'

'Yes, I suppose it is. If you're sure. But promise you'll look me up if you change your mind.'

'You know I won't, but thanks.'

'Cam...'

'Yes?'

Eden wanted to say something to make it better, but she couldn't find the words. She didn't even know what she was supposed to be making better; she only knew that he wasn't himself. Then again, did she even know who that was? Hadn't she only just started to work out who she really was? Sea Glass Bay had done that for her. Was something similar happening to Cam? It had taken her time to adjust, and perhaps he would need the same.

That old film, *Brigadoon*, came to mind again. She didn't even know why or where or how she'd seen it, only that the notion of some magical place that didn't exist in the world unless you sort of needed it had stayed with her throughout her childhood. But it was only here, in the place she was beginning to call home, that she truly understood what it meant. Sea Glass Bay was her Brigadoon. It had been missing from her life for so many years, but it was the place she'd been drawn to, and it had gathered her up and healed her when she'd needed it most. The problem was, strangers never stayed in Brigadoon. She hoped she'd be able to stay here because she was afraid she'd lose everything it had given her if she left.

'You could stay here for a while if you liked. I mean today, with me. We might be good for each other. The company, that is. It might make... I don't know. I know you have work to do, but it was just a thought.'

'Thanks, but I ought to get on. I only wanted to come and see if you were OK.'

'I appreciate that. I'm fine. I suppose I'll go down to the town, try to get more information on what happened, find out whether there are plans for a funeral and stuff.'

'It's a bit soon for that, isn't it?'

'Well, yes, I suppose it is, but...' Eden let out a sigh. 'I don't really know what else to do.'

He gave a short nod. 'There's not much more anyone can do than that. When you do find out the arrangements, would you let me know?'

'You'd want to come to Bilbo's funeral?'

'If you don't think it would be inappropriate. And if I can find the time, of course.'

'I think it would be lovely and not inappropriate at all.'

He finished his coffee and stood up. 'Thanks for the drink. See you around.'

'I hope so.'

A moment later, he was gone, and the house was silent once more. Eden pondered her next move. In a way, things had been settled here. Cam was going to buy the land, but he was going to try to help secure the future of the community café. The bet was over. Cam was leaving, but she was staying. Would he ever come back? With Bilbo's death came the sense that some sort of spell had been broken and nothing would ever be like it had been for the past few strange, unsettling, difficult and yet glorious and amazing weeks. She couldn't quite decide whether she'd won or lost.

One thing became clear, and it took her by surprise that, considering all the tragedy she'd endured in the past few months, it was Bilbo's death that had crystallised the epiphany for her. She had to make peace with her own family. Life was too short, too unpredictable to allow the current situation to continue. What if something happened to her dad and she hadn't ever made the effort? She'd never forgive herself. As for Caitlin, if she didn't reach out soon, she was going to lose her for good. Whatever their differences in the past, Caitlin was still her sister, and Eden loved her. Eden's dad had forgiven her long before this moment, but Caitlin was going to take more convincing – not that Eden was surprised by that; she hadn't exactly been kind to her. In fact, she'd been a total nightmare – it was no wonder Caitlin got so frustrated.

For a few silent minutes, she stared into space, internally composing the right text to send to her sister, each time abandoning it to try again. But when nothing would come, she wondered if the best thing was simply to call and speak from the heart.

When Caitlin answered on the fourth ring, she was almost surprised. She'd called but half expected to get no answer, wondering if her sister would be out or working. There was surprise in Caitlin's tone too – and perhaps some distrust.

'Hello, Eden.'

'Caitlin, hi, I... Can you talk?'

'Yes, let me...' There was a pause. 'Just turning my laptop off.'

'You didn't need to— Sorry, you were working?'

'It can wait. Sounded as if you needed my full attention.'

'That depends on how you feel about what I'm going to say. I'm sorry. Sorry doesn't even cover it, I know that, but I am. About so much. I'm sorry about how awful and selfish I've been recently, but... God, Caitlin, I'm sorry for my entire life. I'm sorry for being such a horrible sister. Can you forgive me? I can't stand the way we are, and I miss you. I'd even take us bickering all the time over this... nothing. I don't even feel like I have a sister right now, and I hate that. I know it's my fault and—'

'Eden, stop. I never thought you were a horrible sister. I love you, you idiot. Yes, you could drive me mad, and yes, sometimes it was like chastising one of the kids at my school whenever I talked to you, but that's just how sisters are sometimes, isn't it? It never made me love you any less.'

'But that day with Mum... the thing I did.'

'I was angry that day, and I blamed you for doing what you did over the community centre, but it wasn't your fault Mum died. You've got to stop thinking that. Mum had something wrong with her heart – you didn't do that.'

'I made her stressed.'

'You and plenty of other things in her life. Don't you realise that I've felt just as responsible for her death as you have? It takes two to argue, and I was giving as good as I got that day. I contributed to her stress, so if you want to see it that way, then we both have to take the blame.'

'It was never your fault!'

'Both of us take the blame or neither of us. So which is it to be?'

'Cait... it's not your fault.'

'Then it's not yours either. Stop punishing yourself because every time you do that, you punish me and Dad too. I've been angry when I've called because I've been hurting and I've needed you, but I see now my anger only made things worse. I'm sorry for that.'

'You had every right.'

'Maybe, but that doesn't make it better.'

Eden's eyes filled with tears. 'I'm so glad we're talking about this.'

'Me too. So does this mean you're ready to come home, or at least back to Essex?'

'Well, that's the other thing I want to tell you – I've decided to stay here for good.'

'In Sea Glass Bay?'

'Yes.'

'Wow... I never saw that coming.'

'I can imagine,' Eden said with a watery smile, assuming that her dad had told Caitlin where she was. 'But if you get some time off work over the next few weeks, I'd love you to come and visit. And Dad too, of course. I'm making a new life here, one I love, and I've made so many new friends, and I want you both to see how amazing it all is.'

'If that's really true, then I'm glad.'

'It is. So you'll come? I get if you don't feel like you want to, but—'

'Of course I want to! You want me to talk to Dad? Or would you prefer to call him yourself with his invite? I know he'd love to hear from you, and he'd be happy to know you're doing so well.'

Eden watched a fat tear drop onto the kitchen table in front of her and soak into the wood. And then another one. Before she knew it, they were coming thick and fast, and she had to sniff hard to pull herself together enough to answer.

'I'll call him,' she said. 'I'll do it right now.'

CHAPTER EIGHTEEN

A meeting that had involved every single person who'd ever known Bilbo or had anything to do with the community café resulted in agreement that after his funeral, and as more of a celebration of his life than a wake, their next community dinner would be a picnic on the beach. Anyone who wanted to come was invited, and anyone who wanted to contribute in any way was welcome. It would be about so much more than food. They'd be coming together to remember a man who'd been such a huge personality that his absence would be felt for many years to come, and who would have wanted his legacy to be happiness, not sorrow.

Eden, Ralph, Livia and Julia, along with Bilbo's family and friends, took on the task of organising. It was a far bigger event than their usual dinner, and they'd need all the help they could get. But there was a sense of excitement too, of anticipation that it was going to be special, an event unlike anything Sea Glass Bay had seen before.

Caitlin and her dad were coming. Eden wondered if they might find it weird, attending what was essentially a wake for a man they'd never met, but they'd both wanted to support her through it when she'd told them what she was helping to organise, recognising that it mattered to her, that this community was now an important part of her life.

The weather couldn't have been more perfect if Eden had ordered it. Julia said as much as they loaded the van they'd borrowed from Ralph to transport their supplies to the beach. They had so much stock that they'd been forced to store it wherever they could find space: at the ice-cream parlour, at Eden's house, in Ralph's storerooms, at the scout hut and one or two other places. Now they had to remember where it all was and collect it, and that task was proving trickier than any of them had anticipated. They were currently loading up the items Eden had been keeping in her kitchen for the past week. Livia and the children were doing their best to help, though it could have been argued that the children were slowing everything down – not that anyone for a moment would have asked them to stop. In fact, it was entertaining to listen to their conversation as they worked.

'I can carry way more than you,' Levi said to Nancy, at which point she looked faintly outraged and tried to pile another stack of paper plates onto the pile she already had in her arms. Predictably, all she succeeded in doing was making sure she dropped the lot.

'See what you made me do,' she grumbled as Levi laughed at her.

'I told you I could carry more.'

'Grandma!' Nancy whined. 'Tell him! He's laughing at me!'

Eden wanted to laugh too – not because she thought Nancy's predicament funny but because they were both so damn cute. Of course, she realised that was the last thing she ought to do, and it was quite a battle to keep her face straight as she went over to help pick everything up.

'Don't worry about it,' she told Nancy. 'You win some, you lose some. Levi won this time, but you might win next. The main thing is you're trying.'

'But Levi laughed at me!'

'Yes, but you can be bigger than that, can't you? People will laugh at you sometimes when you're trying to do something and it's not working, but you don't have to let it upset you or let it stop you.' Eden put the stack of plates into Nancy's arms again, along with the extra one. 'There, see? You only needed some help because your arms were already full. If you'd picked all these up at first, you'd have carried them easily. When your arms are too full, all you have to do is ask. Someone will always help, but they won't if they don't know you need it.'

Nancy smiled and then trotted off to the van with a new purpose in her stride.

'Nice TED talk,' Livia said from behind Eden. 'You should do it for a living.'

'I'm the last person to be giving out life advice.'

'Oh, I don't know. I think you've got more to offer than you realise. After all, when you've lived it, you can talk about it, right? What time did your sister and dad say they'd be coming?'

Eden gave her a grateful smile. She wondered, not for the first time, why she'd been so afraid to share the events that had led up to her mum's death with Livia because when she finally did, Livia hadn't judged at all. Just as Eden had hoped and as she ought to have known, Livia had listened and then told Eden that she couldn't keep punishing herself for a mistake, no matter how big. She also decided that, in the process of punishing herself, Eden had inadvertently punished her family by disappearing from their lives. Caitlin had said something similar, but Livia's way of putting it had been far gentler.

'I was hoping they'd be here for the start, but Caitlin texted me to say they'd hit traffic so they might be late.'

'That's a shame.'

'Yes, but I suppose it can't be helped. It's a miracle they're coming at all – at least, it's a miracle Caitlin is.'

'Look on the bright side – you were worried you'd be neglecting them while we got set up, so if they arrive later, everything should more or less be ticking along, and you'll be able to give them your full attention. If you need to pop up to Four Winds when they arrive to let them in with their stuff, I can hold the fort here.'

'Actually, Dad booked a hotel for them.'

'Oh.'

'It's OK,' Eden said. 'It's the first time we've all been together since I left, and I wonder if Caitlin had some kind of conversation with him about breathing space. I have to agree, I think it's a good idea we're not all staying at Four Winds. We'll see how this couple of days goes, and then maybe we can move forward together to a day when it will be fine, but until then...'

Livia laid a hand on her arm. 'I think that's probably sensible. But you're really OK with it?'

'Of course. I'm just glad they're coming.'

'So... Have you heard from Cam?'

'Not since he left.'

'You haven't even texted him?'

'I messaged him about this thing today, but he didn't reply, so it's obvious he thinks that's the end of it.'

'I still say you're both being idiots. One of you needs to say something.'

'There's nothing to say. He won the bet – the land will soon be gone and the scout hut with it. I know he said he'd help set something up in its place but...' Eden shrugged. 'Realistically, I don't think that will happen. Out of sight, out of mind. He might have felt that way while he was in the bay, but I doubt he'll remember his promise now.'

'What about the fact that you liked him?'

'I liked him because... I don't know why. Because I was being stupid. It was never going anywhere.'

'He liked you too.'

'It was intense, the drama that was going on between us, and we got swept up in that. It didn't mean anything; it wasn't real. It was just...' She cast around for a way to explain, but she couldn't find one. 'Sexy,' she concluded lamely.

Livia raised her eyebrows. 'Arguing over a scout hut made you both horny? Is that what you're saying? And you're actually standing by that rubbish?'

'I know,' Eden said. 'Whatever it was, he's gone, and that's that. It must not have meant enough to him to come back to the bay, so why would I go chasing it?'

'It's only been a few weeks, and he might have been busy.'

'Yes, busy selling our land.'

'It was never our land. We knew this would likely happen when you started the café up, remember?'

'I know, but—'

'Are you two going to stand there chatting all day?'

Both Eden and Livia looked around to see Julia, arms folded across her chest, grinning at them.

'We're not your hired help, you know,' she continued. 'Poor Levi and Nancy are like child labour here, doing all the work. Let's get moving!'

Livia turned to Eden as she made a move towards the van. 'Call him!' she said sternly. 'That's all I'm saying. Stop trying to guess what's in his head and call him!'

Eden gave a wan smile. It might have made perfect sense to Livia, but it wasn't so simple. She couldn't deny she'd missed Cam since he'd gone, but it seemed theirs were two worlds that should never have collided. He'd gone back to a life she'd renounced, and perhaps it was for the best that he hadn't been in contact since.

What she hadn't told Livia was that she'd emailed him at

work and invited him to today's event, and that he hadn't replied. She wasn't sure why she'd kept this to herself, but perhaps it was because she felt foolish for ever believing there was something between them. As she'd told Livia, on reflection, she'd decided it had all been down to the heat of the moment, the drama they'd both fixated on, a situation that had become charged beyond reason because they'd both wanted to win so badly, and that charge had somehow turned into lust. That had to be it. Maybe it hadn't been quite so simple for Eden, but it seemed that was exactly how it had been for Cam.

When they got to the beach two hours later, every bit of food and equipment collected up, most of their helpers with their own contributions were already there waiting for them. Eden shot a glance of misgiving at Livia and swore under her breath. She ought to have been there to greet them. It wasn't the best start to the day.

Livia seemed to read her thoughts. 'Stop stressing. Nobody is bothered about us being a bit late but you. You don't have to be superwoman all the time, you know.'

'We're more than a bit late.'

Livia folded her arms and shot Eden a wry sideways glance. 'Were you like this in your old job?'

'I don't know.'

'All I can say is God help the people you worked with if you were.'

Livia was right: nobody seemed to be too concerned with their lateness. In fact, everyone seemed more than pleased to see them, eager to get things underway. Some had already set out blankets and chairs on the sand. Ralph had taken time off to bring a huge grill down and was currently trying to get it lit while one of his kitchen staff was pricking mounds of sausages ready to go onto it. At the sight of him, Levi raced over.

'Are you cooking sausages, Ralph?'

'Oh,' Ralph said, with such dry weariness it was all Eden could do not to burst out laughing. 'It's you. The sausage fiend. If I'd have known you were coming I'd have hidden them.' Levi giggled, and then Ralph broke into a grin. 'Of course we're having sausages, Levi. As if we could invite you to a party without any.'

Levi thrust his fist into the air. 'Yes!'

He then set up camp on the sand close to the grill, watching as they prepared the food.

'Three guesses what menu item he's most excited about,' Julia said as she swished past Eden and Livia with tubs of potato salad balanced in her arms. She was followed by Nancy, who cradled a single cheesecake with such love that Eden had to laugh again. They headed for a collection of tables that had been set up on the sand.

'I think we've figured out what Nancy is most excited about too.'

Livia looked across and smiled. 'If she could have put her name on that, she would have done.'

Eden gazed around at the activity and took a deep breath. The breeze drifting across the beach had that peculiar tang of salt that somehow calmed the soul, and that was how Eden felt. She'd been stressed on arrival, annoyed that her schedule was out, but now she was here amongst friends in the most beautiful place in the world, she was happy. Livia and Julia were right: nobody cared if things didn't run to plan. The important thing was they were here, celebrating their community and the life of a man who'd meant so much to them. The important thing was they were together. Eden might have some residual anxiety about the arrival of her sister and dad, but even that wasn't strong enough to diminish this moment of contentment.

'Bilbo would have loved this...'

Eden spun round to see his friend, Mavis. Bilbo's great-grandson, Liam, was supporting her as she walked. Even during the short time Eden had known Mavis, she seemed to have become so much frailer. Perhaps it was because, since Bilbo's death, she'd stopped going to the tea dances they'd done together. The notion that some of the people she'd grown so attached to might not be here for much longer made Eden melancholy, but she tried to shake that feeling as she smiled brightly at the old lady.

'I think you're right.' She looked at Liam. 'How are you?'

'All right,' Liam said.

'And your family? They're all coping?'

Liam gave a vague shrug. He'd always been shy, difficult to engage in conversation, but it was clear he'd adored his great-grandfather, and he was a sweet young man with a good heart. He'd helped out at the community café since the beginning, which was a lot more than many boys of his age would have done. 'They're coming down in a bit.'

'That's good,' Eden said. 'I haven't seen them since the funeral. I've been wondering how they're getting on.'

'Is there anything you'd like me to do?' Mavis asked.

Eden cast around for something that wouldn't be too taxing. The truth was they could probably manage without Mavis's help, but she realised that Mavis wanted to feel useful.

'Perhaps ask at the tables. I think Julia mentioned someone pairing up cutlery in napkins so they're ready for people to pick up. And we need some bins setting up for the rubbish too.'

'Quite right,' Mavis said. 'Don't want it blowing all over the beach. I'll go and see.'

Eden watched her lean on Liam's arm as she toddled away before going back to the van to continue their unloading. There was so much food she'd worried that they'd gone way overboard, despite reassurance from both Julia and Ralph, but looking at just how many people had turned up, their numbers swelling with new arrivals all the time, she wondered whether they'd have enough.

It had taken some extra canvassing for donations in the town – donations most were only too happy to give when she'd explained what the event was – plus some help from Ralph and a chunk of her own savings to put this on, but Eden didn't mind. She didn't even mind that her savings were dwindling faster than she'd anticipated. Money was important, but she hadn't expected hers to last forever.

In the past, money had been everything, despite the fact she'd had more than enough. She'd always wanted more: more money, more things, more holidays, more security. It had been her downfall. But in the end, trying to become someone other than that person had saved her because it had brought her here. So if she struggled sometimes, it was all right. Her friends in the bay would have her back; they'd help her through, as they all helped each other. She looked at Livia and her family and saw that she didn't need money to be happy. She wasn't naive – of course people needed money to live, but having more than you needed didn't always equate to a better life. Now that she'd made the decision to stay in Sea Glass Bay, it was something she was certain she'd work out along with everything else.

Livia followed her to the van. 'I've just seen the owner of Four Winds walking along the promenade. At least, it looked like her. I haven't seen her in ages, not since the house was sold. I wonder why she's here.'

Eden's gaze went to the stretch of road that followed the line of the beach. 'Margery? I don't see her.'

'Must have gone into town. I wondered if she might be coming up to check on you, see if you've got everything you need.'

'Maybe. It's a shame she's had a wasted journey if she's been up there while I've been down here. She'll message me if it's important, and I suppose she has a key if she wants to go in and check around. I've got nothing to hide, so...'

'Have you spoken to her about giving up the house early?'

Eden shook her head. 'I don't want to do that until I've found somewhere else. I've seen a couple of apartments for rent... I don't suppose you'd like to come and view them with me? In fact, one has a spare room... the kids could come and stay whenever you and your mum needed a night off. And before you say I don't need to do that and all the other rubbish, I'd love to have them over – they're so much fun.'

Livia blinked. And then she grabbed Eden in a huge hug. 'I can't tell you how glad I am you're staying in the bay!'

'Me too,' Eden replied, her grin so wide it threatened to break free of her face. 'I think it's going to be the best decision I've ever made.'

As they hugged, Eden felt something wrap around her legs and looked down to see Nancy clinging on to them both.

'Group hug!' Livia cried, breaking free to scoop up her niece and fold her back into the embrace.

'Group hug!' Nancy giggled.

Eden pulled her in. She couldn't remember a hug in her entire life better than this one. If there hadn't been so much else going on, she might have been tempted to stay in it all day.

'Right.' Livia was the first to break it up, kissing Nancy on the head and setting her down. 'Come on – we've got lots to do, and it won't get done while we're being all soppy.' She handed Nancy another box of cakes. 'You know what to do.'

Eden was still smiling as she watched Nancy dash off with it. 'You know, you're an amazing not-quite-mum.'

'I try,' Livia said. 'Sometimes I don't mind admitting it's hard, but then I think about my sister, and I realise I'm lucky.'

'You gave up a lot; it's bound to feel hard sometimes.'

'I don't think I gave up all that much, and if I did, I got back something that was worth far more.'

'Nobody would blame you if you sometimes got angry. Losing your sister, then your dad, not getting Four Winds when it had been promised to you as an inheritance...'

Livia shook her head. 'What's the use in getting angry about any of that? I couldn't change it, no matter how angry I got. As for Four Winds, if I had inherited it when my uncle died, I'd have been living in it and you wouldn't have rented it. You might not even have come to the bay at all, so...'

Eden couldn't quite believe that her friendship was worth so much to Livia, but if it was worth even a tiny fraction of that, she was happy.

'I don't let it worry me,' Livia continued. 'Everything works out eventually, doesn't it? Even if we have to get round a few obstacles on the way.'

Eden was about to reply when she noticed a car parking up on a designated spot on the promenade, a few spaces away from where they'd set the van. Her heart stopped as she watched Caitlin and her father get out, her good mood suddenly evaporating to be replaced by anxiety, the likes of which she hadn't known since her arrival in Sea Glass Bay. Things had been cordial enough on messages and phone calls, but seeing them in the flesh brought the whole awful time around her mother's death bowling back at her.

'Oh, God,' she murmured.

Livia followed her gaze and must have guessed what was going through Eden's mind. 'It'll be fine. I'll leave you to it. Come and find me if you need to, OK?'

Eden nodded vaguely, not even noticing Livia go. Her gaze was fixed on the two people she'd left behind, the two people she'd most wronged in the world as they came towards her.

To her amazement, Caitlin broke into a run, throwing her arms around her.

'You silly little cow!' she cried. 'I thought I'd never see you again!'

Eden floundered in her embrace, sudden tears springing to her eyes. Of all the scenarios she'd anticipated, this had not featured in any of them. A moment later, she could see her dad, tears in his eyes too as he waited for his turn.

'I'm sorry,' Eden sobbed as he folded her into his arms. 'I'm so sorry for everything.'

'You have nothing to be sorry for,' he said gently. 'You never had.'

Eden wanted to believe it, but she couldn't. She would have to be content with the fact they were there, willing to forgive, willing to try to be a family once more. And this time Eden would deserve their love and faith. This time she would be the daughter her dad deserved and the sister Caitlin needed and wanted.

She dried her eyes as he let go. Caitlin was doing the same thing. Then Eden's pragmatic sister seemed to collect herself, the sensible, no-nonsense member of the family once more.

She glanced over to all the activity on the beach. 'That's surely not your community thing?'

'Yes,' Eden said, a sense of pride swelling in her. She could see why Caitlin might be surprised. She supposed it might have sounded like quite a haphazard affair, a few stragglers from the local area getting together to have a plate of chips every now and again. But more than a hundred people were gathered on the beach, working like a well-oiled military machine to get the picnic ready. There was a seating area, equipment and furniture, and smoke coming from Ralph's impressive-looking grill. More importantly, there was a sense of love and belonging radiating from the beach that was hard to ignore. Here were people from all walks of life, all demographics, some with money and some with less, some old, some young, some born and bred in the bay and some who'd made the choice to live there, but all with one thing in common: a desire to be part of it all.

'Wow,' Caitlin said, staring at the comings and goings. 'The whole town must be here. When you said a picnic, I thought it would be a couple of your mates on a blanket.'

'Not quite the whole town, but...' Eden smiled. 'Come on – there are people I'd love you to meet.'

By the time Eden had taken her dad and Caitlin around to chat to everyone who mattered and a few more besides, most of the picnic preparations had been done without her. She'd apologised to just about every one of her helpers, who'd all told her not to worry and that she had every right to take an hour off for the arrival of her family. Many had heard that she'd been estranged from them for a while, even if they didn't know why, and they all seemed delighted that her broken relationships had been mended. Caitlin fell in love with Nancy and Levi, of course, because it was impossible for anyone not to, and seemed to instantly warm to Livia. Julia and Eden's dad got on brilliantly, and Julia was only too happy to chat to him while Eden did other things.

'This is my boss at the pub. Ralph...' Eden took Caitlin and her dad over to the grill. Ralph looked up at the mention of his name. 'Ralph... this is my dad, and this is Caitlin, my sister.'

'Oh...' Ralph turned over a sausage. 'So you're responsible for her,' he said, angling his head at Eden.

Caitlin and Eden's dad both looked confused for a moment. Even Eden was thrown, and she was accustomed to Ralph's dry humour. All was right again when Ralph smiled and held out a hand.

'Pleased to meet you both. She's a cracker, this one. You should be very proud of the difference she's made to this town.'

'Ralph, I...' Eden began, but he fixed her with an affectionate look.

'Don't you dare,' he said. 'Always doing yourself down. Take a look around today and tell me you're not a bit proud of yourself for what you've done here. All these people are here because of you.'

'Because of Bilbo, mostly,' Eden said, though she was warmed by his words.

'Mostly because you decided to do something for Bilbo. Don't forget that.'

'We are proud,' Eden's dad said, threatening to make her cry again.

She sniffed it back – she'd cried today more times than she could remember, and it was getting faintly ridiculous.

All four of them turned at the sound of an excited squeal along the beach, the pitch so high it might have confused the dolphins out in the bay. Nancy tore across the sand to a figure who was walking across it. The next moment, she collided with the man's legs, wrapping her arms around them in a hug, and Eden suddenly knew who it was.

What was he doing here? She'd invited him, of course, but...

'There's a turn-up for the books,' Ralph said, shaking his head. 'That's never your Cam, is it?'

'*Your* Cam?' Caitlin aimed a pointed look at Eden. 'Is that... the partner at the company you used to—'

'Yes,' Eden said.

'You're not... you two aren't...?'

'No. It's nothing like that. We just...'

Eden paused. She didn't even know what they were. She didn't even know how they'd left it, not really. Were they friends? Ex-colleagues? Business associates? Or something more? They'd certainly shared something more, but what did any of that mean now?

'I invited him,' she said. 'You know, because he agreed to help with a new venue for the community café. He never replied to the email, though, so I didn't expect...' She turned to Caitlin. 'I'm sorry, do you mind if I go and talk to him? I ought to.'

'Don't worry,' Ralph said cheerily. 'I'll look after them for a minute if you need to go and say hello. As you say, probably a good idea to keep him onside if you want that new centre.'

As Eden left them and started across the beach, Cam looked up and saw her. Nancy was skipping along at his side looking pleased with herself. It was funny, Eden had never noticed his effect on the children, who'd been pottering about somewhere or other for many of his shifts at the kitchen, but clearly he'd had one.

'Cam's here!' Nancy called to Eden, tugging at his sleeve. 'Look!'

'I can see,' Eden said, smiling, pretending that he wasn't having an effect on her, but her heart was beating so fast it was making her dizzy. 'Well done for finding him.'

He'd dressed down for the day in jeans and a checked shirt, so this wasn't business. She tried not to think about how good he looked, but his dark eyes and curls that were slightly more unruly than the last time she'd seen him wouldn't let her do anything else. Had he been working out, or was that just her imagination? Either way, it looked good on him, and she was forced to try even harder not to think about what he looked like beneath that shirt.

'I didn't think you'd come,' she said as they met on the sand.

'I didn't know it was on until this morning. And before you say anything, I know you emailed me last week, but I must have missed it. My PA was clearing my inbox and told me I'd got some unread stuff, and yours was in it. Sorry.'

'You don't have to be sorry. I only invited you on the off-chance; I expected you to be too busy to come, quite honestly.'

'I would always come,' he said with such earnestness that her legs almost gave way. How he looked at her... what was that? Her mind was playing tricks, surely? 'I mean...' He cleared his throat and seemed to realise what he was doing. 'Bilbo was a great bloke – why wouldn't I come?'

Eden allowed herself to breathe again; of course it was all about Bilbo – why else would he have come? 'Let's go and say hello to some of the volunteers,' she added, nodding for him to follow. 'They'll be so pleased to see you.'

'Will they?' He seemed genuinely confused by her statement.

'Are you kidding? They haven't seen you since you left the bay.'

'Even so, I thought... well, the scout hut...'

'You said it before – it was a foregone conclusion the minute the land went up for sale. Nobody blames you for that. If you hadn't bought it, someone else would have.'

'Even you? You don't blame me?'

'Especially not me. I've learned since I've been here that life might not go the way you want it to – in fact, it rarely does – but what matters is how you deal with that.'

He stuffed his hands in his pockets, fixing her with a look that was... intense? 'I like to think you have a certain amount of agency. If you really want something, you can have it.'

'That may be true to an extent, but I think we've established that we're never going to agree on that point. I say it all depends on your starting point, but... never mind. What's the use of trying to explain it again, eh? While we're on the subject, do you have any news on our new community centre?'

He chuckled at that. 'It's good to see there's still a bit of the old Eden left in you. Never let an opportunity go to waste.'

'Well, you can take the girl out of the city, but...'

Nancy tugged at her sleeve. 'What are you talking about?'

'Oh, this and that.' Eden smiled down at her. 'Why don't you go and find Livia? Tell her all about Cam being here? I'll bet she hasn't even noticed, she's so busy gossiping somewhere.'

Nancy gave a solemn nod, as if she'd been entrusted with the guardianship of some religious relic, and then raced off.

'She's cute,' Cam said as she tore over the sand towards the serving tables.

'She's amazing,' Eden said. 'They all are.'

'All?'

'Livia and her family.'

'Ah. I thought you meant everyone here.'

'Them too,' Eden said, her smile growing.

'You seem happy,' he agreed. 'Settled. Even more than when I was here last. You haven't changed your mind about staying here permanently?'

She looked up at him again. 'No. I'm staying.'

He seemed to be forcing his own smile as he nodded. 'Good for you. Having seen what you've built here, I don't blame you. Perhaps I'm even a bit envious.'

'You have the life you want in London, don't you?'

'Yes,' he said, but something about it left Eden unconvinced that he meant it. 'I have everything I ever wanted.'

'That's both of us then. Let's go and get a drink, eh? Celebrate us both getting everything we ever wanted, even though for some of us we've only just figured out what that is.'

He followed her across the sand. Every so often, someone would stop them to say hello. Eden was pleased to see she'd been right to think Cam would be welcome. She was pleased to prove him wrong. It mattered to her, despite their differences in the past – and they'd been huge – that people liked him. She didn't know why that would be except, perhaps, because she liked him, more than she'd ever done when they'd worked together. It was more even than that, but she couldn't allow herself to dwell on any deeper feelings.

When they got to Liam, the young man seemed more than pleased to see him. Cam extended his hand, and Liam looked up at him with something like awe as well as affection.

'You came all the way from London for my grandad?' he asked.

'It was the least I could do. Bilbo was a great guy,' Cam replied. 'Why wouldn't I come to send him off properly? I'm sorry I didn't come to the funeral; I was going to, but then...' He shrugged. 'I thought it might be a family thing – you might not want outsiders there.'

'It doesn't matter about that. Grandad would be made up if he knew you were here today. Let me get Mavis...'

'Don't worry,' Cam said. 'Don't disturb her – looks like she's busy. I'll catch her later. It's good to see you again.'

Liam nodded, and as Cam began to walk away, Eden followed.

'They would have welcomed you at the funeral. You're not a total outsider, you know.'

'I feel like one. Do you think they'll be all right?'

'Who?'

'Bilbo's family? Are they struggling... you know, for money or anything? Because I could help. They wouldn't have to know; I could do it through you somehow.'

'I don't know about that, but if you really wanted to play secret millionaire, I'm sure the community kitchen could do with funds.'

When he turned to her, he looked offended. Eden wondered what she'd said wrong.

'Are you all right?' she asked uncertainly.

'That's how you see me, isn't it? That's how everyone sees me. I breeze in, throw some money around – money I have plenty of – and then I leave again with my conscience clear. Like some medieval fraud giving money to the church so I'll be allowed into heaven.'

'Of course that's not how we see you!'

He pushed a hand through his hair and stopped on the sand. '*Play secret millionaire.* That's what you said.'

'I didn't mean it like...' Eden sighed. She was messing this up royally. 'I'm sorry. You're right; I shouldn't have put it like that. It was meant to be a flippant comment. I suppose it was a bit too flippant. I'm trying to be better, but I'm far from perfect myself. That's the point – when I first got here, I said the same as you to Livia. I didn't want anyone to think this entitled girl was here to patronise everyone by pretending to be some big saviour. Livia made me see that as long as my intentions were pure, people would forgive the odd misguided mistake. She was right. I messed up plenty, and there were times when I probably did insult people, but I learned along the way. People learned about me too, and I think we all finally understand each other. Things aren't perfect, but they're good.'

She paused as he turned his gaze to the sea, the breeze lifting his hair. He seemed troubled, but she didn't know what to say. Perhaps it was something he was going to have to work out himself, whatever it was.

'I can smell sausages,' she said, for want of anything better. 'Let's go and get some food.'

They were close as they walked back to the grill. Her hand grazed his more than once, and she was gripped by the overwhelming urge to take it, to clasp it in her own. It was odd – they'd slept together not so long ago, and yet she'd never felt the intimacy that she did now. All at once, she felt strange and yet distant; it would only take the smallest leap to show her true feelings, and she was certain he felt them too, and yet that tiny leap seemed so vast and terrifying that she didn't dare make it. And so they walked to get food, and they talked about everything but their feelings, the desire that hung in the air between them both driving them together and yet forcing them apart. On paper, he wasn't right for her, and she wasn't right for him. She'd imagined during his absence from her life that she was over him, over the missed opportunity, over the night they'd spent together and the intense fortnight they'd shared, but now he was here, she realised it had been a lie. She'd never been over him; she'd only forced herself to forget.

. . .

The sun had dipped below the line of the sea as the solar
lanterns dotted around the picnic area began to flicker into life.
The crowd had gathered to watch a spectacular sunset, a
furnace of bronze and gold that set fire to the sea, and everyone
agreed it felt like a sign that Bilbo was somehow there with
them, that the most perfect and fitting tribute should appear on
this day of all days when they were gathered to celebrate his
life. Even shy and reserved Liam looked moved to tears as Eden
glanced his way. Cam stood at one side of her, and Caitlin and
her dad at the other, with Livia and Julia and the children next
to them, and Eden felt lucky to be witnessing such a spectacle
with the people who mattered most all around her.

Once they'd watched it disappear, there was a round of
applause, and then someone started to play an old guitar, and
someone else started to sing old songs Bilbo used to sing, and
everyone gathered round to listen. Eden sat on the sand, and
Cam settled next to her, while Nancy insisted on curling up on
his knee.

'You've got a fan,' Eden said with a smile. 'I think she might
be a bit in love.'

'God only knows why,' Cam replied.

'Kids can sense good vibes, maybe?'

Cam said nothing to this; he only grabbed Nancy's hands in
his and made her clap along, which started her giggling uncontrollably.

Once the guitarist had gone through his repertoire, a trio of
guests pulled out violins and began to fiddle a lively jig.

Cam laughed. 'I did not see that coming! I didn't even see
anyone with violin cases!'

Eden turned to him. 'I bet you think it's the lamest thing
you've ever seen. You don't have to stay, you know. Nobody
would notice if you snuck off.'

'I know, but I want to stay. I've come all this way, after all.'

'It's getting late. Do you have a room booked somewhere?'

'No; didn't think I'd need one. It doesn't matter – I'll drive back when it's done.'

Livia ran over and gestured to Nancy. 'Come and dance with me! Country dancing: come on – you love this at school!'

Nancy scrambled to her feet and raced off.

'That's the other thing about kids,' Eden said. 'They're fickle. A better offer and you're forgotten.'

'I can't say I blame her,' he said, his gaze going to where Livia was holding hands with Levi and Nancy and skipping around the sand with abandon.

She looked across at Eden. 'You too!' she yelled. 'Come on – get up!'

Eden shook her head.

Livia laughed. 'You've got to! What would Bilbo say if he could see you not dancing?'

Eden groaned and got to her feet, unable to find an argument. But then she held out her hand to Cam. 'If I'm dancing, then you have to come too. Like Livia said, what would Bilbo say if you sat it out?'

'He'd say there's a sensible man.'

'You don't want to be a sensible man every day of your life, do you? Take a day off from that guy. Here, just today, you can be whatever you want. Don't worry – I won't tell anyone in London about it.'

He hesitated and then gave a sheepish smile. 'God help me, I need more alcohol if the night is going to go this way.'

'No you don't. Just let those inhibitions go.' Eden was sly as she looked at him. She'd perhaps had more drinks than she ought to have done, but she was far from drunk. She was, however, emboldened by it. 'I know you can let your inhibitions go – I've seen it first-hand.'

He stared at her and then shook his head, smiling. 'You're... I don't know what you are.'

'I know,' she said, grabbing his hands and putting them on her waist. 'That's why you like me!'

'I do...' he said, using his grip to stop her dancing and pulling her closer. 'I do like you. God knows I've tried not to.'

'Am I supposed to be flattered by that?' she asked, laughing. But when he replied, he wasn't laughing.

'You can't tell me you haven't done the same? You turned me down, remember?'

'I suppose I might have done.'

'Have you asked yourself why?'

'Yes, many times.'

'And what was the answer?'

'I didn't have one.'

'Me neither. So why are we bothering trying not to like each other when we do like each other?'

'Haven't the foggiest.'

They began to sway, but where everyone else was dancing with a pace that matched the music, Eden and Cam were moving slowly, locked together. For all she knew, at this moment, they could have been alone.

'When you asked me for that drink and I said no...' she began after a few minutes had passed in this way. 'I wish I'd said yes.'

'It's not a limited-time offer, you know. You can change your mind.'

'Yes, please. I'd like to change my mind. I'd like that drink. In fact, I'd love it.'

'Good,' he said. 'When?'

'Soon. Do you have to go back to London tonight?'

'I don't suppose I do, but if you recall, I have no hotel booked.'

'I'm sure we can figure something out.'

He broke into a slow smile. 'Is that an offer?'

'Might be.'

'I ought to do the decent thing and take you out for a drink first.'

'Since when were we ever decent?'

He laughed softly and pulled her closer. 'Let's give it a try – we might like it. Seriously, Eden... I don't want this to be some here today, gone tomorrow affair. I like you, and I want to do it properly. Is that... Do you feel the same way?'

She looked up at him, those dark eyes holding her prisoner, and she nodded. 'Yes, I do. I know I joke, and I pretend I don't care, but I want that more than anything – I just wasn't sure if you did.'

She let her head fall to his chest as they danced, her gaze going out to the crowd on the beach. There was her dad and Caitlin, chatting and laughing with Julia. Eden was happy to see them making friends. Ralph, her friend, boss and mentor, was tapping his foot as he sat on a camping chair with his beer. Livia was with Nancy and Levi, whirling over the sand and laughing like loons as they danced. The lights of Sea Glass Bay shimmered in the distance, and on a far-off clifftop stood the dark outline of Four Winds Cottage. She'd arrived there looking for something, not even sure what that was. And today, finally, she felt as if she'd found it.

A LETTER FROM TILLY

I want to say a huge thank you for choosing to read *Eden's Comfort Kitchen*. If you did enjoy it, and want to keep up-to-date with all my latest releases, just sign up at the following link. Your email address will never be shared, and you can unsubscribe at any time.

www.bookouture.com/tilly-tennant

I hope you enjoyed *Eden's Comfort Kitchen,* and if you did, I would be very grateful if you could write a review. I'd love to hear what you think, and it makes such a difference helping new readers to discover one of my books for the first time.

I love hearing from my readers – you can get in touch on my Facebook page, through social media or my website.

Thank you!

Tilly

https://tillytennant.com

facebook.com/TillyTennant
x.com/TillyTenWriter

ACKNOWLEDGEMENTS

I say this every time I come to write acknowledgements for a new book, but it's true: the list of people who have offered help and encouragement on my writing journey so far really is endless, and it would take a novel in itself to mention them all. I'd try to list everyone here, regardless, but I know that I'd fail miserably and miss out someone who is really very important. I just want to say that my heartfelt gratitude goes out to each and every one of you, whose involvement, whether small or large, has been invaluable and appreciated more than I can express.

I firstly want to mention all the good friends I have made and since kept at Staffordshire University. It's been fifteen years since I graduated with a degree in English and creative writing, but hardly a day goes by when I don't think fondly of my time there.

Nowadays, I have to thank the remarkable team at Bookouture for their continued support, patience and amazing publishing flair, particularly Lydia Vassar-Smith – my incredible and long-suffering editor – Kim Nash, Noelle Holten, Sarah Hardy, Peta Nightingale, Mandy Kullar, Lizzie Brien. Alex Crow, Louisa Pagel and Alba Proko. I know I'll have forgotten many others at Bookouture who I ought to be thanking, but I hope they'll forgive me. Their belief, able assistance and encouragement mean the world to me. I truly believe I have the best team an author could ask for.

My friend, Kath Hickton, always gets an honourable mention for putting up with me since primary school, and

Louise Coquio deserves a medal for getting me through university and suffering me ever since, likewise her lovely family.

I also have to thank Mel Sherratt, who is as generous with her time and advice as she is talented, someone who is always there to cheer on her fellow authors. She did so much to help me in the early days of my career that I don't think I'll ever be able to thank her as much as she deserves. My fellow Bookouture authors are all incredible, of course, unfailing and generous in their support of colleagues – life would be a lot duller without the gang!

I'd also like to give a special shout-out to Jaimie Admans, who is not only a brilliant author but is a brilliant friend. There's also an honourable mention for my retreat gang: Debbie, Jo, Tracy, Helen and Julie. I live for our weeks locked away in some remote house, writing, chatting, drinking and generally being daft. You are all the most brilliant women, and my life is better for knowing you all.

I have to thank all the incredible and dedicated book bloggers (there are so many of you, but you know who you are!) and readers, and anyone else who has championed my work, reviewed it, shared it or simply told me that they liked it. Every one of those actions is priceless, and you are all very special people. Some of you I am even proud to call friends now – and I'm looking at you in particular, Kerry Ann Parsons and Steph Lawrence!

Last but not least, I'd like to give a special mention to my lovely agent Hannah Todd and the incredible team at the Madeleine Milburn Literary, TV & Film Agency, especially Madeleine herself. I'm so lucky to be a part of such a dynamic agenting powerhouse!

I have to admit I have a love-hate relationship with my writing. It can be frustrating at times, isolating and thankless, but at the same time I feel like the luckiest woman alive to be doing what I do, and I can't imagine earning my living any other way.

It also goes without saying that my family and friends understand better than anyone how much I need space to write and they love me enough to enable it, even when it puts them out. I have no words to express fully how grateful and blessed that makes me feel.

And before I go, thank you, dear reader. Without you, I wouldn't be writing this, and you have no idea how happy it makes me that I am.

PUBLISHING TEAM

Turning a manuscript into a book requires the efforts of many people. The publishing team at Bookouture would like to acknowledge everyone who contributed to this publication.

Audio
Alba Proko
Melissa Tran
Sinead O'Connor

Commercial
Lauren Morrissette
Hannah Richmond
Imogen Allport

Contracts
Peta Nightingale

Cover design
Debbie Clement

Data and analysis
Mark Alder
Mohamed Bussuri